GUILD BOSS

Titles by Jayne Ann Krentz writing as Jayne Castle

Guild Boss	*Canyons of Night*	*After Glow*
Illusion Town	*Midnight Crystal*	*Harmony*
Siren's Call	*Obsidian Prey*	*After Dark*
The Hot Zone	*Dark Light*	*Orchid*
Deception Cove	*Silver Master*	*Zinnia*
The Lost Night	*Ghost Hunter*	*Amaryllis*

THE GUINEVERE JONES SERIES

Desperate and Deceptive
The Guinevere Jones Collection, Volume 1

The Desperate Game
The Chilling Deception

Sinister and Fatal
The Guinevere Jones Collection, Volume 2

The Sinister Touch
The Fatal Fortune

Specials

The Scargill Cove Case Files
Bridal Jitters
(writing as Jayne Castle)

Anthologies

Charmed
(with Julie Beard, Lori Foster, and Eileen Wilks)

Titles written by Jayne Ann Krentz and Jayne Castle

No Going Back

Titles by Jayne Ann Krentz writing as Amanda Quick

Titles by Jayne Ann Krentz

THE FOGG LAKE TRILOGY

GUILD BOSS

Jayne Castle

BERKLEY
NEW YORK

BERKLEY
An imprint of Penguin Random House LLC
penguinrandomhouse.com

Copyright © 2021 by Jayne Ann Krentz
Penguin Random House supports copyright. Copyright fuels creativity, encourages
diverse voices, promotes free speech, and creates a vibrant culture. Thank you for buying
an authorized edition of this book and for complying with copyright laws by not
reproducing, scanning, or distributing any part of it in any form without permission.
You are supporting writers and allowing Penguin Random House to continue to
publish books for every reader.

BERKLEY and the BERKLEY & B colophon are registered trademarks of
Penguin Random House LLC.

Library of Congress Cataloging-in-Publication Data

Names: Castle, Jayne, author.
Title: Guild boss / Jayne Castle.
Description: New York : Berkley, [2021] | Series: A Harmony novel
Identifiers: LCCN 2021000692 (print) | LCCN 2021000693 (ebook) |
ISBN 9780593336991 (hardcover) | ISBN 9780593337011 (ebook)
Classification: LCC PS3561.R44 G85 2021 (print) | LCC PS3561.R44 (ebook) |
DDC 813/.54—dc23
LC record available at https://lccn.loc.gov/2021000692
LC ebook record available at https://lccn.loc.gov/2021000693

Printed in the United States of America
1   3   5   7   9   10   8   6   4   2

Book design by Kristin del Rosario

For Otis: A star is born!
(Okay, so stardom is fleeting.
Don't worry, there will always be pizza.)

And for my wonderful editor, Cindy Hwang, a true star.
It is a joy and an honor to work with you.

A NOTE FROM JAYNE

Welcome back to my Jayne Castle world—Harmony. You're invited to join me on another adventure in Illusion Town. This is Las Vegas on Harmony but way more weird. The local slogan says it all: *The thrills are real.*

Turns out the glitzy town sits right on top of the latest Underworld discovery: the mysterious, legendary ruins known as the Ghost City. The eerie, long-dead metropolis is awash in violent paranormal energy, making exploration and mining extremely hazardous. Oh, and the long-lost museum of the Arcane Society known as the Midnight Carnival has recently been found in the tunnels below the Shadow Zone.

Illusion Town is filled with mysteries and dangers, but, as usual, the real trouble is caused by humans.

GUILD BOSS

CHAPTER ONE

The Lord of the Underworld showed up with the dust bunny and a pizza.

Lucy Bell decided she was probably hallucinating again. She ignored the figure looming in the arched doorway and focused on the dust bunny.

"Right on time, Otis," she said. "I'm hungry."

The dust bunny chortled a greeting and bounced across the glowing green quartz floor. He stopped in front of the massive quartz throne where she lounged, the black skirts of her bridesmaid dress draped over one arm of the grand chair.

She leaned down and scooped him up. Clutching his warm, fluffy body steadied her nerves and her senses. Otis, at least, was real. She risked another glance at the doorway. The Lord of the Underworld was still there. He was the one with the pizza box. Usually Otis carried it in two of his six paws.

"Hades, I presume?" she said, going for cool and polite. She had discovered the hard way that strong emotions tended to exaggerate the visions, making them more intense.

Hades held out the pizza box and smiled a slow, satisfied smile. "I've been looking for you, Persephone."

"Why?" she asked, deeply suspicious. "I'm already in hell."

"I'm here to take you back to the surface."

"Is that right?" You had to be skeptical when it came to hallucinations. The brain was easily deceived by the heavy paranormal atmosphere in the Underworld. Best to run a test. "Let me have a slice of pizza first."

Hades raised the lid of the pizza box. "Looks like cheese and olive."

"My favorite. Mostly because that's the only kind Otis delivers."

"The small size, I'm afraid."

"That's probably because Otis can't carry the large size. He's small, too."

She sat up, plopped Otis on her shoulder, and rose from the quartz throne. The skirts of the long black gown fell to her bare feet.

Hades walked toward her and stopped a short distance away. She sensed he was wary of alarming her. He was treating her like a wild creature that he did not want to scare off.

He held out the pizza box. She glanced at the label. OLLIE'S HOUSE OF PIZZA. ALL FOUR FOOD GROUPS IN EACH DELICIOUS BITE. That was reassuring. Everyone in the Dark Zone agreed that Ollie's was the finest pizzeria in the neighborhood.

"Help yourself, Ms. Bell," Hades said.

Cautiously, half expecting the Lord of the Underworld and the pizza to vanish at any second, she reached into the box and picked up a slice. She took a bite. The tang of cheese and olives and Ollie's unique tomato sauce hit her senses.

She took another slice of pizza out of the box and gave it to Otis, who accepted it with his usual enthusiasm. He gripped it in one paw and went to work, devouring it in quick, efficient bites.

"Okay, the pizza is real," Lucy said.

"You're lucky the whole pizza made it all the way to this chamber," Hades said. "There were several times along the way that I thought seriously of helping myself to a slice. By the way, I'm real, too. Gabriel Jones. Guild security."

His voice was rich and resonant, not at all like the ghostly howls of the apparitions that blocked the entrance of the quartz chamber every time she tried to leave.

Close up, Jones certainly looked like a Guild man. He wore boots and a lot of khaki and leather. He carried a flamer on his gear belt and an impressive knife, the only weapons that worked in a reliable manner in the heavy paranormal atmosphere of the Underworld. And then there was the amber. It was embedded in the buckle of his belt, in his Guild signet ring, and in the knot of the leather cord he wore around his neck. She knew there was probably more hidden in the heels of his boots.

If he was the real thing, the amber would be tuned. You couldn't navigate the Dead City and the maze of underground tunnels the long-vanished Aliens had left behind without tuned navigation amber. The members of the Ghost Hunters Guilds, the monopolistic organizations that handled security in the Underworld, were obsessive when it came to nav amber.

She was obsessive about it, too, because most of her work was done belowground. She never went anywhere without at least a few pieces on her person. She had worn a tuned amber bracelet, tuned amber earrings, and a dainty ankle chain of tuned amber with her black gown. She would have worn an amber necklace as well, but the bride had insisted that all the bridesmaids wear the black crystal necklaces she had given them.

The bride was a clothing designer. She had chosen black and white as her wedding colors. She had thrown a tantrum when Lucy had shown up with the amber. Lucy had removed the obvious pieces for the ceremony and then put them back on for the reception.

When she had awakened in the Underworld of the Dead City, she had discovered that all of her tuned amber had vanished. The only item of jewelry left was the black necklace. She had given it to Otis, who adored it. Every time he showed up in the chamber, it was dangling around his furry neck. She glanced at him and saw that he was no longer wearing it. What did that signify?

Now Gabriel Jones was standing so close she could feel his body heat and an aura of energy. That was reassuring. It was also disconcertingly intriguing. Her senses stirred.

He looked formidable and dangerous, but he had very nice shoulders. Everything about him radiated power and control. She liked his amber-brown eyes. Fierce but not in an intimidating way, at least not at the moment. More like the eyes of a man who has been looking for someone for a very long time and has just found her.

He studied her while she munched the pizza.

"I take it the after-party didn't end well," he said.

She glanced down at the crushed skirts of her long gown and sighed. She didn't have a mirror, but she knew she probably looked as if she had spent a hard night in a dark alley. Possibly several nights. Time had become fluid. That happened when you got lost in the Underworld. There was no day or night in the tunnels. The maze of quartz corridors and chambers radiated an eerie acid-green light day in, day out. As far as the experts could tell, they had been doing so since the long-vanished Aliens had disappeared.

"The after-party was a disaster," she said. "Long story."

"When did the dust bunny show up?" Gabriel asked.

"I don't know. I made it to this chamber and collapsed. The dust bunny appeared at some point. I've seen dust bunnies from time to time in the ruins but I've never had one approach me. I could tell he expected me to follow him but I . . . couldn't. He vanished. I assumed I'd never see him again. He came back with a pizza. That's when I named him Otis. I know he's been trying to lead me back to the surface, but I can't get through the psychic gate blocking the door."

Gabriel glanced at the entrance. "I didn't have a problem entering."

"Neither did I, obviously." She glared. "It's getting out that's the big issue here. Do you think I'd still be hanging around in this horrible chamber if I could break through the barrier?"

Gabriel glanced at the entrance again. When he switched his attention back to her, there was a thoughtful expression in his eyes.

"No," he said.

"Let's hope you can get out," Lucy said.

She sounded pissed off, but she didn't care. It was probably not a nice way to treat the man who said he had come to rescue her, but she was not in a good mood. She was irritated, because she was pretty sure she knew where the conversation was headed. Gabriel—assuming he was real—was concluding she was delusional because she had spent so much time in a strong paranormal environment without the steadying influence of nav amber.

What really annoyed her was that he was right. True, she wasn't delusional all the time, but she was definitely suffering recurring bouts of nerve-jangling visions. Deep down she was terrified that she was in danger of getting lost in a world of paranormal nightmares. When she got scared, she got mad.

Otis finished the last of his pizza and chortled.

The dust bunny resembled a large wad of dryer lint. He looked adorable because only his innocent baby blue eyes and the tips of his ears were visible at the moment. His second set of eyes, the ones he used for hunting, were closed and hidden by his gray fur. Dust bunnies were cute and cuddly. Until they weren't. As the saying went, by the time you saw the teeth, it was too late.

Lucy finished the last of the pizza slice, dusted crumbs off her hands, and looked at Gabriel. "How did you find me?"

"Finding people who get lost down here is one of the things I get paid to do," Gabriel said. "Illusion Town doesn't have its own Guild yet, so the local authorities coordinate with the Cadence organization. When they realized you had vanished into the tunnels, the police asked us for assistance. I pulled the assignment."

She took another slice of pizza and narrowed her eyes. "I didn't just vanish, you know. I was kidnapped."

She waited to see how he would take that news.

He watched her with an unreadable expression. "I was told you'd had too much to drink at a wedding reception, did some drugs—Chartreuse—at an after-party, walked home alone, and wandered into the Dead City ruins. The theory is that you got disoriented from a combination of booze, drugs, and the heavy paranormal currents inside the ruins. You went into one of the towers and found a flight of steps that took you down into the tunnels."

"Everyone believes I got stoned and fell down a dust bunny hole? That's crap. I'm a professional weather channeler. Do you really think I'd be that stupid?"

"The energy inside the Dead City is . . . unpredictable."

"I'm well aware of that. I can handle it." She ate some pizza and gestured toward the box. "There's another slice. Help yourself."

"Thanks." He took the last slice of pizza out of the box. "There is also a theory that you were depressed because your ex recently filed for divorce."

"It was an amicable divorce."

"Didn't know there was such a thing."

"It was just an MC, okay? Not a real Covenant Marriage."

An MC—Marriage of Convenience—was little more than an affair with a few legal provisions attached. Either party could end it simply by filing the paperwork. A Covenant Marriage, on the other hand, was extremely difficult to terminate. It was not unheard-of for some people to conclude it was easier and a whole lot cheaper to arrange for an unwanted spouse to suffer a lethal accident.

The last thing she wanted to talk about was the fact that she had been dumped. Time to move on.

"I assume you found me because you followed Otis?" Lucy said.

Gabriel took a healthy bite of pizza. "He certainly got my attention."

"How?"

"He approached me in the Dead City ruins near the Storm Zone Wall about an hour ago. I was trying to locate the staircase you might have used to go into the Underworld."

She thought about that for a beat. "You knew where to start the search? Sounds like my message to Veronica got through. Amazing. The kidnappers drugged me at the reception, you know."

"Did they?" Gabriel said, his tone a little too polite.

She knew disbelief when she saw it. She sighed and reminded herself he had no reason to believe her version of events.

"By the time they put me in a cab I was hallucinating wildly," she continued. "When I got out of the cab I was at the edge of the Storm Zone, so I ran for the nearest hole-in-the-wall. I managed to get on my phone long enough to leave a message for my friend Veronica. I knew she was working that night. I only had a few seconds. No time for a detailed message, so I texted my location."

"Storm Zone Wall."

"Right."

"The cops told me that much. They said that when your friend saw the text she didn't know what to make of it at first. She thought maybe you were at an after-party that was being held near the Storm Zone. When she got home in the morning, she realized you hadn't returned. She filed a missing persons report, but the police wanted to wait the usual twenty-four hours before they got serious about opening a case. Evidently your friend insisted they send a search and rescue team into the ruins to start the search immediately."

Lucy smiled. "People, especially men, tend to do what Veronica wants them to do."

"I haven't met the lady, so I'll take your word for it. Your father was notified, and he put pressure on the locals, as well. The result was that after forty-eight hours of searching the ruins and the nearby neighborhoods, the authorities decided they needed outside help. The Cadence Guild was contacted."

"And here you are. I must admit this is pretty damn impressive rescue work."

"I lucked out when Otis showed up with the pizza. He was wearing this around his neck." Gabriel reached into the pocket of his leather jacket and took out a dainty black crystal necklace.

A thrill of relief splashed through Lucy. "That's mine. The bride gave identical necklaces to all of the bridesmaids. After Otis showed up with the first pizza delivery, it occurred to me that someone might notice the necklace and follow him down here. I gave it to him."

Gabriel nodded appreciatively. "It was a good plan. It worked."

"I couldn't think of anything else to do. I was trapped in this room. The kidnappers took my handbag, my wrap, and every piece of nav amber that I had on me. They didn't bother with the necklace, because it wasn't amber. How long have I been gone? I've lost track of time."

"The wedding reception was three nights ago."

Lucy glanced at the stack of empty pizza boxes. There were five of them. "That's what I was estimating. Otis arrived soon after I crashed in this chamber. I've been waiting for the effects of the drug to wear off before trying to follow him back to the surface. But every time I think I'm coming out of the fog, I get hit with another wave of hallucinations. The visions are absolutely unbearable when I get close to the entrance."

Gabriel dropped the necklace back into the pocket of his jacket and studied the arched opening in the quartz wall. With the slice of pizza in hand, he walked to the doorway. He moved out into the hall and then returned.

"Nothing," he said. He took a bite of the pizza.

Lucy contemplated the doorway. "Damn."

"You said you were drugged?"

She massaged her temples with her fingertips. "They caught up with me when I ran into the ruins. Shot me full of some kind of hallucinogen. I was taken down into the tunnels. I managed to escape, but I barely made it to this chamber before I collapsed. Maybe I'm going through withdrawal?"

"Any idea why you were kidnapped? Your father and stepmother said there have been no ransom demands."

She could tell from his neutral tone of voice that he was trying not to agitate her further. The kid-glove treatment was irritating. Also scary. How badly screwed up were her para-senses?

"No, I have no idea why I was grabbed," she said. "My memories are blurry. I remember a bunch of creepy men in khaki and leather. At first I thought they were ghost hunters, but I decided at some point they were probably ex-Guild men who had gone rogue."

"It happens," Gabriel said. "The Guilds are changing. Hunters who are considered problems are being let go. There are a lot of them out on the street these days. Can you describe the ones you say grabbed you?"

"No, I was really out of it because of the drug. It distorted everything, including faces. But aside from the khaki and leather, I'm almost certain that at least some of them wore pendants set with stones that glowed a deep, dark blue."

There was a long silence while Gabriel finished his pizza.

"You don't believe me, do you?" she said.

"I believe you think you were kidnapped. What I know for sure is that the atmosphere down here can generate a lot of weird visions and hallucinations, especially if it's combined with drugs."

She nodded, resigned. "I knew it. You don't believe me."

"What do you say we get back to the surface before we try to figure out exactly what happened to you?"

She eyed the arched doorway. Just thinking about getting through the Alien nightmares was enough to make everything inside her go ice-cold. Her pulse kicked up, and not in a good way. But, damn it, if a ghost hunter could get through the doorway, she could, too.

"Can't wait to get out of here," she said. "I've spent enough time in hell. Good to know there's pizza delivery here, though."

She went back to the throne and picked up her black stilettos. She hesitated before she put them on.

"How far to the nearest exit?" she asked.

"It will take us about an hour," Gabriel said.

She elected not to put on the very high heels. The quartz floors of the tunnels were smooth and pleasantly warm. It would be easier walking out of hell barefoot.

Gabriel did not head toward the entrance, however. Instead, he went toward the back of the chamber and studied the sparkling, crystal clear water flowing from an ethereal green quartz fountain. The water splashed into a quartz trough and disappeared into a concealed opening.

"You had water," he said.

Lucy watched him for a moment. "Yep, running water and pizza. All the amenities."

Gabriel pulled out a small gadget and dipped it into the bowl of the fountain. After a moment he raised the instrument and examined the reading.

"This is the water you've been drinking?" he said.

"I didn't have any other option. Turns out you get really thirsty when you eat a lot of pizza. Otis drank out of that fountain, so I figured it was safe." Lucy got a queasy feeling. "Why?"

"There's a moderate level of paranormal radiation in it. Otis is probably immune because he's a dust bunny. They are native to Harmony and evolved to handle the energy down here. But there's enough of a vibe in this water to cause serious problems for humans."

Lucy sighed. "In other words, I've been poisoning myself? That's why I'm still dealing with the hallucinations?"

"Probably. But I'm sure the effects will wear off once we get you back to the surface. In the meantime, you'd better have some of the water I brought with me."

Gabriel took a canteen out of his pack and handed it to her. She uncapped it and took a long, healthy swallow. A weird jolt of awareness flashed through her. Drinking out of his canteen was a disconcertingly intimate experience. It wasn't the first time she had shared a canteen with a colleague in the Underworld, but this time was . . . different. Very different.

Startled by her reaction, she hastily capped the canteen and handed it back to him.

"Thanks," she said. She steeled herself to face the doorway. "Let's go. I can't wait to get out of here. My dad and my friends must be worried sick."

"I'm sure they are." Gabriel looked at Otis. "You lucked out when Otis found you."

"And then he found you. Not everyone would have paid attention to a dust bunny."

"I'm not so sure about that. A dust bunny carrying a pizza box and wearing a necklace is not a common sight."

"How did you know the necklace Otis was wearing belonged to me?"

"I studied the photos that were taken the night of the wedding reception. You were a bridesmaid, so there were a lot of pictures of you. I recognized the necklace."

Otis chortled and scampered through the doorway.

"I charted the route when I followed Otis down here," Gabriel said. "We'll take the same way out."

He switched on an amber-powered locator. The screen glowed, indicating the path.

Lucy made herself walk toward the entrance, bracing for the nightmares. *If a ghost hunter can get through it, I can get through it.*

The nightmares seared her senses between one step and the next.

She froze, shivering with raw dread. "I can't."

"Here, hold the locator," Gabriel ordered.

She took the locator and looked at it, dazed and disoriented and really, really pissed off.

"Okay," she said, "but I don't think it's going to help. You'll have to go back to the surface and get medication that will knock me out."

"I carry some emergency meds that would do the job, but it would be a bad idea to use them on top of whatever hallucinogenic substances you've been ingesting. No telling what the side effects might be. I don't think such drastic steps will be necessary. Let's try it one more time."

Before she understood what he planned to do, she was in his arms and his mouth was on hers in a fierce kiss that shocked and overwhelmed her senses. The sensation of sensual intimacy was a million times stronger than what she had experienced when she had sipped water from his canteen. *Lightning.*

The hallucinations flickered. An instant later they were vaporized. Gone.

Gabriel raised his head. She came out of the trance and discovered that she was outside the chamber looking back at the quartz throne and the fountain.

Gabriel had carried her through the doorway on a rush of heat that was stronger than the psychic barrier.

He set her on her feet and watched as if waiting to see if she was going to lose it altogether. As far as she could tell, he was completely unaffected by the kiss. He had delivered it as a form of shock therapy. Nothing personal. Just doing his job.

She took a couple of deep breaths, found her balance, and managed to dredge up some attitude.

"Thanks," she said. "Obviously I needed that."

"Sometimes distraction works in these situations."

"Right. Distraction." She frowned at the doorway. "Do you think I could have escaped if I'd been strong enough to force myself to crash through the barrier?"

Am I that weak now? she wondered. It was an unnerving thought.

Gabriel shook his head. "I don't think you could have made it through as long as you were drinking that water. There's a good chance you would have ended up unconscious in the doorway. If that happened, the forces that were being generated would have hit you every time you started to awaken. Eventually you might have gone insane or died."

She shuddered. "Which was probably why my intuition warned me not to try that tactic. I wonder what the chamber was designed for?"

"Who knows? That thronelike chair and the water are unusual features. I've never seen an underworld chamber like it. Maybe it was a place for royalty or religious ceremonies. It could have been designed to enhance dreaming or meditation. There's just no way to know."

"One more Underworld mystery."

"Ready to go home?" Gabriel asked.

"Oh, yes, please."

They followed Otis down a corridor that appeared slightly warped to the human eye.

"I'm impressed that you trusted a dust bunny to lead you through these tunnels," Lucy said.

"A dust bunny wearing your necklace and carrying a box of pizza." Gabriel smiled. "I figured the worst-case scenario was that I would have pizza for dinner."

CHAPTER TWO

An hour later they climbed a glowing spiral staircase to the surface and moved out into the ruins of the Dead City. Lucy was so relieved to see the night sky studded with stars that it was all she could do not to sob in relief. Once again she summoned some attitude. She was exhausted and still seeing fragments of the drug-induced hallucinations, but her head was clearing.

She paused to slip on her stilettos. Unlike the maze of tunnels belowground, the aboveground ruins of the Dead City were littered with green quartz rubble.

Evidently satisfied that she and Gabriel could make it out of the Dead City on their own, Otis scampered off to investigate the ragged chunks of the ruins inside the Great Wall. He was soon lost to view in the green shadows.

Lucy watched him go, aware of a sense of loss.

"I'm going to miss him," she said wistfully. "Now that I'm safe he'll probably disappear."

"Not if he's bonded to you," Gabriel said. "Sometimes dust bunnies form strong connections with humans. One of my cousins, Marlowe Jones, has a dust bunny pal named Gibson. There's definitely some sort of psychic link between them."

"One thing I've learned is that dust bunnies love hide-and-seek games. Finding me may have been nothing more than a game to Otis."

"We'll see."

The stilettos proved hazardous in her still-unsteady mental state. When she tripped over a quartz pillar that had fallen centuries earlier, Gabriel caught her and scooped her up in his arms again.

"It's all right," he said. "I've got you."

He carried her out of the Dead City and into the ominous yellow fog that blanketed the abandoned buildings of the Colonial-era town. It wasn't far to the invisible border of the Storm Zone. The paranormal mist thinned out quickly and dissipated altogether when they reached the edge.

Gabriel walked through the last of the fog—and straight into a blaze of blinding camera lights. A hoard of journalists and a crowd of onlookers were waiting just outside the Zone.

Lucy groaned. "This is so embarrassing."

"Don't worry about it," Gabriel said. He strode through the crowd with Lucy in his arms. "It'll blow over within twenty-four hours. A one-day story."

"You can put me down now."

"You're sure?"

"Positive."

Gabriel set her down carefully on her stilettos.

"Lucy, Lucy, are you okay?"

Lucy looked at the young man running toward her. He was dressed in a leather jacket, jeans, and sneakers. He had a rez-bike helmet under one arm.

"Hey, Runner," she said. "I'm okay."

"Me and my crew looked everywhere for you in the Dark Zone. Thought you might have gotten disoriented on the way home."

"Thanks," she said. "I ended up in the tunnels. Mr. Jones found me, as you can see."

Runner switched his attention to Gabriel. "Name's Runner, Mr. Jones. I operate a delivery service over in the Dark Zone. Lucy's from the neighborhood. She's a regular customer. Thanks for saving her."

Gabriel smiled at Lucy. "Anytime."

A woman called out from the group of onlookers. "Lucy, it's me, Veronica. Are you all right? We've been so worried."

"I'm okay," Lucy said. "See you when I get home."

"Lucy," a man shouted. "Lucy, darling, your mother and I have been very worried."

Lucy watched her father make his way through the cluster of journalists and flashing cameras. Heywood Bell was the distinguished and successful CEO of a high-flying corporation. He moved in upper-class circles that were as close to aristocratic as things could get in an officially classless society. Power and authority radiated from him. When he moved through the crowd, everyone automatically stepped aside.

He reached her and pulled her close for a quick hug. "Do you have any idea how scared Deborah and I have been?"

As usual, he implied that his wife had been equally concerned, and as usual, Lucy did not bother to correct him. They both knew the truth. If Deborah Bell cared that her stepdaughter had disappeared, it was only because she was furious about the publicity. Having a member of the Bell family go into the weather channeling business, a career that was only a couple of steps up from the ghost hunter profession, was bad enough. Having that same family member get drunk and lost in the tunnels was downright embarrassing. It certainly did not reflect well on the Bell dynasty.

Theoretically, the inheritance laws protected children born out of wedlock financially, but they could not erase the social stigma of illegitimacy. Lucy knew she had been lucky. When her mother had died, her father had insisted on bringing his thirteen-year-old daughter into his home. A lot of kids in her situation ended up in orphanages or foster care.

In fairness, Deborah had not been a wicked fairy-tale stepmother, but it had been obvious from the start that she would never get past the humiliation of being forced to allow her husband's illegitimate daughter to live under the same roof as her own legitimate sons.

The solution had turned out to be boarding school. It had worked for both of them, Lucy thought. She had been dreadfully lonely at the fancy academy she had attended, but she and Deborah did not have to sit across from each other at breakfast and dinner and pretend to have a relationship. Deborah did not have to attend school functions or help her stepdaughter deal with the problems involved in surviving the teens and learning to be a woman.

"I'm okay, Dad," Lucy said.

"What a relief." Heywood released her and immediately turned to Gabriel. "We can't thank you enough, Mr. Jones."

"She was holding her own down there," Gabriel said.

A journalist thrust a microphone at Gabriel. "I'm with the *Curtain*, Mr. Jones. Tell us about the rescue operation."

"It was pretty straightforward," Gabriel said.

A couple of medics with a gurney made their way through the crowd.

Lucy panicked. "I don't need an ambulance. Really. I just want to rest."

"The doctors and your mother insist," Heywood said. "I agree that it would be best for you to go to a para-psych clinic for observation. You've been through a lot. After all, you were down there for three days without food or water."

"The water wasn't so hot, but the pizza delivery was great," Lucy said. "I'm okay. I just want to go home."

One of the medics came up on her left side. She ignored him.

"I refuse to go to a clinic," she said. "I know my rights."

She felt a sharp sting and realized that someone had given her an injection. She turned quickly and saw the medic slipping away into the crowd.

Another medic took his place. "It's all right, Ms. Bell. We'll take good care of you."

"No, damn it," she said.

She started to struggle, but her words were slurring and she was fading into a dark place. The last thing she saw was Gabriel Jones. He leaned down and touched her hand.

"It's all right," he said. "You're going to be okay. I've got another assignment. High priority. But I'll see you when I finish. Good-bye, Lucy."

Things were definitely not okay.

She woke up and found herself in a nightmare of hallucinations that were as bad as those she had endured in the Underworld.

A man in a white coat and a surgical mask leaned over her bed.

Demon, she thought.

"Don't worry, Ms. Bell," he said. "A couple more injections and you'll forget everything."

Another demon in a white coat and a surgical mask entered the room. This one had a gravelly voice.

"Hurry the fuck up," he said. "We don't have all night."

"Yeah, yeah. Give me a minute," the first demon said.

He leaned over the bed. His white coat fell open. Lucy caught a glimpse of glowing blue amber. The stone dangled from a chain around his neck.

She tried to raise a hand to ward off the needle. That was when she discovered she was tied to the bed. She screamed, but there was no sound.

The needle bit into her flesh. Another wave of hallucinations hit hard and fast. She was once again in hell, and this time she was pretty sure the Lord of the Underworld wasn't going to show up with a pizza. She was on her own.

CHAPTER THREE

Two months later the Lord of the Underworld returned.

Gabriel Jones was waiting for her at the entrance of the Storm Zone Adventure Tours gift shop. He was dressed in a lot of khaki and leather again, but in addition, he wore a pair of mirrored sunglasses. He was not holding a box of pizza this time.

"You're two months too late, ghost hunter," Lucy said.

But she said it under her breath because she was at the wheel of the packed tour bus and she had a full load of passengers seated behind her. The goal was to keep them in good spirits until they got off the bus and funneled into the gift shop. A cheerful bus driver was more likely to get tipped than one who turned surly.

For two months she had been telling herself that Gabriel Jones was the last man she wanted to see, but there he was, one broad shoulder propped against the wall of the gift shop, arms crossed; larger-than-life and looking every bit as formidable and as dangerous as he had when he had carried her out of the ruins.

She wondered if he even realized he had single-handedly destroyed her professional reputation and the career she loved. It wasn't just her finances that were in ruins. Her personal life had also suffered. She now wore an invisible warning sign: *Psychically Unstable Talent.*

She brought the big glass-and-mag-steel-plated tour bus to a halt, got up from behind the wheel, conjured what she hoped was a bright, vivacious smile, and turned to address the passengers.

"I hope you enjoyed today's tour of the Storm Zone," she said. "Otis and I thank you for joining us on this unique, exclusive adventure. Isn't that right, Otis?"

She glanced at the dust bunny perched on the dashboard. Otis knew the drill. He went into full-adorable mode and waved his favorite new toy, a tiny, stuffed, sequined dust bunny. He chortled enthusiastically.

There was a chorus of *oohs* and *Isn't he cute?* The kids giggled excitedly. Everyone smiled. In the six weeks that Lucy had been working for Storm Zone Adventure Tours, Otis had become her single biggest asset. The tourists loved him. More importantly, Otis sold toy dust bunnies.

Burt Luxton, the owner of Storm Zone Adventure Tours, had been obliged to increase the orders for toy dust bunnies every week for the past six weeks. The gift shop was flourishing.

"Don't forget to stop by the gift shop to pick up a souvenir of your tour," Lucy said. She winked at one of the kids. "You'll find storm globes, Storm Zone Adventure games, and maps. There are also lots of stuffed dust bunny toys just like the one Otis has. They come in three sizes and assorted colors."

There was a round of *I want a dust bunny, Mom. Please, please can we get one?*

Otis bounded off the dashboard and continued with his routine. He moved from kid to kid, giving each youngster a chance to pet him and admire the toy dust bunny. Lucy took the opportunity to go into her next pitch.

"As a reminder, tour guides here in the Storm Zone work for gratuities. Tips are very welcome. Don't forget to check around your seats to make sure you have all of your belongings. The company cannot be responsible for lost items."

Lucy collected Otis, plopped him on her shoulder, and hauled on the big lever that opened the bus doors. She went down the steps to take up a position at the bottom.

The usual procedure was to assist everyone off the bus while Otis did his cute act on her shoulder. The idea was to make eye contact. The theory was that the personal connection made it a little harder for the cheapskates to slope off without tipping. Otis encouraged the gratuities with enthusiastic chortling. The system worked reasonably well. Usually.

Today, however, it all went wrong, because Otis spotted Gabriel Jones and immediately lost interest in gratuities.

With a wildly excited chortle, he bounded down off Lucy's shoulder and raced across the ground to greet the man he evidently believed was a long-lost pal.

The members of the tour group noticed Gabriel at about the same moment.

"It's the new Guild boss," a boy exclaimed. "This is so high-rez. I'm going to join the Guild as soon as I graduate."

"No, you are not," the boy's mother said. "You are going to college."

The kid ignored her and rushed off the bus, heading toward Gabriel.

The rest of the tourists were right behind him. Somehow they all managed to ignore Lucy.

"Jones is the Guild man who rescued that drunk woman from the tunnels a couple of months ago," a middle-aged woman exclaimed as she came down the steps.

She was so excited, she tripped on the bottom step. Lucy caught her and helped her regain her balance. The woman didn't even say thanks. She rushed off to join the growing crowd around Gabriel.

A perky blonde dressed in jeans that looked as if they had been painted on vaulted down the steps.

"The videos of him carrying that dumb bitch out of the Dead City were awesome," she said. "They're making a movie, you know. It's going to be called *Guild Boss*."

"Language, dear," her mother said.

The blonde ignored her and hurried forward to meet Gabriel.

"I heard the foolish woman did some weird drugs in the Underworld and never recovered," an elderly man announced. "They had to lock her up in a para-psych ward, I believe."

"She should have done jail time, if you ask me," a woman declared. "Forcing that brave Guild man to risk his own life to rescue her when it was her fault she got into trouble in the first place. Outrageous. There should be consequences for that sort of irresponsibility."

"Don't worry," Lucy said softly. "There were consequences. Lots of consequences. I can give you a list."

But no one paid any attention. They were too busy hurrying off the bus to meet Gabriel.

The last member of the tour group lumbered down the steps and joined the others clustered around Gabriel.

The perky blonde smiled at Gabriel. "Hi, Mr. Jones. My name is Amie. Do you know who is going to play you in *Guild Boss*?"

"Play me?" Gabriel said.

"In the movie."

"I didn't know there was a movie," Gabriel said.

"They're casting for it now," the blonde informed him. "The title is *Guild Boss*."

"I see," Gabriel said. He looked at Lucy across the heads of the crowd. "That's interesting."

Another young woman studied Gabriel with an assessing look. "What happened to the woman you rescued?"

"Good question," Gabriel said. He did not take his eyes off Lucy.

She pretended not to see him and climbed back onto the bus to make the sweep of the seats. Someone always left something behind.

Fortunately, none of the tour group so much as glanced back at her. People saw what they expected to see, and no one expected to see the drunk, drugged-up, irresponsible woman Gabriel had carried out of the Underworld driving a tour bus.

It helped that she had cut her hair and now wore it in a sleek, sharply angled bob. In addition, she was dressed in the Storm Zone Adventure Tours uniform: khaki trousers, white shirt, and boots. Her dark glasses and the brim of a rakish expedition hat partially obscured her face.

In the news videos and the photos that had hit the front pages of the papers after she had returned from the Underworld, she had been wearing the bridesmaid gown and her stilettos. Her long, dark hair had been a tousled tangle. All in all, she had been the perfect picture of a silly woman who had gotten drunk at the wedding reception, done some drugs, and wandered into the Dead City, where she had proceeded to get lost in the tunnels.

For once she did not find a pair of sunglasses or a kid's backpack under the seats. That was a good thing, because she would not have to leave the bus and find the owner of the lost item in the crowd around Gabriel.

She had not received a single tip. Just one more thing to blame on Illusion Town's new Guild boss. Her only hope now was that most of the people who had taken the tour would pick up a souvenir in the gift shop. She got a small commission from the sale of toy dust bunnies.

The crowd around Gabriel was finally thinning. Luckily, several people headed for the gift shop. That would mean at least a few sales. Otis, however, was perched on Gabriel's shoulder and showed no sign of abandoning his position.

"Traitor," Lucy muttered.

Apparently, unlike humans, dust bunnies did not know how to hold a grudge.

She sat down behind the wheel and rezzed the engine. The tour she had just escorted through the Storm Zone was the last one of the day. Time to park the bus for the night.

She reached for the lever that closed the doors.

Gabriel and Otis were suddenly on the bottom step. So much for trying to shut the doors.

"Hello, Lucy," Gabriel said.

His voice was exactly as she remembered it—compelling, thrilling. It was a voice she heard in her dreams. She also heard it in her nightmares.

"Oh, hello." She managed her brightest smile, the one she reserved for the tourists. "Welcome to Illusion Town, Mr. Jones. Congratulations on the promotion. I understand you're the director of our new Guild. As you can see, we're all terribly excited. We've never had our very own Guild headquarters."

"This town hasn't needed the Guild until recently." Gabriel lounged in the doorway. "The discovery of the Ghost City has changed the situation. Lot of work going on in the Underworld near here now. That requires increased security."

The Ghost City—the ruins of yet another Underworld metropolis that had been built and later abandoned by the long-vanished Aliens—had changed a lot of things in the area, mostly because big money was involved. Access to the vast and largely unexplored complex was via liquid crystal portals in the underground Rainforest. One such portal had been located below the surface a few miles outside of town. Coppersmith Mining, Inc. had acquired the mining rights to the Ghost City, but word on the street was the company had its hands full dealing with rogue prospectors, smugglers, and other unpredictable hazards, to say nothing of the wild and violent paranormal storms that swirled through the empty streets of the ancient city.

"And as we all know, when it comes to security in the Underworld, the Guild has a monopoly on the business," Lucy said politely.

"It's what we do," Gabriel said, equally polite. "It's why the Guild was founded. You could say we're mission focused."

"No shit. Well, a monopoly is a monopoly. Would you mind getting out of the doorway? That was my last run for the day. I'm going home now, but first I have to park the bus."

"Sure."

Gabriel did not step back down to the ground. Instead, he moved into the bus. Lucy stifled a sigh. There was no way she was going to get rid of him. She yanked hard on the lever, shutting the doors, and put the heavy vehicle in gear. Without a word, she drove toward the bus barn a short distance away.

Gabriel leaned against the handrail and appeared to contemplate the view through the double-pane windows. The ominous ochre-yellow light that bathed the Storm Zone night and day was growing more luminous as darkness approached. The dilapidated two-hundred-year-old buildings of the old Colonial-era town were steeped in strange shadows. Soon the fog would coalesce—the same kind of eerie yellow fog that had been waiting the night Gabriel had carried her out of the ruins and into the glare of the cameras.

"Where's your car parked?" Gabriel asked.

"I don't have a car. Can't afford one at the moment. Luckily, I live in the Dark Zone. I can walk to work and back home."

"Long walk around the Dead City to the Dark Zone."

"Not if you cut across the ruins," Lucy said.

Gabriel eyed her as if he wasn't sure how to handle that comment.

"That's a joke, right?" he said. "You don't really walk home through the ruins."

She rolled the bus into the big garage and brought it to a halt. She shut down the engine and turned to face him, one arm draped over the steering wheel.

"I'm sure you aren't here to quiz me on my commuting habits," she said. "What can I do for you, Mr. Jones?"

"I want to hire you. I've got a situation that requires a weather channeler."

Chapter Four

Okay, she had not seen that coming. Had she been silly enough to wonder if he might have come looking for her because he wanted to see her again? She tried to focus.

"What kind of situation are we talking about?" she asked.

"I'm sure you're aware of the recent discovery of the long-lost Midnight Carnival museum down in the tunnels beneath the Dead City ruins here in Illusion Town."

"The news was in the papers and on the rez screen. Someone found a whole bunch of valuable Earth artifacts that were lost after the Curtain closed. A group called the Arcane Society bought the entire collection. They paid a fortune. Something to do with the fact that the relics were associated with the Old World history of their organization."

The vast energy field in space known as the Curtain had opened more than two hundred years earlier, making it possible for humans to explore and colonize other planets. But the Curtain had closed as suddenly and mysteriously as it had opened. The colonists from Earth had been stranded, with the result that, two hundred years later, Old World items had become extremely valuable and had inspired a lively market in antiques and antiquities.

"As far as the members of the Arcane Society are concerned, the relics are literally priceless," Gabriel said.

"Yes, well, it's certainly nice to have that kind of cash to throw around."

"True," he said.

To her relief, he was too polite to bring up the fact that her father had that sort of cash. It was annoying to have to explain that she was living from paycheck to paycheck these days because she refused to go back to Resonance City and admit failure. Deborah would not be pleased to see her standing on the doorstep. There would be lectures about screwing up and embarrassing the family. Again. Also a lot of conversations about how weather channeling was not a worthy career for a Bell.

"What about the Midnight Carnival brings you here?" she asked.

"Last night one of the relics went missing."

"Tsk, tsk. If the collection was so valuable they should have installed better security." A terrible thought struck her. "You think I had something to do with it?"

That succeeded in startling him. He was first shocked, and then she could have sworn something akin to pain flashed in his eyes. Had she somehow hurt him? Impossible. He was a Guild boss. Everyone knew they were as hard as the green quartz the Aliens had used to build their cities and tunnels.

But the ruins were not entirely impervious, she reminded herself. Eons earlier, some unknown force had ripped through the Dead City here in Illusion Town, and there were plenty of fissures in the tunnels. Nothing and no one was truly indestructible, including Guild bosses. She was annoyed to discover that she felt bad about the faint possibility that she had hurt Gabriel. The man had saved her life. She had to cut him some slack.

"No one thinks you took the damn artifact," he said.

"I can't tell you how relieved I am to hear that. Things have been a little rough careerwise for the past two months. I don't need any more bad publicity."

"I, uh, heard some of the talk," he admitted.

"I'm sure you have." The last thing she wanted from him was sympathy. "Let's move along here. I've got plans for tonight."

"Right." He cleared his throat. "Let me just say that, for the record, Arcane has good security in place. The theft of the artifact appears to have been an inside job. Indications are the thief or thieves escaped into the Ghost City."

"That's a tough one. Very few people can track someone down there."

"Pretty sure I can handle it."

She smiled. "Of course."

"But I'm going to need a very, very good weather channeler."

"And you came to me because?"

"Everyone says you're the best."

She shook her head. "You misunderstood. What everyone says is that I *used* to be the best but that's no longer true." She waved a hand to indicate the tour bus. "I've changed careers."

Her talent for being able to channel the paranormal wavelengths associated with the bizarre and often dangerous weather in the Underworld was as strong as ever. She loved the work. The thrill of controlling such powerful energy was unlike any other. She had the ability to save lives and prevent disasters. But handling weather down below was a business, and she was no longer in that business, thanks in large part to Gabriel Jones.

"I'm aware that your reputation took a hit after the incident two months ago," Gabriel said.

"My reputation was shot to green hell, Mr. Jones. No security team wants to work with me. I'm bad luck. I suggest you try Roxby Weather Wizards. They're handling a lot of the Coppersmith Mining jobs these days. Big outfit. Lots of strong channelers. They look good, too. Flashy uniforms."

Gabriel considered the empty tour bus seats and then turned back to her. "You're working as a tour guide because of what happened two months ago?"

She gave him a steely smile. "What happened two months ago changed my life. And not in a good way."

"Do you want me to apologize for pulling you out of the Underworld?"

"Nope. I'm well aware I owe you my life, and I am very glad to be alive. So, thanks for that."

"But?"

"But if you're here because you think you can do me a favor by throwing some weather work my way, forget it."

"I'm offering you a contract," Gabriel said evenly. "I'm here because I need your skills and your talent."

She shook her head. "You're wasting your time. Even if I took the job, you wouldn't be able to find a team that would be willing to work with me. I told you, I've got a reputation now. I'm the channeler who got drunk at the wedding, did drugs at an after-party, and got lost in the Underworld. Had to be rescued by a Guild security agent who risked his life to haul me back to the surface. Afterward I went crazy because of the alcohol, the drugs, and the trauma of three days in a hot paranormal environment."

"Lucy—"

"Hey, could happen to anyone, right? But no one wants to go down into the tunnels with a weather channeler who got into that kind of trouble. In my business it's all about reputation. I don't have one to speak of anymore."

"You partied a little too hard and you got in over your head," Gabriel said gently. "It happens. But the experience didn't drive you crazy."

"I did not party too hard," Lucy said through set teeth. "I was drugged and kidnapped."

Gabriel regarded her in silence for a moment. His jaw tightened.

"I was told that after I left, the Illusion Town police conducted an investigation," he said, speaking quietly. "There was no evidence to support your version of events."

"The police couldn't even find the driver of the cab that took me away from the hotel that night. Talk about incompetent." Lucy drummed her fingers on the steering wheel. "I went a step further."

"A step further?"

"Hired my own private investigator. Cost me a fortune, but I wanted the best, and that's what I got. Keele Investigations is the go-to agency for the biggest casinos and corporations. They've even handled jobs for Coppersmith Mining. They use the latest and greatest technology, and they've got connections with the Federal Bureau of Psi Investigation."

Gabriel's eyes tightened at the corners. "I wasn't aware that a private investigation agency had looked into your case."

"I kept it quiet, because nothing good came of it. Unlike the local police, the Keele agency was able to track down the cabdriver. Turns out he left town right after I was grabbed. Evidently, he ran because he had been driving without the proper license. That's a major offense in this town. He was terrified of being drawn into a missing persons investigation. He knew that if I turned up dead, he would have been the last person to see me alive. He wouldn't have been able to prove his innocence."

"What did he tell the Keele investigator?"

"Nothing useful." Lucy exhaled slowly. "He confirmed the theory the police and everyone else believed—I got into his cab drunk or high, he wasn't sure which. I said something about a party. I insisted on getting out of the cab when we were near the Storm Zone Wall. The last thing he saw was me running into the fog. The Keele report says there was no evidence of foul play. The investigator concluded that I had become disoriented by the paranormal radiation or the drugs—or both. Even my own father and his wife think I hallucinated the story. That night after you dumped me, I was locked up in a para-psych clinic."

"I didn't dump you. I handed you off to the medics and your father."

She gave him her iciest smile. "From my perspective it sure looked like I was dumped. I guess you had to be there."

Gabriel's jaw clenched, but he did not lose his temper. You had to give him credit for control.

"There seems to be some confusion about what happened at the clinic," he said in an excruciatingly neutral tone of voice. "Apparently you walked out against the doctor's recommendation."

"I didn't walk out," Lucy said. "I escaped. Big difference."

She waited for Gabriel to question that story, too, but he let it go.

"Are you fully recovered now?" he asked.

"Yep. Not that anyone believes me."

"I do. I would like to hire you for the Ghost City job."

"Thank you. That is very nice of you."

Gabriel narrowed his eyes. "Nice?"

"Kind? Generous? Whatever, I appreciate it. Really. Sorry I can't project more enthusiasm and gratitude. It's been a tough couple of months."

"I'm beginning to understand that. Okay, you're welcome. Now, if we could get back to my offer of a contract—"

She shook her head. "I was serious when I said you won't be able to put together a team that will trust me. Stuff happened after they took me away in that ambulance."

"I heard you suffered some kind of post-traumatic psychic stress trauma."

"Oh, there was trauma," Lucy said evenly. "I was shot full of more hallucinogenic drugs, Mr. Jones. It took me a while to figure out what was going on. If it hadn't been for Otis, I would have no memories left of what happened. Those I do have are still blurry, although things are getting clearer."

"Are you telling me they gave you more of the hallucinogen at the clinic?"

"Someone tried to make me forget everything. I guess whoever it was decided killing me to make sure I didn't talk might be a little too risky." She paused. "It might have made people, including a certain Guild hunter, suspicious."

An eerie stillness settled on Gabriel. His eyes heated with a dangerous energy.

"Otis?" he said.

"He showed up later that same night. He was the one thing I knew for sure was real. My father told me later that he wasn't allowed to see me because of the hallucinations. The doctors thought a visit would agitate me. He believed them and returned to Resonance. I phoned him after I got back to my apartment and told him I had discharged myself and that I was okay."

"You didn't tell him you thought you had been injected with more hallucinogens?"

She shrugged. "There was no point. He wouldn't have believed me. After all, the doctors had assured him I was hallucinating—which happens to be the truth."

"Because of the drugs."

"Yep."

"You were about to tell me how you escaped," Gabriel said.

"It was a process. We waited until after dark the following day. Then Otis chewed through the restraints—"

For the first time the vibe of anger shivered in the atmosphere around Gabriel. "They tied you to the bed?"

"Well, sure. I was hallucinating, remember?" She knew sarcasm dripped like acid from each word. "I had a little trouble getting out of the room. Just as I was about to make my exit, the fake doctor showed up to give me another dose of the drug. Otis went for his throat. I bashed him in the head with a metal bedpan. It all turned out for the best, because I was able to borrow the creep's white coat, cap, and face mask. No one noticed me in the hallway. Otis led me out through the loading dock entrance. I made it home to my apartment in the Dark Zone and collapsed."

Gabriel started to say something and then stopped. "Huh."

"Huh?"

"There was no report of an injured doctor."

"That is very insightful of you, Mr. Jones. No, there was no report that a doctor had been injured and a dangerous patient had escaped. That is most likely because the demons weren't real doctors."

"Demons," Gabriel repeated, his voice once again unnervingly neutral.

"Sorry. I've tried to break myself of the habit of using that word to describe the creeps, because it just makes people think I really am suffering some serious trauma. But under the influence of the drug, that's how they appeared to me."

"What happened after you left the clinic?"

"What do you think happened? I went home to my apartment and took a long shower. Then I contacted the hospital and informed them I had checked myself out against medical advice. I called Dad and told him not to worry about me. The effects of the drugs wore off after a couple of days. My friend Veronica looked after me. Made sure I ate. Took time off work to stay with me for the first two nights. Nights were bad. They still are, but things are much better now."

For the second time that day, she thought she saw pain in his eyes, but he did not interrupt.

"When I finally had full control of my senses again, I discovered my professional reputation had been destroyed," she continued. She patted the steering wheel. "I was lucky to get this cool job as a tour guide here in the Storm Zone. Mr. Luxton loves me because I make sure every tour gets to drive through a real storm."

"A storm you generate?"

"Usually. The natural ones are unreliable. Tourists want a little thrill for their money. I'm reliable. With all the energy in the area, it's relatively easy to channel some of it into a small dust devil or a little whirlwind. Luxton sells tickets for my tours at twice the amount of the regular tours. My tours are exclusive. The storm experience is guaranteed."

"Does he pay you extra?"

Lucy almost laughed. "Are you joking? I'm still on probation. The only money Otis and I make is in the form of tips and a small commission from the toy dust bunnies Luxton sells in the gift shop."

Gabriel studied her intently for a long time. The energy in his eyes was feral now.

"I tried to contact you after I got back from my last assignment a month ago," he said. "You weren't answering your phone, and you weren't online."

"I asked Runner—he operates the Dark Zone Delivery Service—to ditch my phone and my computer in the Fire Zone. I was in hiding for the first couple of weeks. I was terrified the kidnappers would come looking for me. I've got a new phone now, but I don't take any unknown calls."

"Any reason to believe that someone has come looking for you?" Gabriel asked.

"No. We have an excellent neighborhood watch in the Dark Zone. People would notice strangers in the area."

Gabriel glanced out at the ruins of the Dead City. "Don't you feel vulnerable here at work?"

"At first I was worried about taking the job, but it turns out you can't eat or pay the rent if you don't work. I'm no longer so concerned. Otis comes with me every day. He would sense a threat."

Gabriel switched his attention to Otis. "I think you're right. It's obvious he has bonded with you."

Lucy smiled at Otis. "We're pals."

"When I couldn't get hold of you I called your parents' house. Mrs. Bell said that you were all right but that you were still recovering from your experience in the Underworld. She said it would not be a good idea to try to get in touch with you."

"That sounds like Deborah. She views me as an embarrassment to the family."

Gabriel was silent for a moment.

"Do you trust me?" he asked.

She thought about that, remembering the dreams and the nightmares. "I guess I sort of trust you."

"Sort of?"

"Well, you did rescue me from the Underworld, but then you turned me over to the demons. I realized that was not your intention, but I also knew I was no longer at the top of your list of priorities. You had completed your mission and you were off to the next one."

"So the jury is still out on whether you can trust me?"

Gabriel didn't sound offended now. She got the feeling he was in working mode—collecting facts for a file.

"Otis likes you, so that means I'm leaning in your favor," she said.

"Obviously you've given the issue of whether or not you can trust me some serious thought."

She sighed. "Okay, I realize you weren't working for the kidnappers."

Irritation flickered in his eyes. "I can't tell you how thrilled I am to hear that."

"I was just another mission for you—admit it."

Gabriel's expression hardened. "You were a mission. Right after I brought you up to the surface I was tasked with another assignment. I spent four weeks in the Rainforest tracking a serial killer. You know as well as I do that high-tech communication devices don't work down there. And even if they did, I wouldn't have been able to risk contacting you or anyone else. The killer knew I was hunting him. I had to disappear for a time."

"I understand. You're a professional. You had a job to do."

He looked irritated again, but he did not contradict her.

"Let's get back to the demons at the hospital," he said. "The ones who gave you the drugs."

"There were two of them that first night," she said. "Both male, but that's all I can tell you. On the second night only one returned. That was a win for me. Taking out one demon was hard enough for Otis and me. Two would have been a problem. I mean, we're good, but we didn't have mag-rez pistols, just a bedpan."

"You're sure the demons weren't on the staff at the clinic?"

"Yes, for the same reason you mentioned. There was nothing in the papers about an injured doctor."

"Do you have any proof of what happened in the clinic?"

This time she gave him a knife-edge of a smile. "Of course not. I hallucinated the whole thing, remember?"

He did not take the bait. He just waited. She hesitated, and then, because Gabriel Jones was the one person who might just possibly be persuaded to believe her, she unfastened the top two buttons of the safari shirt and showed him the pendant she wore on a chain-link necklace. The stone was a skillfully cut and polished chunk of smoky gray amber.

"The demon I beaned with the bedpan was wearing this under his lab coat," she said.

Gabriel studied the pendant. "You took it?"

"It would be more accurate to say I stole it. He was unconscious at the time."

"I see." Gabriel raised his eyes. "Why did you take it?"

She shifted a little in the seat. "Remember me telling you that the kidnappers wore necklaces set with glowing blue stones?"

"Yes, but this stone is gray. What is it, by the way? Looks like amber, but I've never seen gray amber."

"It's amber." She refastened the top two buttons of her shirt. "When the second demon walked into the room that first night, this stone glowed blue."

"Think it's been tuned to be a signal stone? Clubs, sports teams, and gangs sometimes use them to show affiliation with a group."

"Maybe. I haven't dared take it to a tuner who might recognize it and notify the demons—I mean, the bad guys." She really did have to break the habit of thinking of the kidnappers as demons. "The pendant has been cold and gray the whole time I've had it."

"Can I take a look at it?" he asked.

She hesitated. "All right, but I want it back."

"Do you really believe I'm going to steal it?"

She felt the heat rise in her cheeks. "No. It's just that I'm afraid of losing it. It's the only proof I've got that someone tried to kidnap me and then, later, tried to make me forget everything."

"I understand."

Well, at least he wasn't telling her he thought she was crazy.

She took off the chain and handed it to him. Gabriel held the pendant up to the light. She felt energy shift a little in the atmosphere and knew he was trying to rez the amber.

She shook her head. "You can't make it glow—at least, I couldn't rez it, and I'm pretty strong. But there's some heat in it."

Gabriel closed his hand around the pendant. Energy shifted around him. After a moment he opened his fingers and took another look at the amber.

"It definitely has been tuned," he said, "but I don't know what it would take to activate it." He handed the necklace back to her. "You've kept a low profile, but you're not hiding out under a different name. You're still living at the same address in the Dark Zone. Aren't you afraid whoever owned that pendant might be looking for you?"

"I told you, I've got friends and I've got Otis." She paused, trying to decide if she should confide one additional fact. What the heck, why not? "I've also got a gun."

Gabriel did not look delighted to hear that. "What kind of gun?"

"Just a small mag-rez pistol."

"Mag-rez pistols of every size are restricted to law enforcement. Civilians are not allowed to own one."

"Uh-huh. Well, I have some news for you. This is Illusion Town. The rules are a little different here."

"I am, of course, shocked to hear that."

"It's been two months now," Lucy added quickly. "I think the kidnappers have concluded I'm no longer a threat."

"But you haven't been able to get your career back on track."

"No."

"If you take the job I'm offering and we're successful, it would go a long way toward reestablishing your professional status," Gabriel said.

"I told you, you won't be able to put together a team."

"There won't be a team involved in this job," Gabriel said. "Just me."

It was her turn to be startled. "You're going into the Ghost City alone?"

"No. The weather down there is highly unpredictable. I'm hoping to have the best channeler in the business with me. But yes, I will be the only one on the team. I don't want to have to worry about protecting a lot of other people while hunting for the thief. We'll be able to move faster and more efficiently if it's just the two of us."

"I see."

"Do you like your tour guide job?" Gabriel asked.

"No. I don't get a paycheck. I work for tips and commissions off the stuffed dust bunny toys. I can barely make the rent. The only people who bother to fill out the comment forms are the whiners and complainers. Parents let the kids run wild. I live in fear that one day someone will wander off to take photos and get lost just as a storm hits."

Gabriel's eyes heated a little. "Does that mean you're interested in my offer?"

"Maybe. When did you want to leave to go after the thief?"

"The sooner the better," Gabriel said. He seemed to relax a little. "This afternoon."

"Sorry, that's impossible. I've got an engagement party this evening. It's the Covenant Marriage season, remember? Lots of weddings and formal engagements."

Gabriel looked like a man who had just run straight into a quartz wall. Staggered.

"You're getting engaged?" he said, his voice rasping a little.

"No, my ex is. To a friend of mine. It is a Covenant Marriage engagement. You know what that means: big, formal event."

"Let me get this straight," Gabriel said. "Your ex's engagement party is more important than recovering a priceless artifact and the opportunity to recover your reputation?"

"That artifact is priceless only to the Arcane Society, which, I assume, is paying the Guild a lot of money to find it. The relic doesn't mean a damn thing to me. And as for my reputation, one job in the Ghost City may not be enough to get me back into the game." She stopped as a thought struck her. "You called the artifact priceless, but it sounds like just another Old World antique. There are a lot of those floating around. Are you a member of the Arcane Society? Is that why you're so eager to find the thing?"

"The Jones family has always had a strong connection to Arcane. The organization was founded by a Jones back on Earth. You could say I was born into the Society. The relic isn't of any special interest to me, but it is apparently quite dangerous, and this is Guild territory now—my territory. I'm responsible for managing security issues in the Underworld. We've only just begun to explore and chart the tunnels down below. The Ghost City is almost entirely unmapped, and no one knows what the hell happened in the aboveground ruins here."

His eyes sparked with energy. The man was definitely mission-driven, Lucy thought. But then, she had already guessed that much about him. He was the type who put his dedication to his job ahead of everything else, including personal relationships. His private life was probably a hot mess, or maybe simply nonexistent. He was not good husband material, because his work would always come first.

Not that she cared about whether he would make a good husband. Not that she even knew what good husband material looked like. For a time she had believed that Tony was good husband material.

"I appreciate the offer of a contract," she said. "But if you feel you must begin the search for the thief this afternoon, you'll have to find another channeler."

"I want the best. I'll wait."

"Fine. Where do I meet you tomorrow?"

"I'll pick you up in the morning."

"No, I'll meet you somewhere. GPS and the mapping programs don't work in the Dark Zone. You'll never be able to find my address."

Gabriel gave her a slow, cold smile. "The first thing a new Guild boss does is become familiar with his territory. I know where you live."

She tensed. "Is that supposed to be a joke?"

"No, it's the truth. How do you think I found you today? I stopped by your apartment building. Your landlady told me you were working here."

Lucy groaned. "Mrs. Briggs. Of course she told you where I was."

Few people said no to a Guild boss.

"I'll pick you up at five," Gabriel said.

"Are you kidding? I told you, I'm going to a full Covenant Marriage engagement ball. I won't be getting home until two or three in the morning."

"Five a.m. if you want the job."

She tapped one finger against the steering wheel. Okay, the bottom line was that she really, really wanted the job. Maybe there was a slim chance that she could somehow recover from the career disaster. It was a long shot, but at least it offered a spark of hope. She did not want to spend the rest of her days driving tourists around the Storm Zone. The only other alternative was going back to Resonance as a failure.

"All right, five o'clock," she agreed.

She could slip out of the party early. No one would notice. She would get her gear together and maybe grab a few hours of sleep before Gabriel Jones showed up at the door.

In spite of her mood, she was aware of a little thrill of excitement. She was going back into the Underworld. The Ghost City was riddled with wild paranormal weather. She would have an opportunity to employ her talent for something more challenging than navigating the Storm Zone.

"I'll have to notify Luxton, the owner of this operation, that I won't be in tomorrow," she said. "He won't like it."

"He didn't raise any objections when I told him the Guild would be grateful if he would let me borrow you for a couple of days."

Lucy sighed. "Of course he was delighted to do a favor for the new Guild boss. I should have known you'd already taken care of that hurdle. How much did you promise to pay him?"

"Let's just say the Guild will compensate him for any loss of revenue."

"Right. Well, for what it's worth, my advice is to take a close look at the bill when he submits it. Luxton is very entrepreneurial."

"Meaning he'll inflate his invoice? Don't worry, I factored that into my offer."

"He won't be the only one who will be happy to do business with the Guild. It's no secret that the organization pays well, and everyone from the casino owners to the shopkeepers will jump at the chance to do a favor for the new Guild boss."

"Things are changing in the Guilds," Gabriel said.

"Yeah, I've heard that. Whatever. In this town, you pay to play. I'm sure the Guild will flourish here."

The Ghost Hunters Guilds were supposedly in the process of being reformed by strong, professional management at the top, but the old ways and the old attitudes died hard.

A hundred years ago, the ghost hunter organizations had been founded to defend the colonists from Vincent Lee Vance and his followers. According to the history books, Vance had been a charismatic megalomaniac who had convinced himself and the cult he created that he was destined to rule the struggling colonies.

Vance had managed to build what amounted to a militia of people with various talents. His followers had waged a guerrilla war from the tunnels. One of the city-states fell within days. Disaster loomed.

In a desperate attempt to fight back, the ghost hunter organizations had been formed. The only viable weapons were the balls of unstable dissonance energy that floated randomly throughout the tunnels. They were called *ghosts* because they could appear anywhere in the Underworld. They were dangerous, potentially lethal. Those with the ability to manipulate the balls of seething paranormal fire were recruited to do battle with the rebels.

Vance and his minions had finally been defeated at the Last Battle of Cadence. His followers had surrendered but Vance and his lover had vanished into the tunnels. According to the legend, the pair had made a suicide pact but in the end they had died because they had blundered into a lethal energy trap. The period of violence was now known as the Era of Discord.

A hundred years ago the men of the Ghost Hunters Guilds had been hailed as heroes. But decades of operating what had proven to be a monopoly on security in the Underworld had reduced the Guilds' social standing to a level that was just a step or two up from mob organizations.

But as it happened, Illusion Town was unique when it came to the social ladder. After all, the city had been founded by a consortium of individuals who operated in the shadows, and most of the big casinos were run by CEOs who occupied what could only be described as a gray zone when it came to respectability. In Illusion Town, that was the top of the social hierarchy.

It had been ever thus in communities that thrived on gambling, nightclubs, and racy entertainment. There had always been dangerous power brokers in Illusion Town. As the director of the new Guild territory, Gabriel Jones was now officially one of those power brokers. People would be tripping over their feet to do him a favor.

Lucy checked the time. "I've got to get going. I need to go back to my apartment and get ready for the party."

"I'll drive you home," Gabriel said.

"That's not necessary."

"It will save time."

She sighed. There was no point arguing with the logic. It was a long walk home, even though she did take the shortcut through the ruins.

"All right," she said.

"You're welcome."

She ignored the sarcasm and slipped out from behind the steering wheel. Gabriel stepped down to the pavement, Otis still on his shoulder, and moved aside. She locked up the bus and started toward the parking lot. Gabriel caught up with her.

"You said it was your ex and one of your friends who are getting engaged tonight?" he said.

"That's right."

"None of my business, but isn't that going to be a little awkward?"

"Horribly awkward. I'm dreading it."

"So why go?"

"I don't have a choice. Illusion Town is a small community in all the important ways. I need to put in an appearance tonight to make sure everyone knows I wish the couple well. No hard feelings. I've moved on. Blah, blah, blah."

"Again, none of my business," Gabriel said, "but have you considered that maybe it's all for the best?"

"Sure. I tell myself that whenever I think about it. And it's true. But, let's face it, getting dumped is always humiliating."

"True. So you're determined to attend the engagement party to show there are no hard feelings?"

"Right."

"Is the invitation a plus-one?"

"Yes. So?"

"Are you taking a plus-one?"

Lucy glanced at Otis and smiled. "Otis is going with me. My friend and neighbor, Veronica, made a little tux for him. It's covered in sequins. He's going to look adorable."

"I can't pull off the adorable look, but do you think you might be able to get me in as your plus-one?" Gabriel said. "Not to replace Otis, of course. But in addition. A plus-one-and-a-half?"

She stopped abruptly. "You want to attend the engagement party with me?"

"I was planning to head straight down into the Underworld this evening. But it turns out I find myself at loose ends tonight. I'm new in town. It would be nice to meet some people."

She slanted him a suspicious look. "For your information, you don't do innocent well. You want to keep an eye on me, don't you?"

He shrugged. "I don't know who or what I'm chasing. We may be after a simple thief, but my gut tells me we're dealing with a more sophisticated operation. If someone is watching me, which seems likely, that individual now knows that I've contacted you and has probably figured out why."

"You think I might be in danger?"

"I don't know," Gabriel admitted. "I'd rather not take any chances."

"The ball is a formal affair at the Amber Palace, one of the biggest hotel-casinos in the city. You'd need a tux. I doubt if there's time—"

"I'm a Guild boss. Of course I've got a tux. Aiden ordered it for me."

"Who's Aiden?"

"Aiden Shore is my new administrative assistant. He's very keen on making sure the Guild upgrades its image. He calls it *branding*. It's becoming obvious that he sees the establishment of a new Guild headquarters here in Illusion Town as a golden opportunity for him to carry out his cunning plans. Pretty sure that, as far as he's concerned, I'm just a useful pawn in his scheme. He came out of the public relations department at the Cadence City Guild."

"Aiden went so far as to select a tuxedo for you?"

"Aiden has a genuine talent for organization." Gabriel smiled a stunningly cold smile. "Don't worry, the tux is cut to conceal a mag-rez pistol."

"That is not amusing."

"You know what they say about Guild bosses. No sense of humor."

Chapter Five

The instructions from the client came in the form of another blocked text. Dillon Westover opened his phone with a sense of dread. Every time he thought he had things under control, the project got hit with a new twist. Nothing had gone right since Jones had pulled Lucy Bell out of the Underworld two months ago. It had been one disaster after another.

The message was short. **The deadline is tomorrow night. No more delays.**

He sent back the only reply that was acceptable. **Understood.**

He shut down his phone and went to stand at the tall windows of the living room. The big house was situated in an exclusive residential neighborhood. From where he stood he could see most of the Amber Zone, including the bright, gaudy lights of the Strip.

The client had approached him anonymously four months earlier. The money had seemed too good to be true, but he had been unable to resist because the job appeared simple and straightforward. All he had to do was put together a team. With his old Guild connections, that had been easy to do.

These days there were a lot of Guild men retiring earlier than they had planned, thanks to the new management that was taking hold at the top. The old-school bosses were being eased out—in some cases, pushed—in favor of new directors who were hell-bent on refurbishing the image of the organizations. The new bosses were sending a clear message that the Guilds intended to resurrect the proud, heroic traditions of the past while simultaneously employing the latest technology to do their jobs in the Underworld.

One of the ways they were sending the message that the Guilds were changing was by getting rid of the hunters who were deemed problems. The result was a growing pool of disgruntled mercenaries who had decided to move into what they liked to call *security work*. Freelance muscle.

The mercs were proving useful to a number of people like him who preferred to do business in the gray areas. Mercs asked no questions. All they cared about was getting paid.

He had taken the concept to the next level. He now had his own team of *security specialists*. That term was so much more respectable than *mercenaries* or *freelance muscle*. He paid well, and he got the best—at least he thought he was recruiting the best. But they had botched the job two months ago.

His phone pinged again. He took it out and saw the familiar **Number Blocked**. He opened the message.

One more thing. It's obvious that Jones is the problem now.

No shit, he thought. He sent his response.

Yes.

The return text was predictable.

Remove Jones.

Dillon groaned. Sure, take out a high-profile Guild boss. He wondered if the client had any idea of the risk involved.

Consider it done, he texted back.

You had to sound cool, confident, and professional when dealing with a client. It was all about image.

CHAPTER SIX

The driver's name was Joe. He could have been sent from central casting to play the part of a Guild boss's chauffer/bodyguard—big, tough, and wearing an ill-fitting suit that did not disguise his shoulder holster. Joe didn't believe in wasting money on expensive tailoring. Gabriel was surprised that Lucy appeared to like him. Maybe it was because Otis took to him at first sight.

Whatever else you could say about Joe, there was something rock-solid and authentic about him. What you saw was what you got. Take it or leave it, but don't mess with him.

Joe brought the big limo to a halt outside the grand, glittering entrance of the Amber Palace and met Gabriel's eyes in the rearview mirror.

"Is this okay, Boss? If you want, I can drive around to the back. You and Ms. Bell can slip in through the service entrance."

Gabriel glanced at the gaggle of photographers and journalists clustered at the front doors of the flashy casino. He shook his head.

"It won't do any good," he said. "It's obvious the media knows I'm expected to show up tonight. I'm still something of a novelty here in Illusion Town. The fascinating thing is that the local media seems to know my every move before I make it."

"I told you, in a lot of ways this is one very small town," Lucy said. "You're officially a local power broker now. The media pays attention to people like you."

Gabriel looked at her, uncertain of her mood. She was cool and reserved; unreadable. In the shadows of the back seat of the limo she was a mysterious, witchy figure in black, just as she had been the night he had followed the dust bunny into the eerie green chamber and saw her lounging on a glowing green quartz throne. Queen of the night.

She had been barefoot that evening, her sexy high-heeled shoes neatly placed next to the big chair. Her long, dark hair had been tossed and roiled by the powerful currents of paranormal energy that saturated the chamber.

She had cut her hair at some point in the past two months. Now she wore it in a glossy, edgy style that somehow managed to enhance her already arresting hazel-green eyes.

Tonight she was wearing a gown that resembled the one she'd had on when he had found her in the Underworld, a long column of midnight-black satin that swirled around her ankles with every move she made. Her high-heeled shoes were studded with obsidian crystals. She wore amber in her ears and around her throat—*tuned* amber. He had caught a glimpse of an amber ankle chain when she had stepped into the limo. He suspected there was more hidden under her gown. She had not been working in the Underworld for the past couple of months, but she still took precautions. Once you had worked down below, you took navigation amber seriously.

He could not believe the medics, the media, and her ex had all concluded she was psychically unstable. Evidently they did not recognize real strength and power when they encountered it. He still did not know how or why she had ended up lost in the maze of tunnels, but he knew one thing for certain—no weak person could have survived what Lucy Bell had survived. Strong men deprived of their nav amber were known to go mad within forty-eight hours inside the endless green corridors.

Until he had arrived in Illusion Town to take up his new position, he had been unaware of how her disappearance and rescue had wreaked havoc on her life. For the past couple of months he had actually dared to hope she would be happy to see him again. For weeks he had been anticipating their reunion.

He had been working toward his new post as director of one of the big Guild territories ever since he had joined the organization. He had been focused on becoming a hunter since childhood. He had researched the Era of Discord obsessively. Read all the memoirs of the determined men who had founded the Guilds. Studied the heroic traditions of the organizations. He could draw every battle plan that had been used to defeat Vincent Lee Vance. The day he had taken the Guild oath was the proudest day of his life.

When the Illusion Town territory had been offered to him, he had jumped on the opportunity. The fact that Lucy lived in the city had been the icing on the cake. Everything was falling into place in his well-ordered, well-planned life.

He had known something was wrong when he returned from the month-long mission in the Rainforest and discovered Lucy was no longer available online or on the phone. He had finally taken the drastic step of contacting her father and stepmother, who had assured him that she was well but that she was still recovering from her ordeal.

It hadn't taken much digging to discover the gossip about her mental instability. That was when he had finally realized her experience in the tunnels had destroyed her career. Okay, she had a reason to be pissed. Sure, he had saved her life, but then he had left her alone to confront both financial and personal disaster. She was right—a weather channeler's reputation was everything when it came to working in the Underworld. So, yes, she was grateful to him, but that did not mean she was going to fall into his arms.

What in green hell had made him think he could walk right back into her life and pick up where they had left off?

Offering her a contract had struck him as a brilliant way to ease back into her world, but things were not going smoothly. At least she was still speaking to him. Under the circumstances, that seemed to be a good omen. The dust bunny was the only one who was genuinely thrilled to renew their acquaintance.

Tonight Otis was dressed in a small, sequined black jacket trimmed with a red bow tie. He had his toy dust bunny clutched in one of his six paws. Lucy was dreading the evening, but Otis was excited. Life was simple for a dust bunny. Party time was party time: meant to be enjoyed.

A valet wearing the livery of the hotel-casino opened the rear door of the limo.

"Welcome to the Amber Palace, Mr. Jones," he said. "Mr. Smith has given instructions to make sure you have everything you need."

"Please tell Mr. Smith I appreciate the courtesy," Gabriel said.

Aiden had briefed him earlier on the local power brokers. Maxwell Smith, who owned the Amber Palace, was a member of the exclusive Illusion Club, the group of movers and shakers who ran the town.

Gabriel climbed out of the rear of the limo and reached back to take Lucy's hand. She slipped gracefully to her feet, Otis tucked under one arm.

The valet escorted them toward the glass doors, forging a path through the reporters. Lights flashed and video cameras hummed. Tourists who had been strolling down the brightly lit sidewalk stopped to see who had emerged from the limo. Murmurs of *It's the new Guild boss* rippled across the growing crowd.

"Sorry about this," Gabriel said quietly.

"No need to apologize," Lucy said. She smiled graciously for the cameras. "I agreed to take your contract because I'm hoping it will restore my professional reputation. As far as I'm concerned, this is all free publicity."

"Don't try to spare my feelings. Just tell me straight out that you're in this because you're using me. I can handle it."

She gave him a glowing smile. "I'm in this because I'm using you."

"Okay, that's harsh."

"You're a Guild boss. I'm sure it would take a lot more than that to wound your feelings."

You'd be surprised, Gabriel thought. But he kept his mouth shut. It was becoming increasingly clear that he really had screwed up during the past two months.

More cameras and lights fired. Otis chortled. Evidently looking for a better vantage point, he bounced up onto Gabriel's shoulder and waved his toy dust bunny.

The tourists loved it. So did the journalists.

There were squeals of delight and some amused laughter.

"Isn't he adorable?" a woman said. "Love that little tux."

Gabriel stifled a groan. "I'm not sure this is quite the image Aiden was going for."

Lucy smiled. "After all these weeks of being photographed during the tours, Otis has decided he loves to have his picture taken. He gets excited when he thinks he's the focus of attention. He likes to play to the crowd."

A determined-looking man thrust a microphone in front of Gabriel's face.

"Welcome to Illusion Town, Mr. Jones. I'm with the *Curtain*. Any comments about your plans for the new Guild organization you're establishing here?"

"I look forward to working with the mayor, the city council, and the citizens of Illusion Town," Gabriel said. "The Guild is here to serve the community."

Aiden would be proud, he thought. He had remembered his lines.

The journalist switched the microphone to Lucy. "You must be Mr. Jones's date for the evening, Ms.—?"

"Bell," Lucy said firmly. "Lucy Bell. Professional weather channeler."

The journalist's eyes lit up like a casino sign. "You're the woman he rescued a couple of months ago, aren't you? Thought I recognized you. Looks like the *Curtain* can confirm the rumors."

"What rumors?" Lucy shot back.

"That you and the new Guild boss developed a personal relationship after he carried you out of the tunnels. Wow. This is going to make the front page. People will love it, especially now that the studio is casting for the movie *Guild Boss*."

"My relationship with Mr. Jones is strictly business," Lucy said. The words were carved in glacial ice. "I am currently under contract with the Guild."

The reporter opened his mouth to ask another question, but two more members of the casino staff stepped forward to open the glass doors. Gabriel seized the opportunity to whisk Lucy into the glittering casino.

"I was just getting started," Lucy grumbled.

"I know," Gabriel said.

A man wearing a sleek suit and a name tag that identified him as a concierge materialized.

"Welcome, Mr. Jones. I understand you and Ms. Bell are here to attend the Spence-Newport event." The concierge eyed Otis with a politely blank expression. "I see you have a pet dust bunny, Mr. Jones. I assume the animal is well trained?"

"Otis is not a pet," Lucy said coldly. "He's a pal. My pal. And his manners are excellent."

The concierge nodded quickly. "Of course. If you will follow me, I will show you to the ballroom."

He spun smartly on his heel and headed across the crowded gaming floor.

Heads turned and the curious paused briefly at their slot machines and card tables to watch Gabriel, Lucy, and Otis make their way toward the gilded doors of the ballroom.

"Okay, this is weird," Gabriel said.

"Get used to it," Lucy warned in low tones. She sounded amused. "You're a player in this town now. This is how we do things here."

"I'm used to being in security," Gabriel said. "That sort of work is pretty low profile."

"You are no longer low profile."

"I'm getting the picture. This is definitely going to take some getting used to."

"Relax. You look like you were born to wear that tux."

He slanted a wary glance at her, but he couldn't tell if she was being sarcastic or giving him a compliment. He decided it would be a bad idea to ask her to clarify. He was already on shaky ground.

The scene inside the Amber Palace was classic Illusion Town glamour. Crystal chandeliers cast showers of sparkling lights on sequined gowns and elegantly cut tuxedoes and dinner jackets. The buzz of energy in the atmosphere reminded him that there was a reason the term *gambling fever* had been coined back on the Old World centuries earlier.

A few cameras appeared. Otis posed. There were some muffled giggles from the crowd. Gabriel heard a woman murmur, "Isn't he adorable?"

The concierge opened the imposing doors of the ballroom with a flourish and stood back. Gabriel paused briefly at the entrance to get his bearings. Lucy halted beside him.

The music did not stop, but it might as well have. A curious hush gripped the crowd. Every head turned toward the doorway.

Lucy tightened her grip on Gabriel's arm. "Wow. I've always wondered what it would be like to make an entrance. I can't decide if this is very cool rez or simply terrifying."

"Personally, I think I'll go with terrifying," Gabriel said.

Without warning, Otis bounded down off his shoulder and disappeared. That was probably not a good thing, Gabriel thought, but before he could tell Lucy about the disappearance, a uniformed host moved forward to greet them.

"Welcome, Ms. Bell, Mr. Jones," she said. "If you will come with me, I will escort you to the receiving line."

The ballroom unfroze. Everyone went back to their cocktails and conversations. Gabriel felt Lucy's tension escalate a couple of notches as they approached the attractive couple greeting well-wishers.

The host stopped. "Mr. Anthony Spence and Ms. Emeline Newport, allow me to present Ms. Lucy Bell and Mr. Gabriel Jones."

"Lucy." Emeline's eyes widened with delight and something that looked a lot like gratitude. "I'm so glad you could make it. Thank you."

"Wouldn't have missed your engagement party for the world, Emeline," Lucy said.

Gabriel watched, impressed, as the two women did the air-kiss thing. The affection between them appeared genuine.

Lucy stepped back and smiled. "Gabriel, this is my friend Emeline."

"A pleasure," Gabriel said.

He smiled at Emeline, aware that Anthony Spence was watching him with an uncertain expression.

"And this is Tony," Lucy said smoothly. "Another longtime *friend*."

Tony nodded, acknowledging the introduction, and promptly turned to Lucy. "Thanks for coming tonight. We appreciate it. Means a lot, believe me."

He, too, appeared relieved, but Gabriel noticed that no air-kisses were exchanged.

"I wanted to wish you both all the best," Lucy said.

"We're both very glad," Tony said. He shot Gabriel another glance. "We didn't realize you were bringing a . . . friend."

"It was a last-minute thing," Lucy said. "The invitation said plus-one. I hope you don't mind. Mr. Jones is a new client."

"No, of course we don't mind. Just glad you could make it." Tony gave Gabriel another assessing glance. "A client?"

"That's right," Lucy said. She smiled. "Congratulations on your engagement, Tony. I wish you and Emeline a lifetime of happiness."

The best wishes sounded heartfelt, Gabriel decided.

Tony smiled. "Thanks." He turned to Gabriel. "Welcome to Illusion Town, Mr. Jones. It's about time we had our own Guild here."

"Thanks," Gabriel said. "I'm looking forward to joining the community."

"This really is a surprise," Emeline said. She looked at Lucy. "We had no idea the two of you were seeing each other."

"Oh, there's nothing personal involved here," Lucy said. "As I just explained to Tony, it's a business arrangement. I've agreed to help Mr. Jones with an investigation."

Emeline stared at her, anxiety in her eyes. "You're going to go back underground?"

"First thing in the morning," Lucy said.

Tony frowned. "Are you sure that's wise?"

"Did the doctors say it was okay for you to return to your weather work?" Emeline asked. She sounded deeply concerned.

"I didn't ask the doctors," Lucy said.

Emeline looked more anxious than ever. "But—"

Gabriel decided it was time to intervene. "I need a first-class channeler to help with a security matter down in the Ghost City. Fortunately, Ms. Bell is available."

"Yes, of course," Emeline said quickly. "It's just that after what happened—"

"Mr. Jones and I will be leaving early in the morning, so we won't be staying long tonight," Lucy said. "But I couldn't miss this opportunity to congratulate both of you."

"That's great," Tony said. He snagged two crystal flutes off a passing tray. "Champagne?"

"Absolutely," Lucy said. She took one of the glasses and hoisted it in a small toast. "To Tony and Emeline."

Gabriel took the glass, echoed the toast, and drank a little champagne. He set the glass down and looked at Lucy.

"Will you dance with me?" he asked.

She stared at him as if she had never heard of dancing, but she recovered quickly and set her glass down as well. "Sure."

He guided her toward the dance floor and took her into his arms. She felt good, warm and soft; curved in all the right places. She smelled good, too. The whisper of her aura sang to his senses, just as it had the night he had found her in the Underworld. It was so satisfying to have her close again, even if only for the length of a dance. It felt right.

He had spent a lot of time thinking about her during the past eight weeks. Sometimes he had wondered if his imagination combined with the fact that he had been living a sex-free life ever since Angela had dumped him had led him to conjure a fantasy woman. But as soon as he had seen her in the Storm Zone tour bus he had known that the real Lucy was a thousand times more compelling than any woman his imagination could have created.

The band was playing a slow, intimate number. Gabriel tightened his hold and drew her closer. He tried to suppress the question that had been burning in his thoughts ever since Lucy had told him that her ex was marrying one of her friends. But in the end he could not resist.

"Are you okay with what's happening here tonight?" he asked. "Your ex and your friend—?"

She didn't answer for a moment. She glanced across the ballroom to where Tony and Emeline stood greeting their guests.

"Yes," she said finally. "I'm fine, actually. Coming here tonight was a good idea. Tony and I were friends. We had fun together. He's a nice person. But what we had was a flirtation, not a deep, abiding love. That's why I had to show up this evening."

"I understand."

"Ever been married?"

Damn. He should have known better than to bring up the subject of previous relationships.

"Once," he admitted. "An MC. It didn't end well."

"Statistically speaking, they usually don't end well," Lucy said.

"After it was over I decided to postpone any kind of marriage, MC or Covenant, until after I had my own Guild territory. I needed to focus on my job. Personal relationships get messy and complicated. I didn't want to let myself get distracted."

"I assume your need to focus on your career was what caused your MC to crash and burn?"

"It didn't exactly crash and burn. There was nothing spectacular or dramatic about the ending. I came home from a mission one day and Angela was gone. She had moved out and filed for a divorce. I didn't blame her. I spent too much time away from home. She got bored."

"She moved out and you moved up the career ladder."

"Like I said, not exactly a crash-and-burn ending."

"Why the Guild?"

The simple question stopped him cold. Not because he didn't know the answer. He did. He just did not want to have to put it into words. But Lucy was one of the few people who had a right to know. He was responsible for upending her life. She deserved the truth.

"I joined the Guild when I was eighteen," he said. "Right out of high school. My parents were furious. They insisted I was making a huge mistake. I come from a long line of successful scientists, researchers, doctors, and educators. Everyone in our family goes to college and studies a re-spectable profession."

"And the Guilds have always had an image problem."

"Not always. Back at the start, the Guild men were considered he-roes. They saved the city-states from Vincent Lee Vance and his fol-lowers."

"Yeah, well, that happened a hundred years ago," Lucy said. "Old news, as far as most people are concerned. The only reason the Guilds are still powerful is because you can't do business without the kind of highly specialized Underworld security the Guilds provide."

Anger sparked through him. "There were some bad outfits and some bad actors, but things are changing. We can't afford to take the risk of disbanding the Guilds, not now. Every new discovery in the Underworld brings the possibility of unleashing some previously unknown cata-strophic force. Who knows what the Aliens left behind? There's a real possibility they had to abandon their colonies here on Harmony because they came up against something even they couldn't handle."

"Maybe."

"If we stumble into whatever scared them off the planet, we don't have the option of bailing. We're stuck here on Harmony until we get back into space, and that's a long time off. We have to survive here. The Guilds are the only organizations that can provide security down be-low, and—"

He broke off because Lucy was smiling. Her eyes were lit with genu-ine amusement.

"Sorry," he muttered. "I tend to get carried away when it comes to that particular subject."

"It's all right. I like people who have a passion. I find them inter-esting."

"Interesting?" he repeated cautiously.

"Yes. At least for a while."

He winced. "Good to know."

"So what you're saying is that you defied your family to take up a career as a Guild man, and in order to prove yourself, you focused on getting to the top."

"That sounds a bit simplistic, but it's accurate."

"There's one bit you left out, and that's the part that makes you interesting."

"What?" he asked.

"I'm beginning to realize that, deep down, you're a romantic at heart."

"What the hell makes you say that?"

"You joined the Guild because you want to help save the world," she said. "That kind of passion is very romantic."

He came to an abrupt halt in the middle of the floor. "That's ridiculous."

She ignored him. "I should probably go find Otis. The fact that he has disappeared is not a good sign."

"Don't worry about him," Gabriel said. "Otis will be fine. Everyone thinks he's adorable, remember?"

Unlike, say, me.

Lucy hesitated. "I'm not sure it's a good idea to leave him on his own for too long, not in a casino. There's a lot of glitter and sparkle in the vicinity."

"He can take care of himself."

"That's what worries me."

"Relax." Gabriel eased her back into the slow dance.

She allowed him to chart a course through the crowd, but he knew he had lost her attention. She was looking around, searching for Otis. He was losing out to a dust bunny. Time to change the conversation.

"We're probably going to find ourselves on the front page of the *Curtain* tomorrow morning," he warned. "Again."

Lucy immediately switched her attention back to him.

"I suppose so," she said. "But at least this time I'll be upright. I won't look like I fainted in your arms."

"You didn't faint. You were exhausted and dizzy because of the hallucinations."

"Right." She studied him with her intense eyes. "What, exactly, did I tell you that night while we were walking out of the Underworld?"

It was his turn to hesitate. He really, really did not want to get into another discussion about whether or not she had been hallucinating. He doubted it would end well. But refusing to answer her question wasn't an option.

"The same story you repeated this afternoon," he said. "You were convinced that you'd been kidnapped and drugged by some guys who looked like ex-Guild, but you didn't know why. You escaped, but you were trapped in the tunnels."

"Right," Lucy said. "That's exactly how I remember it. At least my story is consistent. Sometimes in the mornings when I wake up from another bad dream, I wonder if I really did hallucinate everything. But then I see the pendant on the table beside my bed and I tell myself that my memories are accurate."

He decided not to remind her that the authorities and her own private investigator had failed to find any evidence to support her recollection of the episode. The last thing he wanted to do was imply yet again that he doubted her story.

A thought struck him, though.

"After you recovered, you must have talked to some of your friends who were at that wedding reception with you," he said. "What did they tell you?"

"They remembered that I left the wedding reception because I wasn't feeling well. One of the hotel staff escorted me out to a cab."

"Is that what you remember?"

"Yes. Most cabdrivers from outside the DZ can't find an address in my neighborhood. I tried to give him directions, but he ignored me. Sure enough, he took a wrong turn. I tried to correct him, but he paid no attention. By then I was hallucinating wildly, so I thought I might have made a mistake. I tried to talk to him."

"Did he say anything?"

"No, the cabdriver never said a word. He took another turn that I was sure was wrong. I tried to get out of the cab at a stoplight. The doors were locked. I decided to climb into the front seat. I think I had some notion of getting control of the car. But a thick plastic shield slid into place. I remember banging on it."

"The driver took you to the Storm Zone?"

"That's right. The cab stopped in the parking lot near the Storm Zone Adventure Tours office. There was no one around at that hour of the night. You can't run tours after dark. Too much energy. There was a big SUV waiting. The cabdriver opened my door. I got out and saw some men coming toward me. I made a run for it. I was really out of it by then but I thought if I could make it into the Dead City, I might be able to hide. I can handle the energy inside. A lot of people can't."

"You sent the text to your neighbor while you were running?"

"Yes. It was so hard to concentrate. I got the words *Storm Zone Wall* out and that was it. As soon as I got inside the Dead City I lost the connection, of course."

"The kidnappers caught up with you inside the Walls of the Dead City?"

"Yes."

"They were strong talents of some sort."

"Because they could handle the heat inside the Walls? I agree."

"The average ghost hunter can't deal with that kind of energy."

"I know. Maybe that's why I concluded they were Guild. I don't remember anything at all after they captured me, not until I woke up in the tunnels. That's when I noticed the blue amber pendants. I managed to escape, but I didn't have any nav amber, so I got lost very quickly. That meant they couldn't find me, but it also meant I was trapped underground. I chose the chamber with the throne to crash in because I saw the water. That's where you and Otis found me."

"Given your memories of that night, I have to tell you I'm amazed you take the shortcut through the ruins to walk to and from work."

Lucy smiled a humorless smile. "I think you know why I keep returning to the scene of the crime."

"You're trying to find some evidence of what happened to you inside the Dead City."

"You could say I'm obsessed."

"No luck so far?"

"No." She searched his face. "You don't believe any of this, do you?"

"I believe you are telling me the truth about your memories," he said, choosing his words with great care. "But you've also told me that you were drugged that night."

"Drugged. Not drunk."

"I understand. But either way, it means your memories are not reliable."

"Well, at least you're honest about it," she said. "You're not trying to humor me. I appreciate that. I think."

So much for the virtues of honesty. The evening was not going well. Gabriel did not know whether to be relieved or disappointed when the music came to an end. He put his hand on the small of her back and guided her gently through the crowd.

Two people were waiting for them at the edge of the dance floor. Both were in their mid-thirties, expensively dressed, and radiating the self-assured vibe of a professional power couple. They wore matching wedding rings signifying a Covenant Marriage.

The woman greeted Lucy with the bright, vivacious smile of a person who had clearly been born for sales, politics, or show business.

"Lucy, so good to see you here tonight," she said. "What a surprise. I heard you were doing tours in the Storm Zone these days. Is that true?"

"Hi, Jocelyn," Lucy said. "Yes, I've been doing a little tour work. How's business?"

"Fantastic," Jocelyn said. "We're constantly recruiting new talent." She turned to Gabriel. "Gabriel Jones, I believe."

"That's right," Gabriel said.

The man held out a business card. "We're Jocelyn and Brock Roxby. Roxby Weather Wizards. We have over thirty high-rez weather channelers on our staff. Let us know if we can be of service to the Guild."

"Thanks." Gabriel took the card and slipped it into the inside pocket of his jacket. "I'll keep your agency in mind."

"We're the largest Underworld weather business in Illusion Town," Jocelyn said. "Coppersmith Mining is our biggest client at the moment, but we can handle more work. We've got a lot of talent and experience on our team, and we're extremely flexible."

"Good to know," Gabriel said.

"Heard you might be in the market for a good channeler, Mr. Jones," Brock continued. "A special project in the Ghost City, I believe."

"I've already hired a channeler," Gabriel said.

"Me," Lucy added with an icy smile.

Jocelyn did not miss a beat. She gave Lucy a concerned look. "Someone mentioned that you had taken a contract with the new Guild director. Do let us know if you need some help. It's been a while since you worked down below, and we all know you went through an extremely traumatic experience two months ago. The weather changes so quickly in the Ghost City. We've got all of the latest charts available. We'd be happy to offer the most up-to-date expertise. Perhaps you should take an outside consultant with you?"

"That won't be necessary," Lucy said. "I'm sure I can handle Mr. Jones's contract by myself."

"Good luck," Brock said to Gabriel. He spoke with deep feeling, as if he suspected a lot of luck would be required. "If you change your mind, give us a call. We're a full-service agency. We've got channelers available twenty-four hours a day."

Brock took Jocelyn's arm and moved off into the crowd. Lucy waited until they were out of earshot.

"You've just met my main competition," she said. "Roxby Weather Wizards moved into town right after Coppersmith Mining took over the Ghost City project. They brought in their own team of channelers and have since hired most of the independents who were already here. There were never many of us because there wasn't much in the way of big corporate jobs. Until Coppersmith opened up the Ghost City, the majority of the clients were small-time prospectors and academic researchers."

"Why didn't you join the Roxby outfit?" Gabriel asked.

"I was thinking seriously about doing just that before my little disaster down below," Lucy admitted. "There would have been some advantages. The Roxbys are getting all the big contracts from Coppersmith, and they pay their channelers well. But in the end I decided I'd rather be able to pick and choose my own jobs. I kept my prices affordable for the small operators who work the fringes—old-fashioned prospectors and the historians and researchers who can't afford to hire Weather Wizards."

"You had a niche market."

"Which I was hoping to keep," Lucy said. "But then stuff happened and I became a pariah."

Gabriel grabbed a couple of glasses of champagne off a tray and drew Lucy into an alcove, where it was easier to talk privately.

"Before we were interrupted," he said, "I was trying to explain that, while I do believe it's possible your memories of what happened two months ago may have been altered by the energy in the tunnels—"

"And the fact that I was drunk and probably doing some illegal drugs," Lucy interrupted much too sweetly. "Mustn't forget that part."

"All right, fine. The combination of heavy drinking, drugs of any kind, and three days in the tunnels isn't a good one. But what I'm trying to tell you is that I don't doubt your ability to handle the weather in the Underworld."

"Is that so? Why not?"

"Because I trust you. If you didn't think you could handle the job, you would tell me. Do you have any doubts about your talent?"

"No."

"Fine. That's settled. We're going down tomorrow morning at five."

But Lucy was not looking at him. She was watching someone in the crowd. He followed her gaze and saw a tall, long-legged blonde making her way toward them. The woman was in her late thirties and dressed for high drama in a bloodred gown.

"Another friend?" Gabriel asked.

"Not exactly. You're about to meet Cassandra Keele of Keele Investigations. She's the owner of the agency I hired to look into what happened to me that night. Like the cops, she came up empty-handed. Unlike the police, she sent me a bill."

Cassandra glided to a halt in front of them.

"Lucy, so good to see you out and about," she said. "I hope that means you're on the road to recovery."

"I recovered as soon as the meds I was given at the clinic wore off," Lucy said.

But Cassandra was not listening. She gave Gabriel a mega-rez smile showing a lot of brilliant white teeth, produced a business card, and handed it to him with a graceful flourish.

"Cassandra Keele, of Keele Investigations. Welcome to Illusion Town, Mr. Jones. We're all delighted to have our own Guild. It's even better than a sports franchise. My firm specializes in high-rez talents who can work aboveground and in the Underworld. Discretion and client confidentiality absolutely guaranteed. Please call if you need our expertise for any reason. We know the local territory."

"Thanks," Gabriel said. He slipped the business card into the same pocket he had used for the Weather Wizards card.

Cassandra looked as if she was about to continue her sales pitch, but a masculine voice interrupted.

"Lucy, I heard you were here tonight." A well-dressed, open-faced man stopped at the alcove. "You look fabulous, by the way. How are you feeling these days?"

"I'm great, Dillon," Lucy said. "Fully recovered."

"Good, good, glad to hear it." The newcomer swung around to give Gabriel a warm, professional smile. He held out a business card. "Dillon Westover. Westover Outfitters. Everything you need to explore the Underworld. We can handle bulk orders for flamers, navigation amber, and Rainforest gear, as well as supplies and equipment for every condition you're likely to encounter down below. We guarantee delivery within twenty-four hours."

"I'll keep that in mind," Gabriel said. He added the card to his growing collection and then made a show of checking the time. He smiled at Lucy. "We should be on our way. We want to get an early start tomorrow."

"Right." She set her unfinished champagne down with some speed and looked around. "We need to find Otis."

A horrified scream echoed across the ballroom. Gabriel realized that everyone was turning toward the buffet table.

"Uh-oh," Lucy said.

She dove into the crowd, heading in the direction of the loudest shrieks. Gabriel followed. The trail led to a table draped in a pristine white tablecloth. A large, multitiered, elaborately decorated engagement cake was displayed on top of the table.

Otis was on the top layer, his rear paws sunk deep in thick frosting.

He was munching his way through the amber-yellow sugar roses that crowned the cake. The path he had used to climb to the top was etched in the frosting on each layer.

When he noticed Lucy bearing down on him, he chortled and graciously offered her a rose.

"Otis, how could you?" Lucy grabbed him off the top of the cake and tucked him under her arm, heedless of his frosting-covered paws.

The head caterer and his staff stared at her, stricken. They were not the only ones in shock, Gabriel noticed. Tony Spence and Emeline Newport were gazing, openmouthed, at the ruins of the giant engagement cake.

Lucy squared her shoulders and gave the caterers a dazzling smile.

"My apologies," she said. "Send me the bill for the cake."

The head caterer pulled himself together. "Your name, madam?"

"Lucy Bell," Lucy said. "Professional weather channeler. Best in the business. Currently under contract to the Guild, but when the job is finished I will be available for consultation. My card."

She opened her small clutch purse, took out a handful of business cards, and scattered them across the buffet table.

"Tony, Emeline, I am so sorry," she said.

She whirled around and went briskly toward the entrance of the ballroom. The crowd parted before her. Gabriel managed to catch up with her just as they reached the gilded doors. He took her arm.

"I'm sure making a dramatic exit is even more effective than making a good entrance," he said.

"You may be right," Lucy said. "But something tells me I won't be getting an invitation to the wedding."

CHAPTER SEVEN

Lucy sank into the richly upholstered back seat of the limo and took a deep breath. Gabriel got in beside her and closed the door. Otis wriggled out from under Lucy's arm and hopped up onto the back of the driver's seat. He chortled at Joe and offered him a sugar rose.

"Thanks, pal," Joe said.

He popped the rose into his mouth and put the limo in gear. Otis leaned over his shoulder and gave an encouraging noise.

"He likes to go fast," Lucy explained.

Joe chuckled and reached up to give Otis a pat. "I like to go fast, too. Not going to happen now, though, not in this traffic. The Strip is always crowded at this time of night."

Joe eased the big car out from under the brightly lit portico in front of the Amber Palace and went down the curved drive. He joined the slow-moving traffic on the Strip.

The silence in the back seat grew heavy.

Lucy risked a quick glance at Gabriel. He was not an easy man to read even in good light. In the shadows it was impossible to figure out what he was thinking. She gripped the armrest very tightly and forced herself to speak in calm, measured tones.

"I know you're concerned about the Guild's reputation," she said. "If you want to change your mind about the contract—"

"I don't think a single dust bunny incident will destroy the reputation of the Illusion Town Guild," Gabriel said. He looked at Otis. "One thing I've wondered about for the past couple of months."

Had he been thinking about her? Wondering how she was getting along? What she was doing?

She held her breath. "What?"

"How did Otis get those pizzas that he brought to you when you were trapped in the tunnels? They were all neatly boxed up. They didn't come from the garbage bin behind the pizza restaurant."

"Oh." So much for whether or not he had been thinking about her. "I checked with Ollie's House of Pizza, and it turns out the staff realized he loves cheese-and-olive pizza, so whenever he showed up at the back door, they gave him a small one. When I realized I'd eaten five free pizzas thanks to Ollie's, I tried to pay for them. Ollie waved it off, but I've made up for it by ordering pizza from his restaurant every day at lunch."

"That explains it." Gabriel checked his watch. "We've got some time, thanks to the cake incident."

"Time for what?"

"Let's go into the Dead City ruins from the Storm Zone Wall and take a look."

"Why?" she asked.

"You said that on the night you disappeared you stumbled through a hole-in-the-wall in the Storm Zone and then got disoriented."

"Because of the drugs someone slipped into my drink at the wedding reception," she said, enunciating each word very clearly.

Gabriel didn't argue. "Right. Can you show me where you went through the Wall?"

"Yes, but it's a dead end. There's no evidence of what happened to me inside the Dead City. Trust me, I've looked. Every damn day when I walk to and from work I go through the ruins. I try a different search pattern each time."

Gabriel's mouth curved faintly. "But you haven't tried a search with me."

"What makes you think it will be different with you?"

"I'm good at tracking people, remember?"

"I know. You found me when no one else could. But it's different inside the Dead City. The energy in there is extremely disorienting even during the daytime. After dark, it's wild. You know that. You went into the ruins after dark to find me two months ago."

"I walked into the Dead City after dark and walked back out with you, remember?"

He had walked back out with her in his arms and afterward *nothing had been the same.*

"Yes," she said. "And I'm very grateful, believe me."

"Forget the gratitude. I was just doing my job."

"Right."

Just doing his job.

"The point," Gabriel said, "is that I'm good at what I do."

She tightened her grip on the clutch purse in her lap, trying to decide what she wanted. It was so tempting to take him up on his offer to conduct a search. Maybe he would notice something she hadn't. But what if he found nothing at all? That was the most likely scenario, and a failed search would convince him once and for all that she had hallucinated the kidnapping.

She *hadn't* hallucinated it, damn it.

She sat very straight in the seat. "All right."

Gabriel didn't wait for her to have second thoughts. He raised his voice slightly. "Change of plan, Joe. Take us to the Storm Zone district."

Joe glanced into the rearview mirror. "You want to go there at night, Boss? I've heard it's not a good place to visit after dark. They say the energy in that zone gets pretty intense."

"Don't worry. I've got a guide who knows her way around the zone."

CHAPTER EIGHT

The ominous yellow light that was the hallmark of the Storm Zone during the day was now infused into the glary paranormal fog. The mist shrouded the Colonial-era buildings right up to the great Wall that had once protected the Dead City.

The paranormal radiation of the zone was stopped cold by the acid-green energy of the quartz that had been used to construct the Wall and protect the towers inside. Unlike the Storm Zone fog, the quartz light inside the ancient city was clear and powerful at night. The vast complex of the ruins outshone all of the casinos in Illusion Town.

A lot of erratic, unpredictable paranormal energy ebbed and flowed in the neighborhoods outside the eight walls that framed the ruins, but the territory on six sides was inhabitable. The Storm Zone and the Fire Zone were the exceptions.

Although the Storm Zone was accessible by day and had become a tourist attraction, it and the Fire Zone were considered off-limits after dark. Only the most desperate criminals, crazy thrill-seekers, and a few idiots high on drugs dared to venture into the Dead City itself at night. Some were never seen again. Many of those who were rescued or managed to find their way out suffered varying degrees of psychic stress for days, weeks, months, or even years afterward.

The exceptions to the rules, as usual, were high-rez talents who could handle the violent paranormal energy. Even they were careful not to stay inside the walls for extended periods of time.

Joe brought the limo to a halt in the parking lot that served Storm Zone Adventure Tours.

"Is this close enough, Boss?" he asked.

"Yes," Gabriel said. "We'll walk from here." He glanced at Lucy. "Ready to do this?"

"Yes, but it's probably going to be a waste of time."

"You never know. I'm good, especially after dark."

A deep shiver of sensual awareness stirred her senses. She flashed on the searing kiss Gabriel had given her when he had carried her out of the chamber of hallucinations two months earlier. She thought about that kiss every night when she was alone in bed and sleepless because she knew there would be nightmares when she finally did fall asleep.

Did he ever think about that kiss? Probably not. He had told her at the time he had used it as a means of distracting her so that he could get her through the psychic barrier at the entrance. But was he subtly hinting at it now? Was he teasing her?

She was overthinking things. She opened her door and climbed out before Joe could extract himself from the front seat.

Excited by the promise of a new venture, Otis tumbled out of the car after her, waving his sequined dust bunny. His second set of eyes popped open. It was night; the energy in the area was hot. He was ready to hunt.

Gabriel opened his own door and got out. He walked around the big vehicle to join her. "Show me where you entered the ruins."

"I used the first opening I could find. It's not far from here."

"Let's go."

She sensed energy shifting in the atmosphere and knew that, like her, he had heightened all of his senses. It brought back more annoying memories of the night they had hiked out of the tunnels. For the past two months, Gabriel had come and gone from her dreams in unpredictable ways. On two memorable occasions, she had awakened from nightmares, certain that he was in grave danger. On other nights, he hovered at the edge of her sleeping senses, whispering to her from the shadows. She wondered if she ever showed up in his dreams.

She led the way along a strip of the cracked pavement that wound through the abandoned Colonial-era buildings.

"Any idea why the founders of Illusion Town tried to establish a community in this zone?" Gabriel said. "It must have been obvious from the start that the energy storms were going to be a major hazard."

"Initially, the appeal of the Storm Zone was that water was more readily available here," Lucy explained. "That mattered because Illusion Town is in the middle of a desert."

Gabriel smiled. "I noticed."

"The First Generation colonists thought they could handle the energy in this zone with the high-tech construction materials and the technology they imported from Earth. That worked until the Curtain closed, stranding the colonists."

"At which point all the Earth-based tech started to fail."

"Yep, including the materials that were used to build the colonies and keep the machines running. The storms proved to be too much for the original community of Illusion Town, so the founders moved to the more hospitable sectors."

"I noticed the tour bus is armored," Gabriel said. "I assume that's because of the storms?"

"Right. The big ones don't come through often during the daytime, but you never know when you're going to run into a little one in an alley or backstreet. We have to be prepared. All of the tour vehicles are clad in mag-rez steel, and the glass is double-paned. Steel and glass are strong enough to withstand the average daylight storm here. If the weather looks too violent we have to shut down until it clears."

Gabriel surveyed structures looming in the yellow fog. "What's the appeal of these old Colonial-era buildings?"

"History. And the fact that there's a lot of hot energy in the area. It gives the tourists a thrill. Everyone wants to experience the kind of storm that happens in this zone."

"And you can make sure that happens."

"I told you, it's not that hard to create one, because there's so much energy in the vicinity." She cleared her throat. "Nothing very big, of course."

"But big enough to impress the tourists?"

"It doesn't take much, because they're primed to anticipate one. They want to experience a storm, so they get excited with just a small weather event." She was starting to get nervous. It would not be a good idea to let the new Guild boss know what she could do with her talent. She stopped in front of a jagged opening in the glowing Wall. "Here we go. I went in this way on that night."

"You're sure?"

Lucy studied the opening, trying to pull up memories. As usual, all she got were bits and pieces of a puzzle. Scenes flashed and sparked and then vanished. Some she was sure were real. Others she suspected were hallucinations and fragments from a dreamscape. She focused on the ones that felt true.

"I can't be absolutely certain, but this would have been the logical place for me to go inside." She turned to look at the mist-bound parking lot. The lights of the limo speared the fog, but she could no longer see the big vehicle. "I remember a dark SUV sitting about where Joe is parked now. When I got out of the cab, I saw figures closing in on me. I started running. I headed straight for the Dead City. This would have been the closest entrance. I must have sensed the energy."

There was no mistaking the currents of radiation that seeped out of the ruins through the crack in the Wall.

"Sounds logical," Gabriel said.

They moved through the tear in the thick quartz wall and walked into the heavy paranormal atmosphere of the moonlit ruins. Excited, Otis scampered ahead of them and began investigating.

Lucy stopped, giving her senses a moment to adjust. Gabriel did the same.

Like the great Wall, the broken and shattered towers were luminous after dark. The handful of structures that had not been destroyed by the ancient catastrophe rose into the night, elegant and graceful, but the proportions struck the human eye as oddly distorted and warped, as if they had been designed in a surreal dream.

There were small, narrow doorways at the base of every building, but no windows. The experts had concluded that the Aliens had initially attempted to colonize the surface of Harmony but something in the atmosphere had proven hostile or, perhaps, downright lethal to them. In spite of their advanced technology, they had been forced to go underground. There they had apparently flourished, at least for a time.

Humans were thriving on Harmony, but the ancient beings who had come before them had either given up and left or, as some archaeologists theorized, perished due to a natural disaster or a virus.

"You said your goal was to hide somewhere inside," Gabriel said. "Did you head for one of the towers?"

She looked at the ruins of a nearby structure. There was a doorway at the base. A sliver of a memory whispered through her.

Run. Run. If you get inside you can go down into the tunnels. You've got your amber. You'll be safe there.

"I tried to get into that tower," she said. "It's the closest to the hole-in-the-wall. I remember thinking that if I could just get down into the tunnels, I could disappear. I had my amber at that point, so I wasn't worried about not being able to navigate. But they caught me before I could get through the doorway."

She started walking across the glowing quartz that paved the ancient streets of the Dead City, dodging broken chunks of stone and toppled structures. Gabriel fell into step beside her. Otis bounced ahead, all four eyes still open.

Lucy stopped just outside the narrow entrance of the shattered tower. Through the doorway she could see the top of a glowing spiral staircase that led down into the tunnels.

"This is as far as I got," she said. "They grabbed me before I went through the doorway. Someone gave me an injection. That's it. That's all I remember until I woke up down below."

Gabriel said nothing. Instead he began to prowl the rubble of green quartz near the entrance of the fallen tower. Curious, Otis bounced over to join him. Lucy watched the two of them for a long moment.

"The thing that I don't understand is the motive," she said after a while. "My father has money, but there was no ransom demand."

"There wasn't much time for the kidnappers to send one," Gabriel pointed out. "You apparently escaped within hours of being taken. Once they lost you, they lost their leverage."

She folded her arms. "Okay, that's true."

"If your memories are accurate—"

She winced. "I know. I can't trust my memories. You don't have to spell it out."

"Ransom money is not the only motive for kidnapping someone. If your memories are accurate to any degree, we should consider the possibility that you possess something the kidnappers wanted."

"Such as?"

He looked at her. "Isn't it obvious? Your talent."

She stilled. "I thought about that. The thing is, there are plenty of weather channelers in town now."

"But how many are available for an illegal operation in the Ghost City?"

Anger sparked through her. "To be clear, Mr. Jones, I'm not available for off-the-books contracts. I have a reputation, or at least I *had* a reputation, for integrity as well as talent."

"Sorry. Didn't mean to imply otherwise."

"That is very good to know."

"I was just thinking out loud. You're an independent and you were—*are*—one of the best, if not *the* best, in town. In addition, your family doesn't live here. If I needed a weather channeler for an off-the-books project, someone whose disappearance might not be noticed for a while, I'd pick you in a heartbeat. You're not affiliated with Roxby's and you are known to work with small-time operators. If you got into trouble in the Ghost City while channeling for an anonymous independent prospector—well, accidents happen in the Underworld."

The temperature of the balmy desert night seemed to plummet. Lucy shivered. Otis hurried toward her and made anxious little noises. She picked him up and held him close. He offered her the toy dust bunny to pat.

"If I hadn't been able to get that text off to Veronica, it would have been at least another day or two before she or my landlady noticed I was missing," she said. "Are you telling me you're starting to believe that I was kidnapped?"

"I think there are questions that need to be answered," Gabriel said. "After we find the thief who stole that Arcane Society artifact, I'm going to reopen your case. As the new Guild boss in town, I've got every right to do that."

"Thank you." She hesitated. "What made you decide that my story might be accurate?"

Gabriel fell silent for a moment. Then he shrugged.

"Damned if I know," he said. "Intuition. Something just doesn't feel right about this whole thing."

She stifled a sigh. Gabriel might be a romantic when it came to his vision of a proud and noble Ghost Hunters Guild, but he certainly wasn't inclined toward romance in other areas of his life.

"I see," she said. "Thanks."

Okay, so she couldn't project a lot of enthusiasm; nevertheless, she was grateful.

He looked at her. "I didn't know about what had happened to your career until I arrived here in Illusion Town, but I realize that I was responsible—"

"No," she said, stricken. "Maybe I've been a little pissed because you dumped me into the hands of those medics who whisked me away to some clinic where I was given more drugs, but—"

"A *little* pissed?"

"Let's just say that I've been experiencing conflicting emotions since that night," she said. "I've tried to be mature and realistic, but I've been running scared for two months, looking over my shoulder because I'm afraid the kidnappers may come looking for me, even though that seems unlikely now. The thing is, only my friend Veronica believed my story. My own father thinks I was hallucinating. My career is in ruins. Tonight I had to watch my ex get engaged to one of my friends. Yes, it's all for the best but—"

"It wasn't much fun."

"It was embarrassing. On top of that, everyone at the reception treated me as if I were a delicate invalid. You heard the Roxbys and Dillon Westover and Cassandra Keele and Tony and Emeline tonight. They're convinced I'm suffering from some kind of severe psychic trauma. *All because of what happened to me that night.* Yes. Okay. I'm a little pissed."

"You've got a right to be angry, Lucy. I should have stuck around to make sure your case was properly investigated."

She straightened her shoulders. "That was not your job. You did what you were supposed to do. You saved my life. You were not responsible for what happened afterward."

Gabriel's eyes burned in the green shadows. "I should have followed up. Should have stayed on top of the case. You save someone's life, you have a certain responsibility."

That did it. Now she really was pissed.

"That is pure, unadulterated ghost shit," she declared in what she hoped were ringing tones.

Responsible. He felt *responsible*. That's why he had come looking for her two months after he had rescued her; why he had offered her the contract. It was infuriating.

"As soon as I handed you over to your dad and those medics, I left to carry out another mission," Gabriel continued.

"I understand," she said coldly. "Lots to do. Track a serial killer in the Rainforest. Get ready to vault up the next rung on your career ladder."

"Organizing a new Guild operation from scratch requires a great deal of time and attention."

She groaned. "I know. I may be a trifle bitter, but I'm moving on. Honestly."

"Look on the positive side," Gabriel said.

"There's a positive side?"

"If I hadn't come looking for you today, you might never have had the opportunity to tell me just how pissed off you are at me."

She blinked, thinking about that. For some reason her spirits lifted. "You're right. There is, indeed, an amber lining here. Plus I can definitely use the money from that contract you're offering. Things have been a little tight lately, and now I'm going to get a bill for a lovely cake. Do you have any idea how much a big engagement cake costs?"

"No, can't say that I do."

"I don't know, either. Never had occasion to order one. I'll bet a cake that size costs a couple of hundred dollars."

"If we could get back on topic here—"

"Right." She pulled herself together. This was not the time to fret about the damned cake. Gabriel was trying to help her find evidence. Time to focus. "Sorry."

He nodded and went back to prowling the area around the tower. He came to a stop near a jumble of tumbled quartz. Energy shifted in the atmosphere around him. He reached out one hand and rested it on the green stone.

"Here," he said. He spoke very softly. "This is where they grabbed you."

She froze. "What? How can you tell?"

"I can read your prints. Fear. Rage. Desperation." Gabriel rose slowly and looked at her. "I can see the prints of the people who took you, too. There's a lot of heat in them. Violent heat."

She looked at him and then at the glowing quartz rubble. "You can see psychic prints?"

He shrugged. "I told you, I'm good at hunting people."

"Can you identify the prints?"

"Not in the sense you mean. I can perceive the energy in them. Pick up some of the emotions. It's like running across the tracks of a ghost. If I meet the person who laid down the energy, I can sometimes make the connection. I know some of these prints are yours, for example, because we've spent some time together and I have a . . . sense of your vibe."

"I thought ghost hunters were only good at—" She broke off, embarrassed.

"Rezzing or de-rezzing energy ghosts down in the tunnels? Traditionally, it was considered a basic job requirement if you wanted a career in the Guilds. But as I keep telling you, things are changing. Other kinds of talents are being recruited. I'm descended from a family that has had a strong psychic vibe in the bloodline for generations. Our ancestors on

Earth had some serious paranormal abilities. The Guild needed my tracking talent."

"I see," she said.

But she wasn't buying that smooth explanation. The Guilds were notoriously big on certain traditions. The uniform hadn't changed much in a hundred years. And everyone knew that within the organizations the ability to deal with ghost fire was traditionally what determined a hunter's advancement through the ranks—well, that plus a streak of ruthlessness and street smarts.

It was unheard-of for someone with another kind of psychic talent to even join the Guild, let alone climb to the top of one of the organizations. But she had other problems at the moment, so she put the matter aside and focused on the important part.

"So now you believe my version of events?" she said.

"You were here," Gabriel said. "There was violence. Yes, I think you were kidnapped."

She took a deep breath. "Thanks."

"Evidence is evidence."

"Right. Evidence."

No leap of faith involved, she thought. He hadn't arrived at his conclusion because he trusted her memories. He was just looking at what he considered cold, hard, paranormal evidence. It was a little deflating, but she told herself it was good enough for now. Better than good. It was the best news she'd had in two months. Finally, someone who was in a position to investigate her case *believed* her story.

"There's nothing else we can do here tonight," Gabriel said. "We both need to get some sleep. We've got a lot of work ahead of us tomorrow."

"Yes," she said.

They turned to make their way back toward the hole-in-the-wall. Otis bailed out of her arms and dashed ahead.

"He's excited to take another ride in your limo," Lucy explained.

"Sometimes it's the little things in life."

Humor? Lucy considered the possibility. Probably not.

She stopped in midstep when she heard Otis growl. She glanced down. In the glow of the quartz pavement she saw that he was no longer in adorable mode. He was crouched at the entrance of the opening, all four eyes gazing into the fog-bound night with fixed attention. He was sleeked out and his teeth were showing.

"Something's wrong," she whispered.

"Yes," Gabriel said.

He moved to the edge of the opening and studied what little could be seen through the jagged slice in the quartz. Lucy felt energy shift around him and knew he had rezzed his senses to another level.

"Stay here," he ordered softly.

Otis growled again.

"I'm not sure this is a good idea," Lucy said. But Gabriel and Otis both ignored her. They moved out through the opening, a couple of hunters stalking prey.

A harsh, masculine voice rang out.

"That's far enough, Jones. Not another step or I'll rez the trigger."

Lucy froze.

"What's this all about?" Gabriel asked, his voice deceptively calm.

"You're coming with us."

"Why?"

"Turns out someone is willing to pay a lot of money to whoever delivers you to a certain party."

"So it's me you're after?"

"Guess you're special. Don't expect any help from the guy driving the limo. We took care of him first. There are three of us, by the way. We've all got mag-rezes."

"If you murdered Joe you can consider yourselves dead men."

"Your driver is just sound asleep. Never a good idea to leave bodies around."

"Especially not the bodies of loyal Guild men. Management doesn't take that well."

"Don't worry, we're not going to kill you," the voice grated. "Right now you're more valuable alive."

"Meaning you plan to kill me down in the tunnels, dump my body there or in the Rainforest, and hope to green hell it never gets found," Gabriel said. "You do realize that kidnapping and murdering a Guild boss is a really bad idea."

Lucy opened her sequined evening bag and took out the small mag-rez pistol she had stashed inside. She moved closer to the opening in the Wall and surveyed the scene.

In the glary fog she could see the silhouettes of Gabriel and three men. Otis had stationed himself next to Gabriel's left leg. She got the sense that he was ready to launch himself into battle as soon as Gabriel gave the signal. They were going to do this together, but they were hopelessly out-numbered. A dust bunny and an unarmed Guild man whose talent was only good for tracking lost people didn't stand a chance against three vicious thugs armed with mag-rez pistols.

"Who said anything about kidnapping?" the man who appeared to be in charge said. "We're just a delivery service. Come along nicely now, or we'll have to kneecap you."

"I've got other plans for the evening," Gabriel said.

Lucy decided her best bet was to go with the element of surprise. The attackers had to know she was in the vicinity, but they were clearly not anticipating trouble from her.

She leaned out of the opening and fired two quick shots. The roar of the small mag-rez shattered the desert silence. It wasn't just the sound of the shot that was startling. The fog abruptly sparked with flashes of wild storm energy. It was as if someone had set off paranormal fireworks.

"What the hell?" Gabriel said.

"*Shit*, there's another bodyguard," one of the men yelled. "Where'd he come from?"

The three attackers swiveled their guns toward the jagged opening and opened fire. Lucy ducked back behind the shelter of the Wall. The bullets pinged harmlessly off the quartz.

"Gabriel, in here," Lucy shouted. "I'll cover you."

"Damn it, Lucy, stay inside."

The night suddenly exploded with ghost fire. Through the opening in the Wall, Lucy watched a seething storm of violent green energy co-alesce in front of the three attackers, brushing lightly against them. She saw their mouths open in shocked screams, but all three went down before any sound could be heard.

Lucy stared, astonished. Ghosts as large as the one Gabriel had just pulled could kill. If the three men were not dead, they were definitely unconscious.

Otis chortled cheerfully and immediately fluffed up. Satisfied that things were under control, he scampered around, apparently searching for something. He found his dust bunny toy and dashed toward Lucy. She scooped him up.

Gabriel went to each attacker in turn, collecting guns and ID. He used his phone to take photos of each face. When he was finished, he turned back to Lucy.

"What did you think you were doing?" he said, his voice low and un-nervingly stern. "Don't you know how dangerous it is to use a mag-rez in this kind of atmosphere?"

He was angry. She had tried to save his life and he had the nerve to get mad?

"How was I to know you could rez a ghost like that?" she snapped. "Aboveground, no less. A few minutes ago you told me you had an en-tirely different talent."

"It's complicated," Gabriel said.

"No, it's not. You're a dual talent, aren't you?"

Statistically speaking, while even young children could rez amber to turn on a light switch or unlock a door, most people were endowed with average psychic ability. The city-states were full of people who could tune amber, produce art, or interpret dreams. Some were good at prospecting for crystal and quartz. Others investigated crimes—or committed them—and some did high-level math or became great chefs or surgeons. Talent came in endless varieties.

But truly powerful talents of any sort were not common. Those individuals usually went out of their way to keep a low profile, because traditionally they were viewed with wariness by the general public. Some off-the-charts talents had proven to be exceedingly dangerous people. Power was power, and all power had the potential for good or ill.

Dual talents—people endowed with more than one powerful psychic ability—were in another category altogether. They were viewed as not simply potentially dangerous but inherently unstable. At best they were delicate. At worst they were human monsters. *Triple* talents usually ended up in locked wards at para-psych hospitals, assuming they did not take their own lives first. Very few triple talents survived beyond their twenties.

The scientists and para-psychologists who studied the phenomena of multitalents were convinced that the human brain simply could not handle the stimulation provided by their additional para-senses.

But whatever else you could say about Gabriel, he seemed stable. It was highly unlikely that he would have been promoted to one of the top jobs in the Guilds if he was suspected of being unbalanced.

She moved out of the shelter of the hole-in-the-wall.

"Well, well, well," she said. "A dual talent. Isn't that interesting."

"We'll discuss it later," Gabriel said.

"Sure."

"Boss?" Joe staggered out of the shadows. He had a mag-rez in one hand. "Are you okay?"

"Yes," Gabriel said. "A little irritated at the moment, but okay. What about you?"

"I'm all right. When the vehicle showed up in the parking lot I got out of the limo to see what was going on. One of those three fired some kind of gas at me. Took me out for a while. Sorry. I screwed up."

"You were outnumbered and outgunned," Gabriel said. "Everything is under control. Call the local cops and have these three picked up for assault with illegal mag-rezes. It's a good bet they'll all have records."

"No problem." Joe surveyed the motionless men. "I'll take care of everything. Were they after you or Ms. Bell?"

"Good question," Lucy said. "But then, I've been a little paranoid lately."

"They indicated they were after me," Gabriel said. "Which means this situation may be connected to the theft of the Arcane relic."

"Makes sense," Joe said. "It's no secret that the museum has asked you to find it." He whistled softly. "Nice work with the ghost, by the way."

"Yes, it was," Lucy said, putting a lot of sugar into her words. "Very nice work. I've seen ghosts that powerful in the tunnels, but never above-ground."

Gabriel shot her another seriously annoyed look. "I didn't get this cool Guild boss job because of my charm and good looks."

"Apparently not," Lucy said.

It hurt that he didn't appreciate what she had tried to do, but she could not blame him. He was a Guild boss. He was used to giving orders, and he expected them to be obeyed. She decided to be gracious and let the issue slide. There were bound to be a few rough spots as they worked out their new relationship.

No, what they had was not a *relationship*, she decided. *Business arrangement* was a more accurate description of their current association.

She started to put the little mag-rez pistol back into her evening bag. Joe watched with professional interest.

"Say, is that the new model five-twelve?" he said.

"Yes, it is," she said.

"Can I take a look?"

"Sure." Lucy handed him the small pistol. "You're using the class four hundred?"

"Yeah." He gave her his weapon to examine. "A lot heavier, obviously, but I like the accuracy."

"The five-twelve is more convenient for me," Lucy said. "Fits into my handbags. Accuracy over distance was the trade-off, but I figure any mag-rez is enough to get a bad guy's attention."

Joe studied her pistol. "Looks like they kept the standard amber-activated trigger mechanism."

"Yes. And the accuracy isn't that bad, really—"

"I hate to interrupt this technical discussion," Gabriel said, "but in case you haven't noticed, we've got more pressing issues."

"Right, Boss," Joe said.

He gave Lucy's gun back to her. She checked the safety, dropped it into her handbag, and handed the four hundred to him without a word.

They both turned toward Gabriel. He gave Lucy an odd look and shook his head.

"I can't believe you carried an illegal mag-rez to that reception this evening," he said. "Why didn't you tell me?"

"I was afraid it would make you nervous," Lucy said.

"No shit." Gabriel turned back to Joe. "Wait here until the police arrive to pick up these guys. After that's taken care of, wake up Aiden and Jared. Fill them in on what happened here. Jared can liaise with the local police. We want them on our side. Give Aiden the IDs and the photos. Tell him I need whatever he can find as soon as possible. These three look like ex-Guild men, so they should be in the files. I'll drive Ms. Bell home."

"Got it, Boss." Joe took a phone out of his pocket. "Are you coming back here after you take Ms. Bell to her apartment?"

"No," Gabriel said. "I'll be staying with her tonight. Think you can find her apartment again?"

"Yep. Memorized the route."

"Good. Be there at five tomorrow morning. Use my vehicle. We'll swap cars. You can pick up the limo and take it back to the garage. Ms. Bell and I will head to the job site."

"Right." Joe turned away to talk to whoever was on the other end of his phone call.

Joe appeared to take the rapid-fire string of orders in stride, but Lucy's head was spinning. She was starting to feel as if she were on a roller coaster. It had been one twist after another today. She tried to focus on what mattered most at that moment.

"What did you mean when you said you were going to spend the rest of the night with me?" she said.

"There are too many questions here. I'm not letting you out of my sight until we know what's going on," Gabriel said.

She searched for a logical reason to refuse. "I don't have an extra bedroom."

No need to mention that she happened to have a sofa equipped with a pull-out bed.

"I'll take the couch or the floor. I'm assuming you've got one or the other?"

She narrowed her eyes. "Both."

"Always nice to have a choice." Gabriel turned back to Joe. "I've got a go-bag in the back of the limo, but I'd appreciate it if you'd stop by my apartment tomorrow morning and grab some clothes. I'd just as soon not go into the Underworld wearing a tux. Not a good look for a Guild boss."

CHAPTER NINE

"This is awkward," Lucy said. She twitched the curtain aside and looked at the long black limo parked on the street in front of her apartment building. "Do you have any idea what Mrs. Briggs and my neighbors are going to think when they see that huge car sitting there all night long?"

Otis vaulted up onto the windowsill to see what had attracted her attention. When he didn't notice anything that was of interest to a dust bunny, he chortled and bounced down to the floor again.

Gabriel glanced out the window and shrugged. "They'll assume you have a friend visiting."

"I don't have any friends who drive around in limousines, especially not in limousines with Guild license plates. Everyone will know the new boss of the local Guild is spending the night."

"Is that going to be a problem?"

She let the curtain fall back into place and turned to glare at him. It struck her that he looked incredibly sexy standing there in her small living room dressed in a tux. The memory of how he had kissed her, scooped her up with easy strength, and carried her out of the Dead City whispered through her.

Focus, woman.

"My professional reputation went down the dust bunny hole after you brought me out of the tunnels," she said coldly. "But there was another issue, as well."

Gabriel raised his brows. "What other issue?"

"Never mind," she muttered. "It was just a three-day tabloid story that faded quickly."

"What kind of tabloid story?"

She waved her hands. "The *Curtain* and some of the other gossipy papers implied that I had disappeared for three days into the tunnels because I was having a wild fling with the Guild agent who rescued me. It was the photo of you carrying me out of the Dead City. They ran with it for a while."

"I see." Gabriel contemplated that for a beat. "I didn't realize—"

"I know. You were busy."

"I had a job to do."

"Right. My point is that two months ago people figured it was just a one- or possibly three-night stand with a Guild agent. It happens. My friends and neighbors forgot about it within a week. Tomorrow morning, however, the rumors are going to fire up again. And this time it will be different, because you're not just a ghost hunter who stopped off in Illusion Town long enough to have some fun. You're the director of the local Guild. You're one of the power brokers here. And you're spending the night at my place. So much for trying to convince everyone that you're just another client."

"I apologize, but security has to be our first priority. Can we agree on that?"

She groaned. "Yes. Damn it."

"Good. That's settled, then."

She lifted her chin, determined to be mature. "Yep. Settled. Got a job to do first thing in the morning."

"Exactly."

Gabriel peeled off the elegantly cut jacket of his tuxedo. Lucy stared at the compact mag-rez pistol he wore in a shoulder holster.

"Good grief," she said. "You weren't teasing me after all. You actually do own a tux cut to conceal a gun."

"Aiden ordered the suit, and he likes the old traditions." Gabriel tossed the jacket over the back of a chair and began loosening the knot of his silk tie. "I told you, Guild bosses aren't known for their sense of humor."

She spread her hands wide apart. "Why didn't you use it tonight when those thugs tried to grab you?"

"Two reasons. First, I wanted information and I've discovered guys like that are more likely to talk if they think they're in control of the situation." Gabriel unbuckled the holster. "The second reason is that mag-rez pistols are dangerous to use in a heavy paranormal atmosphere. Things were going well until you gallantly came to my rescue."

"Sorry about that."

"I was trying to make a joke."

"Fail."

Gabriel nodded. "I get that a lot." He leaned down and opened the well-worn leather backpack he had removed from the rear of the limo. "What do you say we get some sleep?"

Otis bustled over to investigate the contents of the pack.

Lucy gave up. She was stuck with Gabriel for the foreseeable future. And she did owe him her life. Now he was trying to help her restore her professional reputation. She needed to learn gratitude.

"Okay," she said. "Good idea. Big day ahead of us." She paused a beat. "You're a dual talent."

"I think we've already established that. I told you, there have been strong psychics in the family for generations, long before my ancestors came to Harmony. The Joneses adapted quite easily to the paranormal vibe here. There are several dual talents in the family. For obvious reasons, we keep quiet about it."

"Because people might doubt your mental stability?"

"Or be terrified of me. There are too many stories about dual talents turning into psychopaths. Much simpler to let people think I'm just naturally good at reading a crime scene. Which, to be accurate, is the truth."

She folded her arms. "You're not unstable."

"No, I'm not. I might not possess a sense of humor, but I have it on good authority that I'm stable."

"What is the authority?"

"My mom."

"Well, if you can't trust your mom—" Lucy paused. "This is probably none of my business, but do the members of the Guild Council who appointed you director of the Illusion Town Guild know you're a dual talent?"

"Yes, but very few other people know."

"Now I'm one of those people."

"Yes. But I trust you to keep quiet about it."

"Why? What makes you think I won't blab your secret to the press?"

He shrugged. "I just know. Call it a hunch."

Successful Guild bosses did not do things on the basis of a hunch. They were nothing if not strategic in their thinking. You didn't get to the top of the Guild unless you were very, very good at strategy.

Before she could point that out, however, Otis suddenly emerged from the leather pack, chortling excitedly. She could not make out what he had in his paw.

He dashed across the floor and stopped in front of her. She leaned down.

"Sweetie, you can't go around stealing things," she said. "People get annoyed."

An odd stillness came over Gabriel. "He didn't steal it," he said. "He's just returning it to its rightful owner."

Otis waved a string of black crystals.

"What?" Lucy bent down to take a closer look. "It's my necklace, the one I wore to the wedding reception and gave to Otis hoping he could attract someone's attention with it."

"He did," Gabriel said. "He got my attention with it. I was going to give it back to you that night, but they took you away in the ambulance, and, to be honest, I forgot about your necklace until I was in the middle of the Rainforest looking for that serial killer. I knew it wasn't particularly valuable. Figured I'd return it when I saw you again."

"You kept it in your go-bag all this time?"

Gabriel gave her a wry smile. "I think of it as my good-luck charm."

"I didn't know Guild bosses believed in luck."

"Are you kidding? Of course we believe in luck. You know what they say—*better to be lucky than good.*"

"Did the necklace work for you down in the Rainforest?"

Gabriel's brows rose. "The serial killer is awaiting trial and I'm alive, so all available evidence indicates it worked."

On impulse, she held it out to him. "You can keep it if you like. As you said, it's not worth much. Just costume jewelry."

He hesitated. "Are you sure?"

"I'm sure." She shuddered. "Trust me, I'll never wear it again."

"All right, thanks." He dropped the necklace back into his pack. "If you ever want it back, just let me know."

"Okay." In spite of her jumbled emotions, she was touched that he wanted to keep the necklace. She moved to the sofa. "By the way, I've been meaning to ask, what is the missing Arcane relic that was stolen from the museum?"

Gabriel set the holstered mag-rez on the coffee table. "It was de-scribed as a large clockwork doll."

"I assume its value lies in the fact that it's an artifact from the Old World?"

"Think of it as an action figure—a very dangerous action figure. Lethal, in fact."

"A deadly doll?"

"It was designed by a clockwork toy maker named Mrs. Bridewell a few centuries ago," Gabriel said. "Nineteenth century, Old World Date. Apparently it's actually a carefully disguised weapon."

"But if it's an Old World artifact, surely it stopped functioning long ago. Even if the mechanism still worked, which is unlikely after all this time, there wouldn't be any ammunition."

"According to the Arcane Society experts, it wasn't standard Old World technology. It operated on some sort of paranormal power base."

"Amber?"

"No. There was plenty of amber on the Old World, but there is no evidence that it was ever tapped as a power source. Coal and oil were heavily used during the era in which the doll was produced. Later, solar power and other forms of energy became standard on a large scale, but as far as we know, none of it was based on the principles of paranormal physics."

"Interesting." She gestured at the sofa. "There's a pull-out bed. You can have it."

"Thanks. Beats sleeping on the floor."

"We'll have to move the coffee table. Want to give me a hand?"

"Sure."

He took one end of the coffee table. She took the other. They lifted it and moved it to one side of the room. Together they pulled out the bed. It was very cozy and intimate, she thought. A frisson of sensual awareness whispered through her. After all the dreams and nightmares, it was a very odd thing to realize he was going to be sleeping in her apartment tonight. Probably a classic case of *Be careful what you wish for.*

"I'll get the sheets and a blanket," she said.

She started down the hall.

"Lucy?"

She turned around, aware that she was suddenly, and for no apparent reason, holding her breath. "Yes?"

"I enjoyed dancing with you tonight," Gabriel said.

She smiled a little. "All in all, I'd say the evening went well right up until Otis destroyed the engagement cake and those men tried to grab you. But who's quibbling? It was my first date in two months."

"It's been a while for me, too."

"I'll get the bedding stuff."

CHAPTER TEN

Disaster. Again.

Dillon Westover poured himself another glass of good whiskey to calm his rage and frustration. He walked across the vast expanse of the living room, opened the glass doors, and went outside onto the deck. Gripping the railing with one hand, he took a healthy slug of the booze.

He contemplated the glittering Amber Zone spread out before him and the glowing ruins beyond. He had been a fool to rush the job. But the client was really leaning on him. He was in too deep. He had a feeling that if he didn't salvage the project, he might not survive.

The hastily organized effort tonight had ended in failure, just as his intuition had warned him and just as Tuck had predicted. Taking out a Guild boss was always an extremely high-risk endeavor. The men at the top of the Guilds got to their positions of power because they were strong, dangerous, and ruthless. They had survived just about everything the

Underworld could throw at them and managed to navigate the treacherous waters of Guild politics. They were never easy targets.

Arranging for the disappearance of a Guild boss required extensive planning, and above all, it meant making certain there was no evidence left at the scene.

The only sensible strategy was to handle the entire process in the Underworld, where murder could easily be explained as death by natural paranormal causes.

The attempt at a quick grab-and-go on the surface had been a serious mistake, but thankfully, he had been smart enough to outsource the job. There was no connection to his private security team. That meant no link to him.

Next time he would arrange things so that the murder of a Guild boss and the kidnapping of his lover happened in the Underworld. No more relying on out-of-town talent. He would use Blue Amber.

CHAPTER ELEVEN

Gabriel was pouring a second cup of coffee for Lucy and thinking that it was very pleasant to have breakfast with her when the heavy black SUV pulled up in front of the apartment house. Lucy went to the window.

"Another Guild car," she reported. "Can't miss one. Has management ever considered a color other than black for its fleet?"

"No," Gabriel said. He set the pot down. "Tradition."

A short time later the entry buzzer went off.

"That'll be Joe," Gabriel said. "I'll get it."

He set the pot down and rezzed the button.

"It's me, Boss," Joe announced.

"Here you go." Gabriel hit the enter button. "When you're inside the lobby, take the stairs to the second floor. Number five."

"Got it," Joe said.

Otis was on top of the refrigerator, enthusiastically working his way through a bowl of scrambled eggs. He abandoned his breakfast, grabbed his toy dust bunny, and bounced down to the counter. He landed next to the toaster and gave Gabriel an expectant look.

"Sure, you can come with me," Gabriel said.

Otis launched himself up onto Gabriel's shoulder.

Lucy went back to the counter and sat down. "Tell Joe he's welcome to a cup of coffee."

Gabriel paused in the kitchen doorway and looked at her. His blood heated a little. This morning she was dressed for Underworld work in cargo trousers and a loose-fitting denim work shirt. The glamorous, mysterious witch from the night before was gone, but the cool, determined professional weather channeler was just as fascinating, just as compelling. Regardless of what she wore, the seductive power of her aura called to his senses.

He had to make himself continue toward the door.

Joe was standing in the hall. He had a pair of boots in one hand and a duffel bag in the other. "Your change of clothes, Boss. When I went into your apartment, I noticed you didn't have much in the way of furniture yet."

"I've been busy," Gabriel said.

"Right. The rest of your Underworld gear is in the back of your vehicle."

"Thanks." Gabriel stepped back and opened the door. "Come on in. Did Aiden pull up any information on those three guys who tried to get in our way last night?"

"Yep." Joe shook his head in disgust. "Low-rent, out-of-town muscle. The cops didn't recognize them. Definitely ex-Guild men, though. Freelancers who do contract work for anyone who will hire them."

"Who were they working for last night?"

"They claim they don't know. It was a brokered job as far as they're concerned, and the police believe them. I agree. Locating the broker won't be easy. You know how it is with those guys. They're very good at staying in the shadows. It's going to take a while to find whoever put the deal together, but there can't be a lot of guys who would take the risk of arranging the kidnapping and murder of a Guild boss."

"This is Illusion Town," Gabriel said. "I'm told the rules are a little different here."

Joe took the folded newspaper out from under his arm. "Thought you might want to take a look at this. You're famous. Again. So is Ms. Bell."

He thrust the papers into Gabriel's hand and reached up to give Otis a friendly pat.

"How's it going, little guy?" he asked. "You're famous, too."

Otis chortled a greeting.

Gabriel read the headline on the *Curtain. New Guild Boss Dating Woman He Rescued. A Real-Life Love Story in the Works?*

"Well, hell," he said. "Lucy is not going to be happy."

The front-page photo showed Lucy and himself emerging from the limo in front of the Amber Palace. They looked like any other formally dressed couple out for an evening on the town, except for the dust bunny in a sequined tux under her arm.

"Aiden said to tell you not to worry, Boss," Joe said. "This town loves a good celebrity story."

"How bad is it?" Lucy asked from the end of the short entry hall.

"It depends on your point of view," Gabriel said.

He held out the *Curtain* so she could see the headline and the photo.

"Crap." Lucy groaned. "When I was in the shower this morning I got a wild flash of optimism. I thought the press might go with something along the lines of *New Guild Boss Hires Local Weather Channeler for High-Priority Investigation.* But I suppose that was too much to expect."

Gabriel tossed the paper aside on an end table. "I was afraid you would take that particular point of view."

Lucy picked up the newspaper, unfolded it, and turned to the second page. "Guess what. There's another photo."

"Of us?" Gabriel asked.

"No." Lucy raised her eyes to meet his. She looked more grim than ever. "Of Otis."

She handed the paper back to him. The photo showed Otis in his snazzy little tux. He was perched on top of the massive engagement cake, munching on the sugar roses.

Gabriel tossed the paper aside for the second time. "Forget the headlines. We've got a job to do, remember?"

"Right." Lucy squared her shoulders. "Got to stay focused."

CHAPTER TWELVE

"The client doesn't want to wait any longer," Tuck said. He lounged against a workbench and hooked a thumb in the gear belt slung low on his hips. "The experiment will be conducted tonight. The client wants proof of concept before authorizing more funding for your lab."

His full name was Tucker Taylor, but after being kicked out of the Guild he had reinvented himself as just Tuck. It sounded stronger. More dangerous. It suited his new position as an elite operative in the Blue Amber Agency, an exclusive private security business.

"Fine, have it your way," Preston Trenchard muttered. "I've got enough of the liquid crystal to do one full-scale demonstration, but that's it."

"It happens tonight," Tuck said, putting a little more ice into his voice.

"I heard you the first time, all right? But I'm warning you, this will bring my work to a halt until you get me access to more of the crystal. To do that, you're going to have to deal with the weather problem."

"Don't worry, we'll take care of it."

"Don't worry? You've screwed up twice since you lost Bell, and all you've got to show for it are a couple of dead channelers."

"Relax. We brought them in from outside. Independents. None of the locals knew them. Hell, nobody was even aware they were in town." Tuck paused a beat for emphasis. "And nobody so much as blinked when they disappeared."

The implied threat sounded good, he thought. They both knew that no one would bat an eye if Preston Trenchard vanished. Trenchard was an inventor—eccentric, reclusive, obsessed with his theory and his creation. He had submitted one patent after another for decades. Thus far, every application had been rejected as frivolous. No government agency, no corporation, and no research institution would back him.

But a little more than four months ago, an anonymous client had offered to fund the development of a prototype of the machine.

"You must understand that we can't keep using second-rate talent," Trenchard said. "We need the best. I must have more of the crystal. You'll have to pick up the Bell woman again."

"What makes you think Bell is still capable of handling the project?" Tuck said. "By all accounts, she's developed some form of post-traumatic psychic stress. She hasn't worked underground since she escaped from the hospital."

"Because no one will hire her," Trenchard said, exasperated. "Ghost hunter teams and miners are a superstitious lot. They're afraid to work with Bell. But I've researched her psychic profile. I'm convinced she's the only one who might be able to access the pool of liquid crystal."

"The only one? There are hundreds of professional weather channelers scattered around the four city-states, not to mention all the indies who work off the books."

"Sure, but you can't keep kidnapping them at random. You've gone through two already. Bell has the talent we need, and she's an independent. There won't be many questions when she disappears."

"The new Guild boss is fucking Lucy Bell," Tuck said. "He's going to notice if she disappears again."

"So?" Trenchard grimaced in disgust. "Guild bosses go through women like popcorn. Make her disappearance look good and Jones will forget about her soon enough. If necessary you can send another woman around to get his attention. Everyone knows Guild men are very simple creatures when it comes to that sort of thing."

"We don't know how Jones will react if Bell vanishes again."

"Then I suggest you be more careful this time," Trenchard said through clenched teeth. "You're telling me to do my job. You can damn well do yours. You'll get your demonstration tonight. In return I must have more of the crystal immediately."

Tuck shrugged. "If the demonstration goes off the way you say it will, there will be more liquid crystal."

He straightened, opened the door, and went out into the never-ending gray fog that cloaked the Shadow Zone. Trenchard was wrong. The new Guild boss would notice if the woman disappeared. So would the press.

But if Jones and the woman both vanished together in the Underworld... things would be different. Accidents happened all the time down below. Everyone knew that.

CHAPTER THIRTEEN

Trenchard waited until the annoying security man was gone before he gave in to his frustration. He grabbed a wrench off the workbench and hurled it against the nearest wall.

It was infuriating. A man of his genius should have been working for one of the top labs in a major city-state like Cadence or Resonance. Instead, thanks to a lack of appreciation for his bold concepts, he was stuck in the backwater of Illusion Town, reduced to taking orders from an unknown client who hired thugs like the swaggering, bulked-up Tuck.

The only reason he was sticking around was because the client had the two things he required to achieve his goal: money and the vision to comprehend the revolutionary value of the suppressor weapon.

Trenchard had long dreamed of creating the device. For years he had been confident in the theory and the design. The stumbling block had been the lack of the unique liquid crystal required for power.

The unknown client had supplied the makeshift lab and three canisters of the crystal. There was enough left to put on an impressive demonstration, but once it was gone his work would come to a halt. He could not bear the thought. He was so close to perfecting the suppressor. Just a few more tweaks.

He contemplated his mediocre lab. Located in an abandoned house on a dead-end alley in the Shadow Zone, it was not what he had anticipated when he had been recruited. But he understood the need for secrecy and security. Tuck had promised that if the prototype was successful, there would be a state-of-the-art facility and all the liquid crystal needed to refine the invention.

Trenchard crossed the room, raised the shade, and looked out the grimy window. The fog was so thick at the moment that he could barely see the abandoned buildings across the way.

He despised the Shadow Zone, with its sleazy casinos, motels that rented rooms by the hour, and ever-present gray mist. But he had to admit Tuck was right. It had been critical to set up the lab in a location where it would not attract any notice from the authorities. The old warehouse on the fringe of the zone made for perfect camouflage.

Trenchard dropped the shade, clasped his hands behind his back, and considered how he would carry out the demonstration designed to prove the prototype worked. It could be done. He had just enough of the liquid crystal to make a suitable impression on the mysterious client.

Chapter Fourteen

The vortex of paranormal energy struck with very little warning. Otis sensed it first. He had been trotting along the narrow alley of the gray quartz city, darting back and forth, investigating small, glittering stones that captured his attention.

He abruptly froze, sleeked out, and growled a warning.

Lucy picked up the sense of gathering forces almost as quickly as Otis. She had been running hot, her talent at full throttle, ever since she and Gabriel and Otis had gone through the Coppersmith Mining portal located in the Rainforest.

Once safely on the other side, Gabriel had picked up the trail of the thief almost immediately. They had been moving quickly through the deserted Alien city. It was like walking through a dreamscape.

Every structure around them—the paving stones, oddly proportioned buildings, fountains, and plazas—was constructed of a strange, quicksilver-gray quartz. Paranormal energy resonated, whispered, and sparked everywhere. The light, shimmery fog that swirled in the streets and alleys had a muffling effect.

"Stop," she ordered softly.

Gabriel glanced at her and then studied the fog that drifted in the alley. "Storm?"

"Big one. I'm sure I could take it apart, but it's easier to just get out of the way. No sense wasting a lot of energy now. I might need it later for something more dangerous."

"Agreed."

Lucy glanced around. She had been noting possible emergency bolt-holes since entering the city. It was part of the job. Like a pilot who keeps an alternate landing site in mind, she kept track of options for storm shelters.

"That building over there will work," she said.

The storm was sweeping down the alley toward them. It raised the hair on the back of her neck and filled her with a shivery excitement. Most people found the sensation of a big paranormal storm frightening or downright terrifying, but she got a rush out of it.

"*Something wicked this way comes,*" she quoted softly.

Gabriel gave her a knowing look. "You've got a weird idea of fun, lady. Let's get out of here."

Otis growled, reversed course, and raced back to Lucy. She scooped him up and plopped him on her shoulder.

"Don't worry," she said. "We've got about sixty seconds."

"I've never liked the word *about*," Gabriel said. "A little too vague for my taste."

He grabbed her wrist. Together they plunged through the shimmering paranormal door that blocked the entrance to the building. There was some resistance, but the quicksilver door dissolved when they focused a little energy on it. The barrier re-formed immediately after they were safely inside.

Gabriel did not let go of Lucy's hand. Otis crouched on her shoulder. The three of them pressed close together. There was strength in numbers when it came to dealing with dangerous paranormal energy.

The gray quartz walls glowed with an inner light, but unlike the pleasant, senses-lifting energy of the green quartz ruins aboveground and in the tunnels, the vibe was disturbing on several levels.

"Ever heard the old saying *It feels like someone just walked over my grave?*" Gabriel asked.

"I think so, why?" she asked with mocking innocence.

"That must be weather channeler humor."

"Yep."

"No offense, but it also sounds a lot like Guild boss humor."

Lucy had spent enough time in the ancient metropolis to know that the structure in which they were sheltering offered life-saving protection. But no quartz wall could protect them from all of the senses-rattling effects of the storm.

Audio hallucinations whispered and howled in the alley on the other side of the quicksilver door. It was as if the specters of the vanished Aliens were shrieking at the humans, pleading with them, begging them to open the gate and let them inside.

Gabriel tightened his grip on Lucy's hand. She leaned against his chest, pressing close. He put an arm around her. *Nothing personal,* she told herself. Physical contact was standard operating procedure for situations like this. Two auras were stronger than one. Three were even better. Otis's small but powerful energy field added another level of protection.

The wailing became more fearsome. The ghosts were no longer pleading; they were demanding entrance. The door shivered and shimmered and trembled, but it did not give way.

An eternity that was, in reality, more like five minutes passed. The howling abruptly fell silent.

Lucy realized she was still crushed against Gabriel's chest, his arm wrapped tightly around her. Their hands were still clasped. It felt good to be this close to him. It felt right.

After a moment, Otis fluffed up and chortled. He bounced down to the floor and immediately set about exploring the empty chamber.

"I like his attitude," Gabriel said. "Deal with the problem when it hits the top of your to-do list. Forget about it as soon as it's over."

"Humans probably spend way too much time dwelling on what could happen and what almost happened," Lucy said. "Then we worry about what might happen next."

"That's a good description of my job," Gabriel said.

"Mine, too."

Lucy discovered she did not want him to let her go. The fantasies she had allowed herself to indulge in during the last two months whispered to her. She had to concentrate in order to make herself face reality.

Not good. Not smart. You've got a job to do. That's why he came looking for you. He needs your professional skills.

With a small sigh she stepped back. Gabriel released her, but she thought he did so with some reluctance. Probably wishful thinking.

"Never a dull moment in the Ghost City," she said, going for a cool, professional vibe. "It should be safe outside now. I'll go first to check the weather."

"Right." Gabriel studied the locator. "According to this, we should be very close to the doll."

Tentatively, Lucy focused a little energy on the quicksilver barrier. It dissolved. She stepped out into the alley. The fog that ebbed and flowed through the streets of the Ghost City was once again calm. Otis rushed after her, ready for the next stage of the adventure. Gabriel followed, once again checking the locator readout.

"To the left," he said. He took out his flamer. "Next intersection."

She glanced at the weapon. "Do you think we're going to run into that kind of trouble?"

"I doubt it," Gabriel said. "If anyone else had found the clockwork toy it would be long gone. No one, including bad guys, can hang around the Ghost City for more than a few hours at a time. The paranormal environment is too harsh. That's why Coppersmith is running several crews a day in short shifts. Why they set up the mining camp on the other side of the portal in the Rainforest instead of inside this place."

"I heard they are working on vehicles and equipment that can protect the miners."

"If any company can find a way to turn a profit down here, it's Coppersmith. But I'm told it's been one major technical problem after another. Here we go. Left again."

They turned the corner into another narrow lane. The fog elsewhere in the city had been light, but now they faced a wall of gray mist. It was so thick that Lucy could no longer make out the buildings on the other side of the lane. She could barely see her own boots.

Otis had disappeared into the ghostly atmosphere, but she heard him chortling. Every so often he popped out of the luminous gray fog long enough to show her a new chunk of quartz. She had no idea why some of the pebbles and crystals caught his fancy and others did not. They all looked pretty much the same to her—murky and gray.

"Hmm," she said. She stopped and pulled the pendant out from under her shirt. "The stone in this necklace is amber, but the color is almost identical to the gray quartz here in this sector."

Gabriel studied the pendant for a brief moment. "Same color, all right, but I haven't heard of any amber deposits being discovered in the Ghost City. We'll ask the experts at the mining camp about it when we leave."

"All right."

She dropped the pendant back under the shirt.

Gabriel consulted his locator again. "We're very close now. On the right."

This time he took the lead, flamer leveled. They made their way across the narrow passageway, guided by the locator. Sensing that it was time for serious work, Otis scurried out of the fog and joined Gabriel.

Lucy was finally able to make out a quicksilver door. "The doll is inside that building?"

"Looks like it," Gabriel said. "I'll go through first, just in case there's a reception committee waiting."

Lucy got out of the way. This was the kind of work that the ghost hunters got paid to do. She had done her job. The rest was up to Gabriel.

He vanished through the quicksilver door.

Lucy waited. She realized somewhat vaguely that she was holding her breath. Things felt wrong. But then, everything felt wrong in the Ghost City.

Gabriel reappeared in the doorway.

"We've got a problem," he said.

"What kind of problem?"

"The dead kind."

CHAPTER FIFTEEN

"You're sure that's the thief?" Lucy asked.

She made no attempt to take a closer look at the body, but Gabriel was satisfied that she wasn't going to fall apart. She was a professional, and this was not her first trip on the dangerous thrill ride that was the Underworld. He was amazed so many people had been convinced she couldn't handle the work belowground.

"It's Croston," he said. "The museum authorities showed me a photo."

"Was he murdered?" Lucy asked. "Or do you think he got caught in one of the storms and found shelter too late?"

"Hard to tell. There's no obvious wound."

"I'll bet someone murdered Croston for the artifact."

"That's a possibility, but if so, something went wrong. Croston still has his portal key." Gabriel held up a chunk of murky gray quartz. "These things are extremely valuable, especially to thieves and mercenaries.

They are the only way to access the Ghost City portals. I can't see a killer leaving one behind. There's something else, as well."

"What?"

Gabriel glanced at the locator. "This indicates the doll is still in the vicinity."

Lucy surveyed the chamber. "It's definitely not in this room, but there's a hallway. Who knows what's at the other end?"

Gabriel got to his feet and studied the arched opening on the far side of the chamber. The first few feet of a curving corridor could be seen. Shadows shifted and slithered inside the gray quartz walls of the hallway. They were probably optical illusions, but that did not make them any less disturbing on a lot of levels.

"Maybe he tried to hide the artifact," he said. "If so, it's probably in a chamber off that corridor. I'll take a look."

"All right. You know, if Croston had time to stash the artifact in another room, he obviously didn't die immediately."

"No, he didn't."

Otis hissed softly. Gabriel looked at him.

"Is he reacting to the body?" he asked.

Lucy glanced down. "Maybe. I don't know. Something is putting him on high alert."

A whirring sound emanated from the curving corridor. Gabriel spun around, flamer in hand.

The clockwork doll appeared. It was about three feet tall and dressed in an Old World costume, a somber but very elegant black gown with a high neckline and long sleeves. The artifact's dark hair was parted in the middle and tightly bound at the back. A crown of crystals glittered on her head. She gripped a fan in one gloved hand. Her face was set in stern, regal lines. Her eyes glittered with icy energy.

Otis growled.

Lucy was enchanted. "She looks like an Old World queen."

"Victoria, according to the Arcane experts," Gabriel said. "Late nineteenth century, Old World Date."

Otis rumbled a warning.

"She's amazing," Lucy said. "Just look at the detail in the clothes. I think the crystals in the crown are real, not glass."

Lucy started to go closer to get a better look.

"Don't move," Gabriel ordered.

The doll's glittering eyes got hotter. They locked onto Lucy. Gabriel sensed icy energy in the atmosphere.

Lucy shuddered and tried to scramble back out of range, but it was too late. She froze.

Otis sleeked out and raced toward the clockwork doll. He was no longer growling. All of his teeth were showing. Gabriel realized he was going for the queen's throat.

"Hang on, Otis," Gabriel said. "You won't be able to stop the damn thing."

Otis paused, but he didn't look patient. The room was getting colder. Lucy was statue-still.

Gabriel slipped his pack off, opened it, and took out the gadget the museum curator had given him. He rezzed it and aimed it at the clockwork doll.

The device generated a beam of white light. The doll stopped moving. The energy in the crystal eyes faded.

Lucy recovered with a gasp, as if she had been underwater a moment too long. Otis dashed back to her. She scooped him up and held him close.

"Are you all right?" Gabriel said.

"Yes, I think so." Lucy took a couple of deep breaths. "It felt as if I was being sucked down into the coldest part of the ocean. What did you do to stop that thing?"

He held up the small, hand-sized device. "Dr. Peabody, the curator of the museum, gave it to me on the off chance the doll might have been activated. It's designed to jam the thing's frequencies."

"Hmm." Lucy glanced at the body. "Think Croston activated the doll, maybe accidentally, and it killed him?"

"That's what it looks like."

"Well, the good news is that it's mission accomplished for us. We found the thief and recovered the doll."

Gabriel walked closer to the doll and crouched beside it to get a close look at the lethal toy. "Your work is done, but I'm a long way from finished."

"Why do you say that?"

"Because I doubt Croston would have taken the risk of stealing this particular artifact unless he had a buyer lined up."

"Oh, right," Lucy said. "I guess a Guild boss's work is never done."

He looked at her, unsure of her meaning.

She gave him a dazzling smile. "Let me know if you need a weather channeler for the next part of the investigation."

He relaxed. "I'll do that. Always a pleasure to work with a true professional."

She turned abruptly serious. "I owe you for giving me a chance, Gabriel. Because of you, I've got a real shot at rebuilding my reputation. I appreciate it."

"You don't owe me a damn thing. I wanted the best channeler in the business. That's who I got. Give me a couple of minutes to take some photos of the scene, and then we'll head back to the surface with the doll."

"What about the body?"

"I'm not going to haul a dead man through the streets of the Ghost City and try to get him through the portal. Croston's not going anywhere. Coppersmith will send in a team to collect him."

"Sounds like a plan."

High-tech phones and cameras didn't work in the paranormal environment underground, but photography was fundamentally a simple technology. Old-fashioned, amber-based cameras worked fine belowground. Every Guild agent carried one. Gabriel took out his and snapped several shots of Croston and the chamber.

When he was finished he hoisted the doll under one arm. The thing was surprisingly heavy, because it had been built with old-fashioned materials from Earth in an era before plastics and synthetics had been developed. He gripped the flamer in his free hand.

"You can do the navigating," he said to Lucy.

"Sure. Let me check the weather first."

She went to the door. He was aware of energy shifting in the atmosphere as she heightened her talent. The sensation stirred his senses. Everything inside him tightened a little.

He made himself focus on the job at hand. Priorities.

Lucy stepped through the shimmering silver door. Otis bounded after her. A few seconds later they both reappeared. Otis chortled.

"All clear," Lucy reported.

Gabriel tightened his grip on the big doll and followed Lucy and Otis through the shimmering doorway.

A thin quicksilver fog drifted in the empty lane. There was no way to know if it was day or night. In the Ghost City, it was always twilight.

"Now I see why that doll would have been worth stealing," Lucy said. "It's not just a valuable artifact; it's a serious weapon that functions in the Underworld. There are people who would kill to get their hands on that technology. But a large doll isn't what you'd call a convenient weapon."

"Whoever paid Croston to steal the queen must have been convinced the technology could be reverse engineered. Theoretically, once you understand the basic operating principles, you should be able to design a much more convenient version of the weapon."

"Maybe. But paranormal physics is complicated. It's possible that only someone with the same talent as the original engineer—"

"Mrs. Bridewell," Gabriel said.

"Right. There's a good chance that only someone with her talent could re-create the power source in that thing," Lucy said.

"That's Peabody's theory."

Otis fluttered ahead down the lane, pausing here and there to examine a small piece of quartz. As far as Gabriel could tell, nothing he had found so far met his high standards.

The dust bunny darted through a shimmering door and disappeared.

"Don't worry about him," Lucy said. "He'll catch up with us."

She glanced down at the locator. "Turn left."

They rounded the corner into another foggy lane. And stopped.

Two men armed with flamers exploded out of a quicksilver doorway. One got an arm around Lucy's throat. He yanked her hard against his chest.

"That's far enough, Jones," he said. He wore a huge chunk of amber in his belt buckle. "Drop the flamer or I'll use mine on the woman."

"Take it easy," Gabriel said. He crouched and set the flamer on the quartz pavement.

"Thanks for deactivating the damned doll for us," the other man said. His greasy hair was tied back with a leather thong. "We'll take it from here."

CHAPTER SIXTEEN

Lucy had been running hot, concentrating on reading the weather ahead as well as keeping track of the indicator lights on the locator. The man had struck like a snake, wrapping his arm around her throat before she realized what was happening. He stank of adrenaline-fueled sweat. The vibe of his aura was spiked with blood-chilling violence. Psychopath.

"Now put the doll down, Jones," the man with the ponytail ordered.

Out of the corner of her eye, Lucy caught a glimpse of her attacker's belt buckle. Ostentatious, to say the least, she decided.

"Sure," Gabriel said. He lowered the doll so that it was standing upright, deadly eyes pointed at Ponytail. "I take it you paid Croston to steal the queen. Did you kill him?"

"We were going to get rid of him, but the doll saved us the trouble," Ponytail said. "Somehow the machine got activated. We didn't want to get near it. We knew you and the weather channeler were on the way, so we decided to wait and let you do the hard work for us. The client thought you might be able to deal with it."

Otis appeared, racing around the corner. He was sleeked out. Lucy knew he was going to go straight for the throat of Sweat-Stink.

"It's a fucking dust bunny," Ponytail muttered. He aimed the flamer at Otis.

"No," Lucy said quickly. "Please. Don't hurt him."

"Stop that rat or I'll burn it," Ponytail ordered.

"Otis," Lucy said quietly, "it's okay. I've got this."

Otis stopped, but he did not take his four eyes off Sweat-Stink.

Gabriel looked at Lucy. "Do you have it?"

"No problem," she said. "Tons of energy down here to work with."

Ponytail glanced at her and scowled. "What the fuck are you talking about?"

"Just chatting," Lucy said.

She rezzed her talent to the max and went to work. A glorious exultation swept through her. She summoned the energy that was infused into the atmosphere and channeled it.

Ghosts whispered in the lane. The whispers swiftly turned to shrieks and wails. The silvery fog thickened rapidly. Thunder boomed.

"Shit," Ponytail muttered. "Storm. Big one. We need to get inside. Leave Jones and the woman out here. The weather will take care of them for us."

"What about the doll?" Sweat-Stink said.

"Forget it." Ponytail headed for a nearby door. He kept the flamer aimed at Gabriel. "It's lasted this long. It will probably survive the storm."

Sweat-Stink released Lucy and hurried after his pal.

Flashes of energy sparked. Lightning shattered the atmosphere. A senses-dazzling bolt struck Ponytail when he was a foot away from a silvery door. He stiffened, his face twisted into a monstrous mask.

Sweat-Stink collided with him. Another bolt flashed in the fog. For a moment both men looked as if they had been cast in a tableau straight out of a horror film. In the next instant they crumpled to the ground.

The thrill of raw power blazed through Lucy's veins. So much *energy*. And she was channeling it. She was in control, a goddess unleashing lightning.

"Lucy," Gabriel said quietly.

She laughed, because his hair was standing on end. So was Otis's fur. She turned in a circle, savoring the wild storm she had created.

"Lucy," Gabriel said again. Louder this time.

He walked toward her.

"Don't you just love a good storm?" she said.

"Some other time, maybe," he said. "You need to come down, Lucy."

"Why? I'm flying."

"Yeah, I can see that." Gabriel smiled. "You're high on psi, Lucy. Time to come back to the real world."

"I feel real." She put her hand on his shoulder. "You're real, too, aren't you?"

"I think so."

A fierce excitement flashed through her.

"The first time I saw you I thought you were a hallucination," she said.

"Did you?"

"But you're not. You're my very own Lord of the Underworld."

"Uh, Lucy—"

She threw her arms around his neck and kissed him with all the energy flooding her body. He went very still.

"Damn it," he said against her lips. "Wrong time. Wrong place."

But he kissed her back, hard and fierce, and there was so much energy in the physical connection that she knew they were both flying. They stood in the eye of the magnificent storm that whirled around them.

Gabriel abruptly set her aside. "Lucy. Stop. Now."

She took a deep breath. He was right. Wrong time, wrong place. Reluctantly she lowered her senses.

The otherworldly gale dissipated almost immediately.

"Sorry about that," she said. "Things got a little out of control."

"I'll say." Gabriel studied her. "I've never known a weather channeler who could pull a storm like that. There was lightning. The real deal."

"Yeah, well, there aren't many of us who can do the lightning thing. Those of us who have the ability usually keep quiet about it. It's not good for business. Clients get nervous if they think you can turn that kind of energy against them." She cleared her throat. "Didn't mean to scare you."

"My nerves will survive." He looked surprisingly satisfied, as if she had just confirmed something he had suspected all along. "You're not just a strong talent, you're an off-the-charts talent. No wonder finding out that I'm a dual talent didn't worry you."

He turned and walked toward the men sprawled on the ground. She watched him pat them down, removing flamers, knives, and other assorted gear. Otis joined him, watching the process with deep interest.

Ponytail and Sweat-Stink did not move. From where Lucy stood they did not appear to be breathing. A tide of dread descended on her, sluicing away the last of the euphoria.

She cleared her throat. "Are they—?"

"Alive?" Gabriel removed an energy bar from Ponytail's cargo pocket and gave it to Otis. "Yes. Amazing, really, considering they were struck by paranormal lightning."

Otis got very excited—his usual response to anything he considered a treat. He ripped open the wrapping of the energy bar. Gabriel continued with the pat-down.

Lucy took a deep breath. Okay, the good news was that she hadn't actually killed anyone. Ponytail and Sweat-Stink were not nice guys, but she did not want to have the weight of their deaths on her conscience for the rest of her life. Punishing them was the job of the judicial system.

The bad news was that Gabriel now knew what she could do, given an intense paranormal environment. Most clients would be alarmed by the wild side of her talent. Anyone who wanted to employ a weather channeler *because* of her ability to generate a potentially lethal storm was probably not someone she wanted to work for. Generally speaking, there were no legal uses for killer storms.

"Sometimes I get a little carried away," she ventured.

"I noticed." Gabriel stood, removed his camera, and started taking photos. "I'd really like to talk to these two, but obviously they are not in a chatty frame of mind at the moment, and we don't have time to hang around down here. One of them must have a portal key. As soon as I find it, I'll cuff them and haul them into one of these chambers. With a little luck, they'll still be here when the Coppersmith security team comes down to collect Croston's body."

Lucy became aware of a warm sensation between her breasts. She had felt it earlier, but she had been so busy channeling storm energy that she hadn't paid any attention. The entire Underworld had seemed hot for a few minutes.

Alarmed, she hauled the chain out from under her shirt and stared at the amber pendant.

"Gabriel, look."

She held up the pendant. The amber was no longer gray. It was glowing a deep, eerie blue.

"That's the color it was when the fake doctor gave me the injection in the para-psych clinic," she said. "It lit up when the other demon—I mean, creepy bad guy—came into the room. It's the color of the pendants that the kidnappers wore. Maybe using my talent activated it. Or the energy in the doll's eyes?"

"But you just now noticed it?"

"Yes. No. I think it started getting warm a few minutes ago, but I was distracted by those two guys with the flamers. And then there was that storm and the lightning and, well, I wasn't paying close attention, if you see what I mean."

"So you didn't notice it until this pair showed up?"

"Right."

Gabriel tugged the leather jacket off Sweat-Stink, exposing a stained khaki shirt that had seen better days. He opened the front of the shirt.

A portal key dangled from a chain around Sweat-Stink's throat. So did something else: a crystal that glowed blue. Without a word, Gabriel moved to Ponytail and opened the man's shirt. Lucy saw another pendant. It, too, radiated a blue light.

Gabriel snapped the chain that held Ponytail's pendant. Gripping the stone in one hand, he walked several feet away from the unconscious men. The blue glow of the amber faded rapidly. He turned around and walked toward Lucy. The pendant brightened. So did the one that Lucy wore around her neck.

"The ambers are tuned to respond to each other," Gabriel said. "Signal stones. Must be a form of identification for a gang."

"Like a tattoo or a secret password."

"Right."

"Those three men who tried to grab you last night weren't wearing blue crystals," Lucy pointed out. "Neither was Croston."

"No, which is interesting."

"They took a big risk ambushing us down here."

"No," Gabriel said. "It's the perfect spot for an ambush. Lethal accidents happen in the Ghost City. Searchers would have found my body, and it would have looked like I died of natural causes. I think you would have vanished."

"It's me they wanted, isn't it? You were in the way, so they tried to take you out."

"That's what this looks like."

"And to think I always wanted to be one of the popular A-list kids back in boarding school."

CHAPTER SEVENTEEN

"I can't begin to tell you how relieved we are to have the arti-fact back in the vault, Mr. Jones," the curator said. "Obviously we must upgrade our security here at the museum."

His name was Reginald Peabody. He was in charge of the Midnight Carnival, the legendary museum of the Arcane Society. Lucy listened absently to the conversation he and Gabriel were engaged in while she wandered through the enchanting array of exhibits, scaled-down thrill rides, and miniature towns and buildings.

Peabody had explained that the Carnival had been constructed and concealed in the Underworld tunnels soon after the Curtain closed. It occupied a vast chamber and looked like a real, working carnival, right down to a fortune-telling booth and a hot dog stand.

The museum had been designed and built by one Aloysius Jones, a historian who had been obsessed with preserving the Old World history of the Arcane Society. In the chaotic years following the closing of the Curtain, the First Generation colonists had been focused on survival.

When the machines and computers had failed, much of the past had been lost or had morphed into the realm of legends and myths. Aloysius Jones had feared that the descendants of the founders who had ties to Arcane would forget their own secret history. He had concluded that the safest way to preserve it was in the form of a visual story—the Midnight Carnival. His theory had been that, while the historical record might disappear altogether, legends had a way of surviving.

"All security systems are vulnerable to an inside job," Gabriel said to Peabody. "The first line of defense is thorough employee background screening. After that you should review your systems. Unfortunately, none of the high-tech gear will work down here. Normally I would advise you to hire a Guild security consultant to evaluate your situation, but considering that the Carnival is a unique museum, I think you'd be better off bringing in a Jones and Jones consultant."

Peabody sighed. "It's been on my to-do list ever since the Society acquired the rights to the Carnival, but I haven't had time to get to it. Obviously it will now go to the top of my ever-lengthening agenda."

"Yeah, I've got one of those lists, too. Which reminds me, I have a question for you." Gabriel took out the two pendants he had confiscated. "Ever seen anything like this amber?"

Lucy paused to listen to Peabody's response.

The curator examined the glowing amber, brow tightening into heavy lines. "No. Very unusual color. Signal or identification rocks, I assume. Clubs and biker gangs use them. So do scout troops and sports teams."

"Try walking about twenty feet away," Gabriel said. "That will take you out of range."

Peabody walked across the space and stopped next to an exhibit marked, HEADQUARTERS OF NIGHTSHADE. BEWARE THE DRUG. He stopped and held up the pendant. It no longer glowed blue. Instead it had returned to a murky gray.

"Fascinating," Peabody said. "I've never seen amber like this. I wouldn't be surprised if it came from the Ghost City. It's the same color as everything else that has been coming out of those ruins."

"You're sure it's not Arcane?"

"Well, I can't be one hundred percent positive without running some tests, but I don't think so." Peabody paused and closed his hand around the pendant. He concentrated for a moment and then shook his head. "No. It doesn't have the feel of an Old World object. That vibe is very distinctive."

"Thanks," Gabriel said.

Lucy wandered down the main street of a miniature town named Scargill Cove. She stooped to read the small sign in a window. JONES & JONES. PSYCHIC INVESTIGATORS.

She straightened quickly when she heard Otis chortle. He sounded excited. She looked over the rooftops of Scargill Cove and saw a flash of gray fur disappear into what looked like a tunnel ride fashioned of some sort of purple crystal.

There was more chortling, muffled now. Probably not a good sign.

Lucy exited Scargill Cove and headed for the entrance to the crystal tunnel. She went past a full-sized carousel populated with creatures she had only seen in children's books featuring Old World fairy tales. There was something ominous about the crystal eyes of the animals.

More muffled chortling echoed from inside the purple tunnel. When she reached the entrance, she saw a sign: THE SECRET LAB OF SYLVESTER JONES.

The tunnel curved immediately past the entrance. Lucy could not see around the corner, but she could hear thumps and increasingly irritated growls.

"Otis, come out of there. You'll break something. This is a museum. This stuff is super valuable."

Otis growled some more. There was a significant increase in the thumping.

Gabriel materialized at Lucy's side. "What's going on?"

"Otis just went into that exhibit."

The crystal walls of the tunnel started to glow an eerie shade of purple.

"I've got a bad feeling about this," Lucy said.

Peabody rushed across the room to join them. "Did the dust bunny go in there? You must stop him. That exhibit is the most valuable one in the entire collection."

"I'll get him," Gabriel said.

He moved through the entrance and disappeared around the corner.

"Otis?" he called. His voice echoed down the tunnel. "What are you doing, pal?"

Otis chortled enthusiastically, evidently pleased to have assistance.

"Let's see what you've got," Gabriel said. He sounded intrigued. "Huh. Interesting. I wonder what happens if you rez this button?"

"Stop them," Peabody pleaded. "Please, Ms. Bell, tell Mr. Jones to stop."

"Why don't you tell him?" Lucy said. "You're in charge down here."

"He's a Guild boss," Peabody hissed. "One doesn't go around giving orders to a Guild boss, especially when he has just done you a huge favor and you know you'll probably need more favors in the future."

"Oh, right."

A muffled rumble reverberated from inside the tunnel. It was followed by a slow clanking sound. Otis chortled madly.

"Move over," Gabriel said. "I want to sit in front, too."

"Do something, Ms. Bell," Peabody wailed.

"Cover me. I'm going in."

"Cover you?" Peabody gave her a quizzical look. "I don't understand."

"Never mind."

Lucy hurried through the doorway and around the corner. The

glowing walls illuminated a small train that was already in motion. She caught a glimpse of Gabriel and Otis in the front seat.

She opened her mouth to shout *Come back here*, but it was too late. The train was picking up speed, rumbling forward, about to round a corner. Unable to think of anything else to do, she managed to jump aboard. The train jerked. She lost her balance and half fell onto the last bench seat.

The train clattered into a glowing purple chamber. A full-sized figure of a bearded man dressed in a pointed hat and flowing robes hovered over a laboratory workbench. The robes were decorated with stars and ancient alchemical symbols. Sylvester Jones, no doubt.

Sylvester appeared to be intent on a chemical reaction that was taking place in a purple crystal vessel. A leather-bound notebook was on the workbench. It was open to a page filled with what looked like a formula. The symbols were all handwritten. There were more leather-bound books on a nearby shelf. A large glass case filled with dried herbs and small, dark green bottles that appeared to contain mysterious powders stood against the wall.

"Meet my ancestor, Otis," Gabriel said. "The old man is said to have invented a unique formula back on Earth in the seventeenth century, Old World Date. They say it affected his DNA. The Jones family hasn't been the same since."

The train came to a stop. Gabriel and Otis got out and headed for the workbench.

"Don't touch anything," Lucy ordered. "Get back on board, both of you."

Otis chortled and held up a small object he had found on the workbench.

"Put it down," Lucy said. "I mean it, Otis."

"Better do as she says," Gabriel said. "We can take a closer look some other time. Right now we've got bigger problems."

Otis put down his treasure and bounced back to the train. Gabriel got in beside him. The vehicle lurched into motion, heading for another curve.

Gabriel turned in the seat and looked back at Lucy. "I didn't know you had come along for the ride."

"Dr. Peabody is very upset," Lucy said. "But he was afraid to try to order you off this ride."

"Being a Guild boss has its privileges," Gabriel said. "Besides, it's a carnival ride."

"These are valuable and possibly dangerous artifacts. This isn't an amusement park, it's a museum."

"I guess it depends on your point of view."

The train clanked down a short corridor and came to a halt. A sign announced the end of the ride. Gabriel and Otis got out of the front seat. Lucy stepped down from the rear bench.

"This is so embarrassing," Lucy said as they walked out of the purple cave. "I can't take you two anywhere."

Peabody was waiting anxiously. "Did the dust bunny break anything?"

"No," Lucy said. "I apologize on behalf of Mr. Jones and Otis."

Peabody flushed. "I'm sure there was no harm done."

"Very interesting exhibit," Gabriel said. "I'd like to come back and take a closer look one of these days."

"Certainly, Mr. Jones," Peabody said. "Anytime."

Lucy thought his tone of voice lacked enthusiasm.

The big utility vehicle was parked in a narrow lane in the Shadow Zone. Night had fallen. The shabby neighborhood, with its low-end casinos, cheap motels, and discount wedding chapels, took on a noir glamour after dark.

Gabriel opened the door for Lucy. She grabbed a handhold and vaulted up onto the passenger seat. Otis perched on the back of the seat. It gave him a good view out the front window.

Gabriel climbed in behind the wheel and rezzed the engine.

"What's next?" Lucy asked.

"Next we get some sleep."

She wondered how to ask the obvious question: *Where are you going to sleep?* But she had a feeling she knew the answer. He wasn't going to let her out of his sight until they discovered how she was connected to the thugs who had worn the pendants.

"My place," she said, resigned.

"Good choice. I don't have any furniture yet. I've been sleeping on the floor."

"In that case, definitely my place."

CHAPTER EIGHTEEN

Gabriel drove out of the Shadow Zone, which ran the length of one of the eight Walls, and turned the corner into the brightly illuminated Amber Zone.

He was immediately aware of the very different vibe of the neighborhood. The gloom and fog vanished, as did the aura of faded sleaze that characterized the Shadow Zone. Within the Amber Zone it was all bright lights and glittering gambling palaces. Crowds strolled the sidewalks enjoying the clear, balmy night and the buzz of excitement. At the end of the Strip, the recently opened Alien Storm Roller Coaster towered into the night sky.

Lucy lowered the window on her side of the vehicle and smiled. "I love this town."

"Never a dull moment, that's for sure." Gabriel glanced at her, amused by her obviously genuine affection for the town.

"You were born and raised here until you were thirteen," he said. "It's your home. No wonder it's in your blood."

"Mom and I lived in the Dark Zone until she died. She was a dealer at one of the big casinos on the Strip." Lucy stopped abruptly and then turned her head to look at him. "You know about my past?"

He wanted to give himself a head slap. "I did a little research before I went looking for you."

"In other words, you've got a file on me?" she asked.

She sounded suspicious.

"Part of the job," he admitted. "When people suddenly go missing there are usually a few clues in their past that help narrow the search process."

"Right. Assembling a file on me was research for the mission."

There was no need to add that he knew that following her mother's death she had been bundled off to a boarding school. After graduation she had immediately returned to Illusion Town. These days she only saw her father, stepmother, and half brothers at the customary mandatory family gatherings.

"Lucy—" he said.

"Never mind. There's no need for an explanation. You took a perfectly logical approach to my case, and I'm sure you'll apply that same logic when you reopen it. Which I truly do appreciate, by the way."

He tried to come up with a way to change the conversation.

"What made you decide to pursue your weather channeling here in Illusion Town?" he said.

She laughed. "The weather, of course."

He smiled. "Illusion Town does have a lot of dramatic climates."

"Two zones are virtually uninhabitable," she said. "The Fire Zone and the Storm Zone. People can go into both zones under certain conditions, but no sane person would try to live in either zone. I'm sure your new Guild will be fielding a lot of calls from the local police asking you to chase down bad guys, thrill seekers, and the occasional kidnapping victims who disappear into those zones."

"You like interesting weather," he said deliberately. "I like interesting work."

There was a long silence from the passenger seat. So much for his conversational skills.

"Think you'll ever marry?" Lucy asked. "I mean a real Covenant Marriage?"

The question stunned him. He had to take a moment.

"Eventually," he said, feeling his way. "When the time is right. Everyone gets married eventually. Usually. Everyone in the Jones family ends up in a Covenant Marriage. My turn will come. Why do you ask?"

"Just curious. You've made it clear that your job has top priority in your life."

He was a Guild boss. He could sense impending disaster when he saw it. The conversation had taken a harrowing turn.

"I'm serious about my work," he said. He was pleased with his response. It sounded both professional and sincere.

"Yeah, I did get that impression. Guild men usually marry into other Guild families, don't they?"

"It's traditional," he said. "But there's no rule about it. There have been plenty of exceptions over the years." Okay, he was flailing. He needed to level the playing field, and fast. "What about you? Think you'll try another Marriage of Convenience one of these days?"

"I doubt it. Given recent experience, I'm not keen on the idea."

"What about a Covenant Marriage?"

"Like most people, I'd like to find someone to love, get married for real, and have a family."

"I understand."

Thanks to the rigid laws and customs instituted by the First Generation, family was everything on Harmony. Preserving and strengthening the family unit had been a primary goal of the Colonial governments. It had been viewed as the basic building block of society. Strong families meant strong communities. The First Generation had concluded that forging social bonds was essential if the colonists were to have a chance of surviving.

Some traditions had eased over the past two hundred years, but there was no escaping the fact that, sooner or later, everyone was supposed to enter a permanent Covenant Marriage. Sexual orientation was not a factor. You were free to marry anyone you wanted to marry, but you *were* expected to marry.

The longing to have a legitimate family was probably even more powerful for someone who had been born out of wedlock, he thought.

"Got anyone in mind?" he asked quietly.

"Nope, not at the moment. I've had other things to worry about lately."

"Right." He slowed the big vehicle as he joined the traffic crawling along the Strip. "Speaking of which, I can't be with you night and day—"

"Of course not. You've got a lot of work to do—close the case of the stolen doll, establish the new Guild headquarters, et cetera, et cetera. I understand. No problem."

"And because I need time to do some investigation work on your case," he said. He was beyond flailing. He was starting to lose his temper. He *never* lost his temper. "It's not a good idea for you to be alone, not until I find the kidnappers."

"I don't need a babysitter, Gabriel."

"Yes, you do, but we will call him a bodyguard. Jared's feelings will be crushed if you call him a babysitter."

"Jared?"

"Jared Flint. He's a member of my start-up team. He's been complaining about getting stuck with a lot of paperwork. Accompanying you on your Storm Zone Adventure Tours will give him a break."

"What will you be doing while I'm driving the bus with Jared riding shotgun?"

"I'm going to track down the tuner who tuned the amber in the pendants."

Lucy perked up, her interest sparked. "Great idea. How do you go about that? There are a gazillion tuners in Illusion Town."

"The quartz is unusual, and so is the tuning work. Someone in the trade will know who handled the job. When I find the tuner, I should be able to find out who commissioned the work."

"That sounds like a very logical plan."

He wasn't sure if she was impressed or being sarcastic.

"It's what I do, Lucy."

"I know. Got a plan to furnish your new apartment?"

"What? No." He frowned. "Why?"

"I would think it would be high on your list of priorities," Lucy said. "You're moving here. This will be home for the foreseeable future. Seems reasonable that you would want to get some furniture."

"Furnishing my apartment is at the bottom of my to-do list," he said. "In fact, at the moment it's not even on the list. When I've got time I'll have Aiden hire someone to take care of the furniture issue."

"You're going to ask your administrative assistant to oversee the decorating of your new apartment?"

"Aiden is good when it comes to taking care of details."

"The furniture you will be living with isn't a *detail.*"

"Most of my time is spent at the office."

"Of course." She paused. "Why didn't you bring your old furniture with you?"

"I didn't have any. It was all rented. It went back to the agency when I moved. I'm sure I can rent more here in Illusion Town."

"At your age, you should not be renting furniture."

"My age?"

"It's not like you're just starting out in your career," Lucy said. "You're at the pinnacle of success but you're still renting furniture. That's depressing."

Startled, he glanced at her. "Depressing?"

"Never mind. It's none of my business."

"No, it's not."

He stopped talking, because the SUV was slowing down. He glanced at the display screens built into the dash. All of the readouts showed that the engine was shutting down. The headlights went out.

"What's going on?" Lucy asked.

"I don't know, but for now we're going to assume the worst: someone has sabotaged the vehicle."

"Weird place for an ambush. We're in the middle of the Strip. There are thousands of people on the street. Security everywhere."

"Get ready to bail when I give the word."

"Okay."

"I never thought I'd say this, but have you got your little pistol?"

Lucy opened her pack and took out the small mag-rez. "Oh, yeah." She unclipped her seat belt, grabbed Otis, and prepared to open her door. "I assume we're going to head for the closest casino? There will be tons of security inside."

"Right. The Amber Palace."

Gabriel got the mag-rez out of his shoulder rig. The SUV came to a full stop. He put on the parking brake. He was about to order Lucy to jump when he realized that the cars around him were also stopping. Headlights went out by the dozens. Traffic came to a complete halt.

"I'm not so sure this is personal," Lucy said. "Everyone is getting out of their cars. Look, the casinos are starting to go dark, too."

The big glowing signs that marked the entrances to the casinos began blinking. One by one they went out. The lights inside the casinos became faint. People poured out into the street.

A moment later the human-engineered lighting of the Strip disappeared entirely, leaving the streets and darkened buildings in the long shadows and acid-green radiance of the nearby quartz Wall.

"Looks like a power failure," Gabriel said, "not an ambush." He opened the console and took out the flashlight. Nothing happened when he rezzed the switch. "Check the charge in your gun."

"It's dead," Lucy reported. She tucked it into her pack.

"It's not just the local grid that has failed. The amber in our weapons and the flashlight aren't connected to the city's power station. Something has killed all of the amber-based energy in this part of town."

"I've never heard of anything that could do that," Lucy said.

"Neither have I. But this is Illusion Town. Some very powerful forces were unleashed here a long time ago, forces that were strong enough to rip holes in the Wall and topple the towers in the Dead City."

"And now we've started opening up the Ghost City down below," Lucy said. "Maybe we've disturbed those forces."

"If so, I'm going to be very glad I didn't invest in a lot of new furniture."

"Is that another example of Guild boss humor?"

"Sorry."

Screams echoed in the night.

Lucy stiffened.

Gabriel listened for a few seconds. "Relax. It's just the people trapped on the roller coaster."

Lucy shuddered. "They've got a right to scream. I'd be screaming, too. Looks like it's going to be a long walk home, but at least we're on the ground and can actually *walk* home."

"True. I'll secure the vehicle."

"How? Everything in the car is amber-powered. We're lucky the doors are mechanical."

"Standard safety feature. Don't worry, there are other ways to protect a vehicle like this."

He slipped the mag-rez back into the shoulder holster, opened the door, and went around to the rear of the SUV. Lucy jumped down to the pavement, Otis tucked under one arm. She watched curiously.

"What are you going to do?" she asked.

"Leave a note on the car requesting people not to steal it when the power comes on," he said.

"A nice little note *requesting* people not to steal it? You really think that will work?"

"It usually does."

He rezzed his dissonance talent. Because the Dead City Wall was so close, there was plenty of energy available. A small ball of green ghost light burned in the night and quickly coalesced into a miniature fireball about six inches in diameter. He positioned it above the license plate.

Lucy whistled softly. "Okay, that will certainly send a message. *Guild boss's car. Don't touch.* No smart car thief is going to risk stealing it."

"That's the plan. The flaw is that not all car thieves are smart."

People climbed out of nearby cars to see what was going on.

"It's the new Guild Boss and his girlfriend," a man said.

Lucy whirled to face the small crowd. She raised her voice. "The name is Lucy Bell. I'm a weather channeler currently under contract with the Guild."

"Jones and that weather channeler were on the front page of the *Curtain* this morning," a woman exclaimed. "Looks like the press is right. They're dating."

"No," Lucy said. "This is a business relationship, damn it."

Otis chose that moment to wriggle out from under Lucy's arm and hop up onto Gabriel's shoulder.

"He knows an audience when he sees one," Lucy said.

Otis chortled at the crowd.

"Look, there's the dust bunny," a man observed. "Must be the same one that destroyed the fancy engagement party cake last night."

"The article in the *Curtain* said that cake cost a couple of thousand dollars," a woman announced.

Lucy stared at her. "A couple of thousand dollars?"

She sounded as if she had just had the breath knocked out of her lungs.

The woman who had quoted the price spoke up again. "Well, it was a Covenant Wedding engagement party, not some cheap Marriage of Convenience affair."

Lucy looked as if she was in a trance. "A couple of thousand dollars?"

This time her voice was a thin whisper.

"Forget the cake," Gabriel said. He took a firm grip on her arm. "Let's get our packs. It's been a long day, and we've got a hike ahead of us."

"A couple of thousand dollars."

Now she sounded numb.

"Don't worry about the damn cake," Gabriel said. "Put it down as a business expense when you submit your invoice to the Guild."

Lucy snapped out of her trance. "Seriously?"

"Seriously."

"But it wasn't really a business expense—"

"Call it collateral damage."

"Well, if you insist."

"I insist."

He opened the door of the vehicle, hauled out her pack, and handed it to her. A thought occurred to him. He took out one of the amber pendants he had taken off the attackers. It glowed a deep blue.

"Check your pendant, Lucy," he said.

She pulled it out from under her shirt. It was illuminated. "It's still hot," she said. "What does that tell us?"

"That it's not standard rez amber. It isn't affected by whatever shut down the Strip. Interesting."

Before he could pursue the matter, the lights of the casinos and cars flared. Loud cheers went up the length of the Strip.

"Look," Lucy said. "The signs, the casinos, and the hotels. Everything is working again. The power company fixed the problem. Thank goodness. We won't have to walk all the way back to my apartment."

Car engines hummed. Headlights blinked back to life. The Alien Storm roller coaster lurched forward. The casinos blazed and sparkled in the night.

Gabriel dropped his pack on the floor of the car and surveyed the brilliantly illuminated Strip.

"This should take us off the front page of the *Curtain* tomorrow morning," he said. "I'll be interested to know what went wrong at the power station."

CHAPTER NINETEEN

Lucy rezzed the lock of her front door, walked into the hall, and rezzed the lights. With a cheerful chortle, Otis bounced down to the floor and zipped into the living room. He stopped in front of the sliding glass doors that opened onto the balcony and chortled again.

Lucy opened the door for him. He bounded across the small balcony, hopped up onto the railing, and then disappeared over the side.

"Where is he going?" Gabriel said.

"Sometimes he takes off at night for a few hours. He often returns with a little chunk of quartz or amber. I think he hangs out with other dust bunnies in the ruins. When he's finished partying, he'll come home."

"How does he get back inside your apartment? It's two stories above the street. Please don't tell me you leave the balcony doors open at night."

"No, of course not. When he gets back he'll show up on the balcony and let me know he's home. Trust me, he's not subtle about it."

Gabriel looked around, contemplating her warmly lit apartment with a speculative expression. It wasn't hard to guess what he was thinking.

"It's kind of scary to realize that everything can suddenly stop functioning in a heartbeat, isn't it?" she said.

"It's an eye-opener, that's for sure," Gabriel said. "Makes me think about what it must have been like for the First Generation when they realized the Curtain had closed and they were stranded with Old World technology that was crumbling in front of them."

She shivered. "Yes."

She went back into the entry hall, set her pack on the floor, and slipped off her leather jacket.

Gabriel followed her and took off his own pack. His grim expression worried her.

"What?" she asked.

"I'm thinking that what happened tonight makes you realize we may have become too dependent on rez amber to operate everything from our cars to our refrigerators." He shrugged out of his jacket. "The city-states need to consider developing alternative sources of power."

Lucy sat down on the hall bench and went through the process of removing her boots. "Resonating amber has always been cheap, available, and nonpolluting. Pretty much the perfect energy source."

"It's also been extremely reliable. I've never heard of an incident like the one we witnessed tonight. Rez amber has to be tuned periodically. It can melt if you push enough energy through it, but a city's power grid is fueled by thousands of expertly tuned amber bars. They're designed and installed in an alternating sequence on a chain that makes it impossible for a large number of them to fail simultaneously."

"You know what they say—*there's no such thing as impossible.*"

"True." He sat down beside her and unbuckled his scarred and scuffed boots.

"Are you wondering if this might be a problem that will require the Guild's attention?" she asked.

He set one boot neatly under the bench and went to work on the other. "Yes."

"Seems like a problem for engineers, not the Guild."

"You said it yourself, Lucy. Something destroyed the Dead City eons ago. What if the mining operations down in the Ghost City have unleashed that force again?"

She sat back, lounging against the wall, and thought about all that had happened in the past twenty-four hours. "You know, we suddenly have a lot of mysteries tangled up here."

"Yes, we do. And it strikes me that, viewed from a certain perspective, they all involve you."

"Me?" She snapped to an upright position on the bench. "You think I'm to blame for the fact that someone tried to kidnap and murder you? And for the missing clockwork doll? And . . . and those guys who attacked us down in the Ghost City? *And* the lights going out on the Strip tonight?"

"No, I don't think any of those things is your fault. I'm just saying that in one way or another you've been in the picture, starting with the kidnapping two months ago."

She slanted a long glance at him. "I sense a conspiracy theory."

"At this point it doesn't amount to a theory, just an observation."

"You can't possibly connect me to that power outage tonight."

Gabriel didn't answer. He put the other boot under the bench, got to his feet, and went to the jacket he had hung up in the closet. Reaching into a pocket, he took out one of the two amber pendants he had confiscated from the men who had confronted them in the Ghost City. He studied it as if he was trying to read cryptic runes.

"Gabriel?" she said.

He looked up. "I have to find whoever tuned this amber. It's the key."

The cold determination in his eyes told her everything she needed to know.

"You will find the tuner," she said.

His expression softened a little. "You sound very sure of that."

"I am certain of it." She smiled. "You and I may have our differences, but I don't doubt for a moment that you will fulfill your mission. You were born to be a Guild boss—the old-fashioned serve-and-protect kind of Guild boss, not the mobster kind."

"Thanks. I think."

"I was teasing you. Sorry. Couldn't resist." She pushed herself to her feet and started toward the kitchen. "Let's get something to eat. And a glass of wine. Maybe two glasses of wine."

Gabriel got up from the bench. "Lucy?"

She stopped and turned around to face him. "What?"

"I thought about you a lot during the past couple of months. I'm so damn sorry I didn't know how bad things had gone for you after I left Illusion Town."

The bleak pain in his eyes was too much for her. She took a couple of steps forward and touched the side of his hard jaw.

"It wasn't your fault," she said. "None of it was your fault. And to be clear, you were on my mind a lot, too."

His mouth kicked up in a humorless smile. "Because you were so pissed?"

"Probably. But you also showed up in my dreams."

"Your nightmares?"

"Sometimes."

"Figures."

"But sometimes I dreamed you were searching for me. I told myself that eventually you would find me. All I had to do was hold on until you showed up."

Gabriel's eyes heated. "I had a few dreams, too."

She held her breath. "About me?"

"I was looking for you, but every time I got close, you slipped away."

"Why were you searching for me?" she asked.

"In my dreams I didn't have a reason. Didn't need one. I just knew I had to find you."

"What were you going to do once you found me?"

"In my dreams I didn't think beyond the need to find you."

She smiled. "Wow. Even in your dreams you are mission focused."

Anger and frustration flashed briefly in his eyes. "That's a real problem for you, isn't it?"

"It would be if we were planning for the future. But right here and right now, no, it's not an issue."

"Are you sure?"

"Positive," she said. "Why do you ask?"

"Because when I'm awake, I know exactly what I would have done if I had found you in my dreams."

She traced his mouth with a fingertip. "Kiss me?"

"I wanted to do a lot more than kiss you, but I would have started with that. What about you? What did you think would happen if I ever found you in your dreams?"

"We would have started with a kiss and decided where to go from there."

"You can run that experiment anytime you feel like it."

"How about now?"

Gabriel's eyes got very fierce and very hot. "Now would be a good time."

He reached for her with both hands, but she was already hurling herself into his arms. The impact of her body sent a shudder through him. He caught her close and held her with a mag-steel grip. His mouth came down on hers in a kiss that burned so fast and so hot she knew the experiment was already out of control. It was the same kind of kiss he had given her when he had rescued her from the Underworld. Her senses were overwhelmed.

Energy charged the atmosphere in the narrow hallway. She was suddenly flying just as she had in the Ghost City when she had channeled a storm and called down lightning. She clawed at the buttons on Gabriel's khaki shirt. He let her peel the garment off his shoulders and then he went to work on her shirt. It landed on the floor beside his.

He stopped when he realized she had nothing on beneath the shirt except the amber pendant.

"No bra," he said. He smiled and slowly trailed his palms over her breasts. "I like your style."

"I need to be comfortable when I'm working." She threaded her fingers through the hair on his chest. "And when I'm not working."

He gave an exultant laugh, picked her up, and carried her down the short hall to her bedroom.

He didn't rez the lights. The green radiance of the Dead City Wall pouring through the windows was all that was needed. He stood her on her feet beside the bed and removed the pendant. He set the amber necklace on the bedside table and unfastened the front of her trousers.

A moment later she was naked and stretched out on the sheets. She levered herself up on her elbow and watched Gabriel undress in the shadows. He was everything she had known he would be—lean, powerful, sleekly muscled.

He was also unmistakably and seriously aroused. Rigid. And all because of her.

Anticipation thrilled her senses. In her dreams he had been both hero and villain, rescuer and betrayer, thrilling and dangerous. Today she had summoned lightning, and instead of being alarmed he had laughed. He knew her secret and he did not give a damn. She knew his secret and she did not care, either.

They were both riding a psychic buzz generated by the brush with death in the Ghost City. Sooner or later they would both crash, but right now they were running very, very hot. Neither of them was in a mood to contemplate the future. Tonight was all about tonight.

Gabriel came down on top of her, making her intensely aware of his physical strength and the power of his aura. She sank her fingertips into his broad shoulders and gloried in the shudder that went through him.

His mouth closed over hers again. The hunger in his kiss sent a searing pleasure through her senses. She stroked one hand down his chest, through the crisp curls below his flat belly and lower still. She gripped his heavy erection.

He groaned, framed her head with his arms, and looked down at her. "This is how my dreams were supposed to end."

"Mine, too." She tightened her grip on him.

For a few seconds his whole body went taut. She looked up and saw that his eyes were squeezed shut with the effort he was exerting to keep from climaxing. She knew that, given all they had been through in the past several hours, it probably wouldn't have taken much to push him over the edge tonight, but she didn't care. She was the one who was in bed with him, the one who had the power to storm the barricades of his self-control.

She found the sensitive place at the base of his erection and pressed firmly.

"Lucy," he gasped. "Wait."

She ignored him.

He sucked in a harsh breath. "That does it."

He rolled slightly to one side and cupped the hot, wet place between her legs. He leaned over. His mouth closed on one nipple. He tugged gently.

She was so sensitive now that she nearly came off the bed. He stroked relentlessly, his fingers finding all the right places. She stopped breathing for a beat as her lower body tightened and tightened again. She clutched his forearms. He responded by easing two fingers inside her and pressing upward against the small muscles of her core.

She gasped. He started to withdraw. She gripped his shoulder with all of her strength.

"No," she managed. "Don't."

"Hold me," he whispered. "Show me how much you want me."

She could hardly breathe. Her body clenched around his fingers. Tight. Tighter.

"Don't let go," he said.

The waves of her release struck out of nowhere, rippling through her. She was lost in the climax when he shifted position and drove deep into her. The sensual invasion triggered another series of tremors.

She was still flying when he surged into her one last time, his back arching, mouth open on a hoarse roar.

His climax ignited her senses again. For an endless moment an unfamiliar energy charged the atmosphere of the bedroom. She could have sworn that her aura had somehow melded with his. The sensation was indescribably intimate, thrilling, and harrowing. Like walking into a wildly dangerous storm.

Dread sparked through her. She wondered if she was hallucinating or having an out-of-body experience. Perhaps the drugs the kidnappers had used on her had affected her permanently.

What was happening to her?

The unnerving sensation vanished in a few heartbeats. She fell back into the reality of damp sheets and the weight of Gabriel's sweat-streaked body. She listened to his heavy breathing and knew that in some inexplicable way there was now a bond between the two of them. She did not know whether to be terrified or euphoric. Maybe both.

Gabriel stirred, rolled onto his back, and folded one arm behind his head. He rested one hand on her bare thigh.

"I think there was lightning," he said.

"Don't be ridiculous."

"Pretty sure there was lightning."

Chapter Twenty

"Good news, Trenchard," Tuck said. "The client is pleased with the results of the demonstration. I was on the Strip in the Amber Zone last night. I saw the blackout for myself. Got to admit it was pretty damn impressive."

He tossed the early editions of the *Curtain* and the *Illusion Town Times* onto the workbench.

Preston Trenchard adjusted his glasses and studied the front pages of both papers. A rush of exhilaration slammed through him. The *Curtain*'s headline was *Chaos Reigns on Amber Zone Strip. Alien Energy Released from the Underworld?* Predictably, the *Times* had gone with a more sedate headline— *City Officials Investigating Power Failure in Amber Zone.*

"What did you expect?" he snorted. He raised his head, scowling. "I told you the prototype worked. But as I warned you, I had to use the entire supply of the liquid crystal. The suppressor won't work again until you bring me more. To do that you're going to have to grab a first-rate weather channeler."

"Don't worry, we'll grab Lucy Bell again," Tuck said.

"I suggest you don't screw up this time."

Tuck smiled. "We won't. By the way, the client wishes to thank you for your service."

"Just see to it that I get a proper laboratory."

"That won't be necessary. All that was needed was proof of concept. The client will take it from here."

"What are you talking about? This is my life's work. The client needs me to complete it, and I need a real lab."

"The client disagrees."

Tuck reached beneath his leather jacket and took out a mag-rez pistol. He fired two quick shots before Trenchard could grasp what was happening.

Trenchard was dead before he hit the floor.

Tuck holstered the pistol and went to work cleaning up the scene. Bodies were easy to get rid of if you had access to a hole-in-the-wall. Fortunately, cracks in the green quartz maze of the Underworld were fairly common. There was one in the basement of the warehouse. He had made sure of it before he set up the lab. He had known from the start that it would be necessary.

He wasn't concerned with the tools and workbenches—the local scavengers would make them vanish—but he needed to secure the empty canister and Trenchard's notebooks. He collected everything that might constitute a clue to the work that had been done in the warehouse, carried it outside, and stowed it in the back of his vehicle.

When he was satisfied, he slung Trenchard's body over his shoulder and carried it down the old concrete steps into the basement. Green energy seeped around the cracks in the downstairs door.

He opened the door, went through the large, jagged crack in the green quartz wall, and paused to set his locator. When he was sure he would be able to find his way back to the entry point, he strolled a short distance along a glowing corridor. He chose one of the many chambers at random and dumped the body inside. He checked the locator to backtrack to the opening.

The only way the corpse would ever be found was if someone stumbled into the room by accident. It was possible but unlikely. In time, via a process the scientists did not yet understand, most of the biological materials would break down and be absorbed through the stone and disappear. The only things left would be the bones, some clothes, plastics, and metals. The paranormal energy that flooded the tunnels kept the vast maze free of the dead.

He went back upstairs and took one more look around. He was a thorough man, and this had been his assignment from start to finish. He had a reputation to maintain.

Satisfied, he went out into the fog, got behind the wheel, and drove away from the warehouse. Time to deliver the prototype to the client. The suppressor was an incredible invention. It could jam resonating amber. Once it was perfected and access to the liquid crystal pool was assured, the device would be the ultimate weapon on a world that was totally reliant on tuned amber.

Trenchard had found a way to harness the power of the liquid crystal. He had done the basic research and had produced a working prototype. He was no longer needed. From now on it was just a matter of scale. That was merely a straightforward engineering issue, according to the client.

Last night the prototype had shut down the Amber Zone Strip. Soon the client would control the technology that could deactivate anything from a flamer or a mag-rez pistol to an entire city.

The farsighted client had realized that a first-class security team would be required. Blue Amber had been created to serve that purpose. Only the most powerful ex-Guild men had been recruited.

He was finally working for someone who appreciated his talent and his determination.

Fuck the Guilds. They had screwed him and the others. Soon his team would be armed with weapons that rendered flamers and mag-rez pistols useless. They would control the city-states and the Underworld.

Blue Amber was going to become more powerful than all the Guilds combined.

And he was the head of Blue Amber.

Chapter Twenty-One

Lucy's doorbell chimed just as she rezzed the coffee maker. She went down the hall to answer it. Gabriel appeared from the bedroom. He was fastening a fresh khaki shirt he had found in his duffel bag. His hair was still damp from the shower.

"Who's that?" he asked.

"Probably my friend Veronica. She lives down the hall."

Gabriel frowned. "It's a little early for a neighbor to drop in, isn't it?"

"Don't be so suspicious. Illusion Town is like the Guild. It operates around the clock. Veronica works nights at a club. She gets home about this time every morning."

Otis scampered out of the kitchen, where he had been supervising breakfast preparations. He chortled in anticipation of greeting the morning visitor.

Lucy glanced down at him. "See? No need to worry. Otis knows who's out there."

Gabriel looked at Otis and visibly relaxed. "Okay."

Lucy opened the door. A tall, stunning redhead dressed in tight-fitting leather from her low-cut, corset top to her spike-heeled leather boots stood in the hallway. A leather whip was clipped to her wide leather belt. She was in the process of peeling off gauntlet-length leather gloves. She smiled a weary smile.

"Good morning," she said. Her voice was throaty and sensual. "I knew you would be up."

"Hi, Veronica," Lucy said. "Busy night at the Dungeon?"

"The usual. I'm exhausted. Sorry to bother you, but I was wondering if I could borrow some eggs. I realized on my way home that I'm out. You know me. After a long night's work I am absolutely ravenous."

"Sure, come on in." Lucy stood back.

Otis chortled and waved his toy dust bunny.

"Good morning, little guy." Veronica removed a set of velvet handcuffs from her belt and leaned down to give them to Otis. "There you go. Have fun."

Otis could barely contain himself. He rushed back to the kitchen with his treasure.

"Don't lose the key this time," Lucy called after him.

Veronica chuckled. "No worries, I've got an extra key."

"Good to know. The last time he used your handcuffs to make a trapeze swing, it took us twenty minutes to extricate him."

"I remember."

Gabriel appeared. He inclined his head politely. "Good morning."

Veronica gave him a glowing smile. "Mr. Jones. I recognize you from your pictures in the press. I couldn't help but notice the vehicle parked out front. Nice little ghost you've got attached to the plates, by the way. Slick."

"This is Veronica Star," Lucy said to Gabriel.

"A pleasure to meet you, Ms. Star," he said. "You're the person who got the message Lucy sent just before she disappeared two months ago, aren't you?"

"That was me," Veronica said.

"It was very helpful," Gabriel said. "It gave me a starting point."

"I know, Lucy told me. Glad the information was helpful. We were all very worried."

"Gabriel is going to reopen my case," Lucy said. "He believes my story."

"Excellent," Veronica said. "About time someone paid attention." She looked at Gabriel. "Call me Veronica. Apparently we're going to be neighbors."

"For a while," Gabriel said.

"It's a professional relationship," Lucy said quickly. "If you saw the news, you know that I have a contract with the Guild. Gabriel feels I may be in danger until the case he's investigating is closed."

"Right, 'professional.'" Veronica pulled a card out of her leather handbag and handed it to Gabriel. "Welcome to Illusion Town. I'm usually fully booked, but I would be delighted to make room for the director of the Guild. Please feel free to call to make an appointment. By the way, the club will be running a special for members of the Guild. A package of six sessions, half-price. Includes a cocktail. Just our way of welcoming the organization."

"Thanks." Gabriel glanced at the card. "The Dungeon Club."

"That's right. We specialize in discipline."

"I see it's on the Strip in the Amber Zone," Gabriel said. "You must have witnessed the power outage."

"Did we ever. Now I know the meaning of the phrase *As dark as a dungeon.*" Veronica shuddered. "Luckily all of the clients were blindfolded at the time, so they never had a clue. My colleagues and I tried to find the doors so we could evacuate everyone if necessary, but the signs over the emergency exits went out along with everything else. It was really unnerving, and I say that as a true control freak."

"It's not just unnerving," Gabriel said. "It's potentially catastrophic."

Veronica watched him with an uneasy expression. "Do you think it could happen again?"

"I don't see why not," Gabriel said.

"Okay," Veronica said, "you just ruined my day. I assume the Guild will be involved in the investigation?"

"It's on my to-do list," Gabriel said.

Mad chortling from the kitchen interrupted the discussion. Several thumps and rumbles of dust bunny outrage followed.

"I knew it was a bad idea to give him those handcuffs again," Lucy said with a sigh.

She hurried down the hall and went into the kitchen. Veronica and Gabriel followed.

The velvet handcuffs were dangling from the refrigerator door handle. The sequined dust bunny was locked inside one of the cuffs. It dangled a couple of feet off the floor. Otis was on the floor, hopping up and down in increasingly alarmed attempts to recover the toy. Every time he bounced up to seize the dust bunny, he succeeded only in batting the cuff, which sent its glittering prisoner swinging out of reach.

"How in the world did he manage to lock his favorite toy inside the cuffs?" Lucy asked. "Never mind." She looked at Veronica. "Good thing you brought a spare key."

"You know," Veronica said, "this gives me an idea for expanding my list of discipline therapies. Thanks, Otis. You're an inspiration."

CHAPTER TWENTY-TWO

"I'm not sure this is a good idea," Brock Roxby said. "There's a lot of risk involved in your plan."

Jocelyn Roxby had been pacing the office. She stopped and swung around to glare at her husband. Brock was seated behind his impressive desk, cranked back in an equally impressive chair. The desk and the chair went well with the stylishly decorated office.

Her office was just as imposing. The interiors of Roxby Weather Wizards had been designed by Fortune & Associates, one of the most prestigious design firms in town. The goal had been a CEO suite that could compete with the offices of the top casino moguls. Helen Fortune, the owner of Fortune & Associates, had outdone herself.

"There is very little risk if we handle things carefully," Jocelyn said. "Don't be a wimp. This is an incredible opportunity. We can't let it slip away."

"But if things go wrong, we could lose everything," Brock said.

"Here's the plan, Brock," Jocelyn said through her teeth. "We don't let things go wrong. We negotiate. Carefully. We're good at that, remember?" She swept out a hand to indicate the spacious, expensive headquarters of Roxby Weather Wizards. "Look at the business we've built."

Brock regarded her with a grim expression. She couldn't deny that he had reason to be apprehensive. She was nervous, too. This was a deal that had to be carefully managed. There was a lot at stake.

"We have to do whatever it takes to make this happen," she said. "If we pull it off, we'll be able to expand to the other city-states. We will control the entire weather channeler market. We've already got ninety percent of the business down in the Ghost City, and that's just the beginning. Who knows what will be discovered next in the Underworld? Whatever it is, you can bet weather will be a problem."

"I know."

"The Federation authorities and every smart CEO on Harmony who has a stake in the Underworld will want the best channelers. With sharp marketing and financial backing, Weather Wizards will be the number one choice."

At long last there was a spark of excitement in Brock's eyes. "Huh."

"If we play our cards right, Weather Wizards could ultimately become as powerful as the Guilds."

Brock sat forward abruptly. "All right. Call the client. Tell him we'll get Lucy Bell for him."

Jocelyn did not hesitate. She was on her phone, punching in the number, before Brock finished the sentence.

The client answered immediately. Impatient and eager.

Her fingers tightened around the phone. She didn't want to admit it, but she was as uneasy as Brock. They were about to take a very big risk.

But the payoff would be huge. She infused her words with cool, professional confidence.

"Weather Wizards will make it happen," she said. "Trust me, Lucy Bell will not be a problem."

Image was everything.

Chapter Twenty-Three

"A decorator?" Gabriel looked up from the long string of messages on his phone. "Why in green hell do I need a decorator? This is an office. All it requires are a couple of chairs and a desk. I've got those."

He was sitting behind the desk at that very moment, looking straight at the two chairs on the other side.

"All of the office furniture we are currently using is rented," Aiden Shore said. He pushed his glasses higher on his nose and stood his ground in the doorway. "It's functional, but I never intended for any of it to be permanent. I had to get the new headquarters in working order in a hurry. Those were your instructions, sir."

Aiden was young, earnest, and determined. He had joined the Cadence organization two years earlier. He had the basic ghost hunting talent required to handle dissonance energy in the Underworld, but within the first month he and his instructors had concluded he was incurably claustrophobic. He got panic attacks when he went belowground into the maze of tunnels.

He had been offered a desk job in public relations. In that environment he had thrived, displaying a talent for organizational skills. When Gabriel had been appointed director of the new Illusion Town Guild, he had realized immediately that he was going to need someone like Aiden—an administrative assistant who could run the office.

He knew he had selected the right person for the job when he had approached Aiden's boss to request permission to recruit the young man. The head of the public relations department had said, *Shore is all yours. Drives everyone in my department straight up a wall. He's always trying to tell people how they can streamline their process and improve the image of the Guild.*

Gabriel had been pleased with himself when Aiden had accepted the offer of the new post. It was rapidly becoming apparent, however, that his new assistant was drunk with power.

"What's the problem with rented furniture?" Gabriel asked.

"It has no style," Aiden said. "This is not just any business office, Mr. Jones. This is a Guild director's office. It should send a clear message to everyone who enters the space."

"We're not the phone company, Aiden. We don't deliver messages."

"I'm talking about the sort of message that enhances our image, sir. The Guilds are changing. This office needs to reflect that. It should also suit the community. The CEO suite should have style and a certain ambience."

Gabriel studied the interior of his office. He realized he hadn't taken a close look at it until now. It was a big space on the top floor of a sparkling new six-story building. He had put Aiden in charge of acquiring the building and arranging for the special security upgrades. There was a mag-rez steel garage for the vehicles, state-of-the-art power to handle the latest computers and phones, and direct access to the Underworld via the basement.

As far as he could see, that was all that was needed to fulfill the mission of the Illusion Town Guild.

"What sort of style and ambience did you have in mind?" Gabriel asked. "If you're talking about making this room look like a casino or a club, forget it."

"Don't be ridiculous," Aiden said.

Gabriel raised his brows, but Aiden did not appear to notice.

"Mr. Jones, you and I both know the Guilds have a serious image problem," he continued. "The public has forgotten that not only do we have an origin story that is heroic and noble; we perform an invaluable service to the community and the entire Federation of City-States."

"You're going to fix our image by calling in a decorator to furnish my office?" Gabriel asked.

"It's a start, sir."

"I don't have time for this kind of stuff. Do whatever you want with the place. You're in charge."

"Don't worry, sir, I'll take care of everything." Aiden pulled out his phone. "Now, then, I have a few messages for you."

"*More* messages?" Gabriel held up his own phone. "I've already got a few hundred."

Aiden frowned. "You should not waste your time dealing with business correspondence. I'll take over that account and make sure you only see what you need to see. I'll be able to handle ninety-five percent of your email and messages. You'll still have your private account for personal correspondence."

"Uh—" Gabriel looked down at the endless string of emails that had accumulated on his phone in recent days. The thought of not having to go through them and figure out how to respond gave him a genuine thrill of relief.

"Okay," he said.

Aiden glanced down at his notes. "As I was saying, I've got three items to run by you. Dillon Westover of Westover Outfitters would like to invite you to lunch to discuss what he can do for the Guild. He's open any day this week."

"I'm not. Tell him we'll be in touch if we need his services."

"Yes, sir." Aiden made a note. "Next up, Mr. and Mrs. Roxby of Roxby Weather Wizards have, and I quote, 'an exciting opportunity to discuss with you.'"

"We'll be in touch if we need their services."

"Right." Aiden made another note. "Ms. Cassandra Keele, president and CEO of Keele Investigations, would like to invite you to join her for a private business dinner to discuss what her firm can do for the Guild."

"Tell her we'll be in touch if we—"

"Need her services. Got it." Aiden cleared his throat. "Lastly, Mr. Smith, the owner of the Amber Palace, would like to host you at a small gathering of the Illusion Club."

"What's the Illusion Club?"

Aiden looked up. "It's a club that includes the most important, most influential local power brokers. My research indicates that Mr. Smith and his friends run this town."

"Tell Mr. Smith that I'll be in touch—"

"I'm afraid you can't turn down this invitation," Aiden said. "Like it or not, the Guild absolutely must establish cordial relations with the other power brokers here."

"Do I look like a power broker to you?"

"Yes, sir."

Gabriel groaned. "All right. Accept the invitation. Advise Mr. Smith that I will be accompanied by Ms. Lucy Bell."

"Yes, sir."

"Her dust bunny will probably be with us. You had better warn Mr. Smith that he might want to put the hors d'oeuvres behind a mag-steel barricade."

Aiden chuckled. "I saw the photos of the cake disaster at the engagement reception. Cute."

"Not everyone thought so. Is that it? Are we done here? Because I've got some actual work to do."

"What work is that?"

"I have to track down and interview all the really good amber tuners in the city."

"There are amber tuner shops on every corner and in every jewelry store in town. Can you be more specific?"

"That," Gabriel said, "is an excellent question." He got to his feet, walked around the desk, and propped his backside against it. He folded his arms and gave the matter some thought. "I'm looking for a tuner who can handle gray amber. Rez amber, to be specific."

"I've never heard of gray amber, resonating or otherwise."

"Neither has anyone else, apparently. The general consensus is that it probably comes from the Ghost City."

"All right, so we know it's rare," Aiden said. "That's helpful, because only the most skilled tuners can handle rare or unusual rez amber. Anything else?"

Gabriel unfolded his arms, straightened, and crossed the room to the coatrack. He reached into the pocket of his leather jacket and took out the pendants. "Specifically, I'm looking for the tuner who handled these stones."

"They're glowing. That's weird."

"They're glowing because they are in close proximity. Watch what happens when they are separated."

He tossed one of the pendants to Aiden and walked to the far end of the big office. The farther away he got, the duller the amber became.

Aiden studied the pendant he was holding. "Signal stones. We are definitely looking for a very specialized tuner." He looked up, eyes bright with enthusiasm. "I'll get started on the search immediately."

"*You'll* get started?"

"You've got staff now, Mr. Jones. As it happens, I'm very good at finding people."

"Is that right? Is that a skill you picked up in the PR department?"

"You'd be surprised by what you can learn working in public relations."

CHAPTER TWENTY-FOUR

At the end of the second tour of the day, Lucy concluded that Jared Flint was going to be as big an asset as Otis when it came to encouraging tips. People descending from the bus shoved cash at her so fast she had to use both hands, but their attention was on Otis and Jared.

Her bodyguard was a poster boy for the new image the Guilds were trying to create: young, good-looking, and dashing in his khaki-and-leather uniform, boots, and gear belt. He projected strength and competence. Everything about him, from his broad shoulders to his body language and easy confidence, sent a message of professionalism, talent, and dedication to the mission.

"Great tour," a fortysomething woman said. She gave Jared a flirtatious smile. "I would have been quite nervous when that storm came up out of nowhere if you hadn't been on board. It's always good to have a Guild man around in a situation like that."

Jared gave her a polite smile. "Glad to be of service, ma'am. But there was nothing to worry about. Your tour guide, Ms. Bell, is the best weather channeler in Illusion Town. That's why she handles Guild contracts in the Underworld."

"That was so high-rez," a teenage male announced. He gazed up at Jared, eyes glowing with hero worship. "I'm going to join the Guild when I get out of school."

"The Guild is always interested in talent," Jared said.

The young man grinned. His mother, who was a few steps ahead, turned around. "You are going to be a lawyer, Ben, just like your father."

Ben rolled his eyes. His mother ignored him and hurried toward the gift shop.

Jared winked and lowered his voice. "Like every other organization, the Guilds need lawyers."

"Excellent." Ben gave a thumbs-up and took off after his mother.

A little girl dressed in pink gazed up at Otis with adoration. "I want my very own dust bunny."

Otis chortled at her and waved his miniature dust bunny. The kid giggled. Her father pressed some cash into Lucy's hand.

"Guess we're headed for the gift shop," he said.

"There are three sizes of dust bunnies," Lucy said. "And I believe there are some pink ones."

The man laughed and then nodded at Jared. "Good to have a Guild man along for the ride."

"Accompanying Ms. Bell is the best assignment I've had yet, sir," Jared said respectfully.

The last customer off the bus was a twentysomething woman. She shoved some cash at Lucy and then smiled at Jared. "I want my very own ghost hunter."

Jared gave her one of his polite, professional smiles. "Always happy to be of service, ma'am."

She giggled and headed for the gift shop.

Lucy waited until the woman was gone before she quickly counted the take. "This is my biggest day yet. Between you and Otis I could actually make enough to pay off some bills."

Jared laughed. "Always happy to be of service, ma'am."

Lucy chuckled. "You are good. Just what the Guilds need to clean up the brand."

"I'm proud to be working for Mr. Jones," Jared said, turning serious. "I'm lucky he selected me to join his start-up team here in Illusion Town."

"He wouldn't have done that if he didn't think you were the best," Lucy said.

Jared flushed. "Thanks. What's next? Another tour?"

"Nope. Lunch break. I ordered a pizza from Ollie's House of Pizza. It should be delivered any minute now."

Otis chortled.

"He gets very excited about pizza," Lucy explained. "First stop is the parking lot. That's where the pizza will be delivered. We can eat in the storage room behind the gift shop. There's a table inside."

"Sounds good."

A gleaming SUV pulled into the parking lot just as they reached the pavement. The bold sign on the side read, ROXBY WEATHER WIZARDS. GO INTO THE UNDERWORLD WITH THE BEST.

Lucy sighed. "Not our pizza."

The doors on either side of the vehicle snapped open. Jocelyn and Brock Roxby emerged. They were dressed for business in matching tailored uniforms done in the distinctive Weather Wizard colors—maroon with accents of amber yellow.

"Hi, Lucy," Jocelyn said. Her smile was nothing short of vivacious. "This is great timing. We were hoping to catch you between tours." She switched up the smile and looked at Jared. "You must be a friend of Lucy's. I'm Jocelyn Roxby. This is my husband, Brock."

Jared nodded to both Roxbys.

"Jared's new in town," Lucy said, slipping smoothly into the cover story they had invented to explain his presence in the Storm Zone. "He wanted to learn something about the Storm Zone, so I invited him to shadow me on the tours."

"Mr. Jones wants everyone on his start-up team to get to know the territory aboveground as well as down in the tunnels," Jared said.

"Excellent idea," Brock said. He took a business card out of the inside of his jacket and handed it to Jared. "Lucy knows her way around the Storm Zone, but when you're ready to go down into the Ghost City, be sure to call us. We're running special discounted tours for all ghost hunters this month. Just our way of welcoming the Guild."

"Thanks." Jared glanced at the card and then slipped it inside his leather jacket.

Lucy looked at Jocelyn. "I'm assuming this isn't a social visit?"

Jocelyn gave a sparkling laugh that sounded as real as fake amber. "In the middle of a parking lot in the Storm Zone? Of course not. We're here because Brock and I would like to offer you a position on the Weather Wizards team."

"Wow," Lucy said. She rezzed up her own version of a dazzling smile. "That's very kind of you, but I'm under contract at the moment."

"With the Guild," Brock said quickly. "Yes, we know. That won't be a problem. We can make arrangements to transfer your contract to Weather Wizards."

"And take a commission?" Lucy said, careful to keep her tone polite.

"The customary split is forty-sixty," Jocelyn said. She cleared her throat. "But given your unique talent, we're happy to offer a thirty-seventy split. The larger share goes to you, of course."

A sleek black rez-bike pulled into the parking lot. The fenders were emblazoned with the logo of the DZ Delivery Service. There was a large cargo box behind the driver.

Otis got so excited he almost fell off Lucy's shoulder.

"Lunchtime," Lucy explained to the Roxbys. "I'll make this quick. I appreciate your offer, but for now I prefer to continue working as an independent."

Brock looked annoyed. "We're open to negotiation. What's your counteroffer?"

"I don't have one. I'm not negotiating."

Runner got off the delivery bike and took a large pizza box out of the cargo holder. He walked toward Lucy and the others.

"Got your usual, Lucy," he said. "Cheese and olive. Extra large this time."

"Thanks, Runner," she said.

She reached into her pocket and dug out some of the tip money. She peeled off a couple of bills and handed them to Runner. She took the pizza box and gave it to Jared.

Runner grinned at Jared. "Part of the new Guild team?"

"That's right," Jared said with a nod.

"Welcome to Illusion Town."

"Thanks," Jared replied.

Runner dug a card out of his jacket. "If the Guild needs delivery service within the Dark Zone, be sure to call us. We know the zone. Outside delivery services always get lost."

"I'll pass that info along to the boss's administrative assistant," Jared said.

"Great. See you later."

Runner gave Otis a pat on the head and went back to the bike.

Otis gazed at the pizza box with rapt attention.

Lucy gave the Roxbys a blazing smile. "If you'll excuse us, we don't have much of a lunch break today. Got several more tours this afternoon. Business has been brisk lately."

Jocelyn's eyes went cold. "You know as well as I do that working as an independent in the Underworld is dangerous. If you join the Weather Wizards team you'll have backup and protection."

"I don't think I'll need protection as long as I'm working with the Guild, do you?"

"Be reasonable," Brock said. "We all know you can't handle all of the Guild business. No one channeler could do that."

"I'm sure you'll get your share of Guild work," Lucy said. "Thanks again for the offer, but—"

"Think about it," Jocelyn said. She took a breath and appeared to steel herself for what she was going to say next. "We're prepared to offer you a partnership arrangement."

Lucy stared at her. "Are you serious?"

"Very," Jocelyn assured her.

"Twenty percent stake," Brock said quickly. "Not a controlling interest, of course."

"That's an amazing offer," Lucy said. "I appreciate it. I'm satisfied with my business at the moment, but if I change my mind, I'll be sure to get in touch."

Jocelyn's expression tightened. "Everyone knows most miners and prospectors and ghost hunters won't work with a channeler who is rumored to have para-psych issues and possible drug problems. As a Weather Wizard you'll be able to rebrand yourself. You'll no longer be seen as a high-risk independent operator. You'll be viewed as a professional, a member of a high-profile corporate team."

Something in the tone of her voice got Otis's attention. He stopped focusing on the pizza box and looked at Jocelyn. He did not go into full hunting mode, but he gave a warning growl.

Jocelyn yelped and took several steps back. "Control that creature."

Lucy fought the wave of anger that cascaded through her. She realized Jared had gone very still. He watched Brock.

Tension shivered in the atmosphere.

"It's okay, guys," Lucy said quietly. "We're finished here. Let's go have lunch."

She turned and walked swiftly toward the rear door of the gift shop. Otis lost interest in the Roxbys and returned his full attention to the pizza box. Jared, however, kept an eye on Brock and Jocelyn until they roared out of the parking lot.

He fell into step beside her. "How well do you know the Roxbys?" he asked.

"On a professional level, I've been acquainted with them ever since they set up in business here in Illusion Town. They were independents back in those days. Worked together as a team. That changed when Coppersmith opened up the Ghost City. That was when the Roxbys got the idea to form an agency that supplied weather channelers. They hired most of the local talent. Now they dominate the market. It was a brilliant move, to be honest. Wish I'd thought of it first."

They reached the rear door of the gift shop. Lucy opened it. Jared carried the pizza on through and set it on the table. She took some paper plates and napkins out of a cupboard. When she opened the lid, the unmistakable aroma of hot pizza wafted through the room.

"Cheese and olive," she said. "How exciting, right, Otis?"

Otis hopped down off her shoulder and landed adroitly next to the open box. He made happy noises.

Jared looked amused. "Looks good to me, too. But you don't sound too thrilled, Ms. Bell. Don't you like cheese-and-olive pizza?"

"Don't get me wrong," Lucy said. "Cheese-and-olive pizza will always have a special place in my heart." She removed a slice, positioned it on a paper plate, and gave it to Otis. "But I have come to the conclusion that, when it comes to pizza, too much of a good thing may be too much of a good thing."

Otis seized the paper plate with two of his paws and bustled down to the far end of the table.

"Not for Otis, apparently," Jared said. "Why order cheese and olive if you have had enough of it?"

"I do it for Otis. Pizza is the only paycheck he gets. He does a lot of work on the tours. I figure he deserves his favorite treat for lunch. It's the least I can do. But given my budget, it means that I end up eating it, too."

She removed another slice of pizza, put it on a plate, and gave it to Jared.

"Thanks." Jared grinned. "Cheese and olive is fine with me."

Lucy served herself and sat down across from Jared. She took a bite and munched while she considered the mini-confrontation in the parking lot.

"Why did you ask how long I've known the Roxbys?" she said.

He shrugged, but his eyes sharpened. There was a new intensity about him that reminded her a little of Gabriel. Another man on a mission.

"It's pretty clear they're not thrilled that you won't join their crew," he said.

"Obviously they want to add me to their team because they think I've got an inside track to future Guild work."

Jared nodded a little too politely and ate some pizza.

Lucy groaned. "Okay, you don't have to say it. I know everyone thinks Gabriel and I have a personal relationship."

Which was, she reflected, nothing less than the truth. It was a startling thought. She never slept with clients. Oh. Wait.

"The boss's personal life is none of my business, but it's obvious the Roxbys think you could be very useful to them," Jared said. "If you're on their team, the Guild will be hiring a Weather Wizard channeler and, therefore, will be likely to hire more Wizards when security work ramps up. That will be happening soon."

"It's certainly one logical explanation for the Roxbys' sudden interest in recruiting me. But you're wondering if there might be another reason, aren't you?"

"Crossed my mind," Jared said. He ate some more pizza. "Apparently it crossed yours, too."

"I'm a little paranoid these days."

"We are not alone in our paranoia and suspicion," Jared said. "At least, we won't be for long. I can guarantee you the possibility that the Roxbys were involved in your kidnapping will occur to Mr. Jones, too."

"Motive? It's not like I'm the only channeler in town."

"No, but you're good," Jared said. "I watched you handle that storm we ran into on the last tour. It was the real deal, wasn't it? Not just a pesky whirlwind or a small dust storm. It wasn't big, but it was hot, and it was highly charged. I've never seen an energy storm aboveground."

"Welcome to Illusion Town. Like the sign says, the thrills are real."

"I think I'm going to like it here."

"The weather is amazing," Lucy said.

CHAPTER TWENTY-FIVE

Gabriel stopped midway along the sidewalk and checked the directions Aiden had given him. According to the map on his phone, they were only half a block from the tuner's shop.

"Almost there," he said.

It was late afternoon. He and Lucy were in a shabby neighborhood deep in the eternally gray Shadow Zone. Otis was riding shotgun on his shoulder, evidently having concluded the position gave him a better view.

The neighborhood was run-down even by Shadow Zone standards. The fog seemed heavier in the narrow streets and alleys. There were no sleazy casinos, no cheap motels; just a scattering of empty shops, most of which had FOR LEASE signs in the windows. Several were boarded up.

Half an hour ago, Aiden had come through with a name and an address for a very specialized tuner named Stewart Pitney. Pitney was no longer among the living, having died in a suspicious fire that destroyed his shop.

Gabriel had called Lucy to tell her he was going to be late because he wanted to take a look around the burned-out shop. She had insisted on joining him. Jared had delivered her to the front door of Guild headquarters and briefed Gabriel on the Roxby encounter. Gabriel had immediately gotten a ping that told him something was off.

He dropped the phone into his jacket and started walking again. He resumed the conversation he and Lucy were having.

"I don't like the way the Roxbys are suddenly pressuring you to join their organization," he said.

"Relax." Lucy adjusted her pack. "I'm sure it's just a business maneuver. Can't blame them. They know I've got a Guild contract. They want in on the action."

"Got a feeling there's more to it than that."

"Jared and I discussed possibilities, but we couldn't come up with any reasonable explanation."

"What if they've made a discovery in the Underworld but can't get to it because of bad weather?"

Lucy shook her head. "It's hard to believe they're up against something they can't take care of on their own. They're both very, very good, Gabriel. What's more, they can combine their talents and work as a team."

"Maybe they don't want to take the risk of tackling whatever it is that they are after," he said.

"I just can't see them hiring a bunch of thugs to kidnap me."

"That failed, so they're going with a different tactic."

"Offering me a partnership in their business is more their style," Lucy admitted. "But still . . ."

"It strikes me as an act of desperation," Gabriel said. "They must be under pressure for some reason."

"Okay, I agree they seemed more than a little anxious today."

"Do you trust the Roxbys?" he asked.

"Depends on the situation. They wouldn't hesitate to stab me in the back if they thought it would make it possible for them to get an exclusive contract with the Guild. Actually, that's probably exactly what they're trying to do with this move. Even if I took the offer of a partnership, I'm sure they would come up with a plan to ease me out of the way once they had what they wanted. But that would just be business as usual for them. There's no doubt but that they are very ambitious."

"Ambition is a very powerful motivator," Gabriel mused.

Lucy raised her brows. "You don't say."

Gabriel opted to ignore that little dig. He had bigger problems.

He stopped at the end of the block and looked at the sign over the boarded-up shop. It had been badly charred by the fire that had destroyed the interior, but it was possible to make out the lettering—PITNEY'S AMBER TUNING. RARE AMBERS OUR SPECIALTY. Beneath it was another sign—CONDEMNED BY ORDER OF FIRE MARSHAL.

"According to Aiden, this is the place," he said.

Lucy studied the smoke-blackened brick walls. "When did the fire occur?"

"About four months ago. There was an investigation, but they never found the arsonist."

"So we're breaking in?"

"I like to think of it as gaining access by unconventional means. I didn't have time to get a warrant."

"I don't think unconventional means will be much of a problem in this neighborhood," Lucy said. "I don't see any witnesses."

"All the same, I'd rather not attract attention here on the street. Let's try the alley. There's always a back door."

They walked to the end of the block, turned the corner, and entered the shadowed alley behind the row of small shops and businesses. There were a couple of rusted-out trash bins, broken wine and beer bottles, and discarded odds and ends.

Otis surveyed the scene and chortled.

"He likes alleys," Lucy explained.

"Always something interesting in an alley," Gabriel said.

"Please don't tell me you like to hang out in alleys."

"Only on the odd weekend when there's nothing else to do."

Lucy shot him a glare. He paid no attention because he was rezzed. His intuition was shooting small, hot sparks through all of his senses. He was on the right trail.

The rear door of Pitney's Amber Tuning was boarded up. So were the small windows.

"No point crawling through a window when we can just as easily use the door," Gabriel said.

He slipped his pack off his shoulder, took out the small pry bar, and went to work. It didn't take long to get inside.

He switched on his flashlight and splashed the beam around the interior of the charred space. It was filled with the remains of workbenches, cutting and polishing machinery, and cabinets that had once held raw amber. Everything but the mag-steel tools had been burned beyond repair.

"This was one very hot fire," Lucy said, flashing her light around the space.

Gabriel prowled slowly through the room. "Whoever set it wanted to destroy evidence."

Otis abruptly vaulted down from Gabriel's shoulder. He landed on a workbench and hopped down to the floor. Ash billowed around him. He opened all four eyes and bustled about, churning up more ash as he explored the room.

Lucy groaned. "He's going to need a bath when we get home." She looked down at her clothes. "We will, too."

When we get home. She spoke casually, but Gabriel reran the words in his head as he searched the burned-out room. The phrase hummed through him like a line from a song he couldn't quite remember. For him, *home* still meant his parents' house. He hadn't lived there since he had joined the Guild, but none of the apartments he had rented during his climb to the top had ever felt like home.

His current situation—spending his nights at Lucy's apartment—was as temporary as things could get, but for some reason he found it natural to use the word *home*.

Lucy cautiously checked what was left of a cabinet. "What are we looking for?"

"Every tuner I ever knew kept the best specimens stashed in a vault in the Underworld. I'm betting Pitney had a hole-in-the-wall. The problem will be trying to find it. Everything is covered in ash and grit."

Lucy took a step. The floor squeaked and groaned beneath her boot. She jumped back quickly.

"Stay where you are," Gabriel said. "There's a reason the fire marshal put up that condemned sign out front."

He dug the pry bar out of his pack again and used it to probe the ashes.

He found what he was looking for beneath the wreckage of what had once been a small bathroom.

"Here we go," he said.

He applied the pry bar to the trapdoor in the floor. Otis rushed over to see what was going on. Gabriel got the trap open and aimed his flashlight down into the darkness. A flight of cracked concrete steps led to the basement. Tendrils of a familiar energy wafted upward.

Otis chortled excitedly.

"Did you find Pitney's hole-in-the-wall?" Lucy called from the alley door.

"Looks like it. There's definitely a lot of Underworld heat. Come on over, but follow my footprints."

"On my way."

Lucy picked a path through the ash and soot. When she reached his side, he got a pleasant little shiver of awareness and knew she had heightened her senses.

"Definitely tunnel heat," she said. "But even if Pitney had a secret vault down below, how can we find it? We'd need the coordinates."

"Finding things is what I do, remember? If Pitney frequently came and went from a chamber in the tunnels, there will be a trail."

"How will you be able to recognize it?"

Gabriel took one of the pendants out of his jacket. "If Pitney was the tuner who worked this amber, his vibe will be infused into it."

Lucy smiled. "Excellent."

"Let's go."

He went down the steps, senses at high rez. Otis scampered ahead of him. Lucy followed.

Pitney's hole-in-the-wall was easy to locate. He had secured it with an impressive mag-steel door and a serious-looking lock. Green quartz energy seeped around the edges.

"I don't think your pry bar will work on that door," Lucy said.

"It's a frequency lock. I've got a jammer that could open it, but we're not going to have to go to any trouble."

"Why not?"

Gabriel grabbed the steel handle and hauled the door open. "Because whoever went through this door last either did not know how to reset the lock or wasn't worried about locking up. I think we can assume that person was the killer. He was looking for Pitney's vault. The question is, did he find it?"

The heavy vault-style door swung open. Acid-green energy spilled through a ragged, two-foot-wide crack in the quartz wall. A shivery thrill rezzed his senses. He had spent a lot of his life in the Underworld, but he still got the rush.

He glanced at Lucy. There was a gleam in her eyes that told him she felt it, too.

Otis fluttered through the opening first. Gabriel and Lucy followed. Once inside, they stopped to double-check their nav amber and the locator. Otis could always be counted on to lead the way to an exit, but years of professional training and experience ran deep. You never went into the Underworld without well-tuned nav amber and a functioning locator.

"All set?" he said.

Lucy touched the amber in her bracelet and nodded. "Yes."

He gripped the pendant in one hand and focused on the unique frequency of Pitney's tuning vibe. A thread of identical energy appeared on the green quartz floor.

"Got it," he said.

Lucy gave him a curious look. "You can sense Pitney's vibe in here?"

"I can see prints on the floor. It isn't usually this easy, but it looks like Pitney spent a lot of time down here. He left a clear trail, and it's hot."

"Hot?"

"The last time he came this way he was . . . agitated. Scared, maybe."

He started walking, concentrating on the path he was following. If he stopped focusing, the prints faded immediately. Lucy fell into step beside him. After a couple of moments Otis seemed to realize what was going on. He dashed ahead.

"He must have figured out we're following Pitney's vibe," Lucy said.

"He'll probably get us there faster than I can." Gabriel kept his attention on the faint path of energy. It was just barely visible in the glow of the quartz. "The next question is whether the arsonist got there first."

"I doubt it. Not many people can do what you do," Lucy said.

"The killer might have forced Pitney to reveal the location of the vault before he murdered him."

"So whether or not we find something useful is what we here in Illusion Town like to call a *crap shoot.*"

"Trust me, there's always something left at a scene."

Otis disappeared around another corner and then reappeared, chortling.

"He thinks we're playing a game," Lucy explained. "Dust bunnies, I have discovered, are big on games of any kind. They excel at hide-and-seek."

The trail led into a vast rotunda. There were over a dozen arched openings marking the entrances to more tunnels. Otis was waiting for them at one of the openings. He waved his miniature dust bunny and bounced up and down.

Gabriel studied the energy path on the floor. It led straight to where Otis stood on his hind legs, barely able to contain his glee.

"Got it," Gabriel said. He went forward to join Otis. "Now to see what's left."

Pitney's vault was a small chamber to the right inside the tunnel. It had not been cleaned out. Glass and steel cases held heaps of unpolished, untuned amber.

Lucy came up to view the interior of the chamber. "And this is what we here in Illusion Town call *hitting the jackpot.*"

Otis scampered toward a glass case and hopped on top, apparently trying to figure out how to open it.

Gabriel walked slowly through the space, pausing here and there to examine the collection. "This is incredible. I've never seen examples of some of this amber except in museums or in the vaults of the big amber-mining companies. Pitney must have spent his life collecting rare rez amber."

"Probably because he had a talent for working it." Lucy studied the pink amber in one of the cases. "You know how it is. Once you become aware of a psychic ability to resonate with a particular form of energy, you can't resist it. You feel like you have to use the talent, the same way you use your other senses."

Gabriel looked up from a small pile of uncut purple amber. She was studying the pink rocks very intently. Her energy whispered in the chamber. He responded to it in ways he could not describe.

A thumping sound made him turn around. Otis was jumping up and down on top of a small steel lockbox, apparently annoyed because he could not get inside.

Gabriel walked toward the lockbox. He took the old-fashioned lock pick out of his pack. The lock on the box was mechanical, not high-tech.

"Let me see what I can do, pal," he said.

Otis muttered encouragement and hopped off the top of the case. He watched intently as Gabriel went to work on the lock. A few seconds later there was a sharp click.

Gabriel raised the lid. Two velvet bags and an envelope were inside the box. Otis chortled exultantly, as if to declare he had won the game.

"Thanks," Gabriel said. "You saved us a lot of time."

Satisfied with his victory, Otis waved his dust bunny and bounced across the chamber to continue his explorations.

"What did he find?" Lucy asked, hurrying across the room.

"Let's see."

Gabriel picked up the larger of the two velvet bags, rose, and went to a nearby workbench. He loosened the cord and emptied the contents of the bag onto the bench. A dozen chunks of uncut gray amber tumbled out.

He took the pendant from his pocket. It was glowing because it was still in close proximity to the other pendant and to the one that Lucy wore. None of the raw, gray amber stones illuminated in response.

"It's the same kind of gray amber, but it hasn't been cut or tuned," he said.

Lucy picked up the other velvet bag and the envelope. She carried both to the workbench and opened the bag.

There was a piece of cut and polished amber inside. It glowed a deep, dark blue. She plucked it out and set it on the workbench.

"Pitney had one tuned rock left," she said. "I wonder why it wasn't sold to whoever commissioned the pendants?"

"Good question." Gabriel picked up the stone and kicked up his talent. Awareness flashed across his senses. "This one is different."

"How?"

He tightened his grip on the stone. The energy in it pulsed, strong and steady. "It's more powerful than the pendants. I think it's doing more than just sending out a short-distance recognition signal."

"What?"

"I have no idea. Open the envelope."

Lucy unsealed the envelope and glanced inside. "It's one of those small video recorders that journalists use."

"Journalists aren't the only people who like those gadgets. The police and blackmailers are fond of them, too. Easy to conceal. They're sophisticated devices. We won't be able to rez it down here in the tunnels. Let's get back to the surface and see what we've got."

Lucy put the recorder in her pack. "It will probably be password protected."

"That shouldn't be a problem. My administrative assistant is good when it comes to tech security issues."

Lucy glanced around the chamber. "Otis? Where are you? We're going home. Time for dinner."

Otis emerged from behind a crate, made enthusiastic sounds, and fluttered toward the door.

"He's very keen on dinner," Lucy said.

Gabriel watched the dust bunny hustle out into the corridor.

"So am I," he said.

He switched on the locator. *I'm also big on the idea of going home. With you.*

CHAPTER TWENTY-SIX

"We'd better take our shoes off in the car," Lucy said as Gabriel brought the big SUV to a stop in front of the apartment house. "Mrs. Briggs will be pissed if we leave sooty prints in the hall and on the stairs."

"Can't blame her," Gabriel said.

Lucy removed her sneakers, hooked them on two fingers, opened the door, and got out of the vehicle. She tried to remember if there was anything left in her refrigerator. She'd had no time to do any grocery shopping recently. It looked like a takeout night. Not pizza, she decided. Anything but.

She liked pizza—nevertheless, what with one thing and another, she had eaten a lot of it lately, including at lunch that day.

Gabriel joined her, his low boots gripped in one hand. Otis had given himself a good shake when they left Pitney's shop, but his paws were still covered with gray ash, and there was more of it in his fur. He did not appear concerned.

"Here, I'll take him," Lucy said. She reached up to remove Otis from Gabriel's shoulder. "He'll leave paw prints everywhere."

Otis started to object to the change of location. She gave him a pat on the head. "Please, Otis. It's important. We do not want to annoy our landlady."

Otis allowed her to tuck him under her arm. They walked toward the front door of the lobby.

The door opened before Lucy could punch in the code. Mrs. Briggs stood in the opening, a picnic basket in her hands. That was disconcerting enough, but it was the fact that Briggs was smiling that sent a chill of alarm through Lucy.

"Uh, hi, Mrs. Briggs," she said. "Going on a picnic?"

"No." Mrs. Briggs's smile did not waver. "Waiting for you to get home, dear."

Dear? The situation was becoming more unnerving by the moment.

Gabriel nodded. "Hello, Mrs. Briggs. Nice to see you again."

"It's lovely to see you, too, Mr. Jones." Mrs. Briggs's welcoming smile abruptly switched to a frown of concern and, finally, shock. "You're covered in soot and ash." Her eyes widened. "Both of you are. And so is the dust bunny. Were you in a fire?"

"No, ma'am," Gabriel said. "We got too close to a building that had recently been burned out."

"Was there a major fire in town today? I didn't see anything on the rez screen."

"The fire occurred months ago, Mrs. Briggs," Lucy said quickly. "We happened to walk down the street in front of the damaged building. Accidentally brushed up against the ashes and soot. A shower will take care of everything."

Mrs. Briggs scowled at Otis. "See that your dust bunny gets a bath, too. Don't let him get his filthy paws on the lobby floor or the stairs or the hallway."

Otis ignored her, as was his habit.

"We'll be careful," Lucy said.

Mrs. Briggs scrutinized her and Gabriel. "I see you've both taken off your shoes. That's good. Don't touch anything on the way up to your apartment."

"We won't," Lucy promised.

Mrs. Briggs recovered her composure, rezzed up a surreal smile, and held out the picnic basket. "I've been waiting for you and Mr. Jones to return. I know the two of you have been very busy lately. I thought you might like a break from takeout and delivery. I made my special stew and corn bread for you. Just heat and serve. There's a lovely cheesecake for dessert."

Lucy managed, just barely, not to appear completely stunned. She handed Otis to Gabriel and took the basket. It was heavy. "Thank you so much. I've got diddly-squat in the refrigerator."

"You're quite welcome." Mrs. Briggs turned back to Gabriel. "It's so nice to have the director of the new Guild visiting in our neighborhood. Will you be staying with Lucy until you find a place of your own? We would be thrilled to have you as a permanent resident here in the Dark Zone. I've got a vacancy coming up soon. It's on the second floor, not far from Lucy's apartment. Very convenient."

"Thanks," Gabriel said. "I'll certainly keep that in mind."

"If you decide to buy instead of rent, I can give you my son's card," Mrs. Briggs continued. "He's a real estate agent who specializes in this zone. Outside agents can't find their way around our neighborhood. You'll definitely want an expert who is local. He'll get you the best price, too."

"I will remember that," Gabriel said.

Lucy tightened her grip on the basket and flashed Mrs. Briggs another smile. "Got to run. Sorry, can't chat. Thanks again for the meal. Have a good evening."

"You, too, dear," Mrs. Briggs said. "Oh, one more thing. Don't forget that according to your lease you can't have a guest staying in your apartment for longer than a week. After that there will be an extra charge. If Mr. Jones moves in with you, we'll need to sign a new lease, one with both your names on it. The monthly rent will be adjusted accordingly."

Lucy forced herself to smile. "Thanks for the reminder."

Mrs. Briggs stood back to allow them into the lobby. Otis waved his dust bunny, eager to get upstairs. The action raised a small cloud of ashes, most of which landed on Mrs. Briggs's face and the front of her blouse.

She gave a yelp of dismay, stepped back quickly, and brushed frantically at her clothing.

"Gentlemen, let's move," Lucy said. She sprinted toward the stairs. "Fast."

Gabriel followed, taking the stairs two at a time with an easy stride. Otis chortled, sensing a new game.

Lucy was panting by the time she reached the landing. The picnic basket felt as if it was loaded with rocks. It was also awkward.

Down below in the lobby a door slammed. Mrs. Briggs was not happy.

Lucy led the way along the hall and set the picnic basket down long enough to get the door open. She picked up the basket and rushed inside. She dropped the basket and whirled around to seize the sleeve of Gabriel's leather jacket. She hauled him inside. Otis chortled with glee.

She closed the door, locked it, and turned to glare at Gabriel and Otis. "Into the shower. Both of you. I'll wipe down the packs, shoes, and jackets. Gabriel, leave the rest of your clothes on the floor of the bathroom."

"What about you?" Gabriel asked with suspicious innocence. "There's room in the shower for all three of us."

She narrowed her eyes. "No. There is not enough room for all three of us. Don't even think about it."

"Well, we wouldn't need Otis, so—"

"Go clean up. Now."

"Right."

Chapter Twenty-Seven

Forty minutes later Lucy shoved the stew and the corn bread into the oven and poured two large glasses of wine. The sooty clothes were all in the washer. The leather jacket and packs were outside on the balcony. With luck, the smoky odor would be gone by morning.

She took the lid off Otis's pretzel bowl. He hopped up onto the rim and went to work selecting pretzels. She opened a cupboard, took down her own jar of pretzels, and filled two small bowls. She handed the wine to Gabriel, picked up the bowls, and led the way to the sofa.

They sat down. Gabriel propped his sock-clad feet on the coffee table, ate several pretzels, and then leaned back against the cushions. He drank some of his wine and lowered his glass.

"Interesting day," he said.

Lucy ate a few pretzels, picked up her glass, and stacked her slippered feet on the table. "That's one word for it."

They both looked at the miniature video recorder sitting on the coffee table between the two bowls of pretzels. The recorder was not the only souvenir of the day on the table. The two velvet jewelry bags they had discovered in Pitney's private vault were also there.

After a moment's contemplation, Gabriel leaned forward and picked up the recorder.

"Let's see if we can rez it," he said. "If it's locked I'll call Aiden and tell him I need help."

"Okay."

Lucy watched Gabriel rez the start button. To her astonishment, the screen lit up. A blinking light indicated it was ready to record or review previous recordings.

"Huh." She took another sip of wine. "Pitney was big on security. Wonder why he didn't use a password."

Gabriel rezzed REVIEW. There was a brief delay before the image of an aging elf of a man appeared on the small screen. He wore a leather apron over a faded work shirt. His unkempt gray hair was topped by a brimmed leather cap. When he spoke, his voice was strong but laced with urgency and dread.

"My name is Stewart Pitney. I'm an expert in rare amber tuning. If you're viewing this, I am probably dead. I'll keep the message as short as possible. A few weeks ago a man who identified himself only as Tuck brought a handful of raw gray amber stones to my shop. He asked me to tune them so that they would resonate with each other when in close proximity. I didn't like the look of the man—ex-Guild, I think. But he paid cash. I admit the gray amber interested me. I'd never seen anything like it. Tuck wouldn't tell me the source, but I've seen a lot of rocks in my time. I'm almost certain the amber he gave me came from the Ghost City. Here's the video of him that my recorder picked up when he came to my shop."

A short video of a seriously bulked-up man wearing a leather jacket, boots, and khaki cargo trousers popped up. Tuck wore a black cap with the brim pulled down low over his eyes, but it was possible to see the lower half of his face and his jaw.

"Could be a biker," Lucy said.

Gabriel shook his head. "Pitney is right. Tuck is ex-Guild."

"No offense, but how can you tell the difference between an ex-Guild man and a low-rent biker gang enforcer?"

"The way he wears his nav amber," Gabriel said. He never took his eyes off the screen.

Lucy took a closer look. "Damn, you're right. He's loaded with it, right down to his earring and belt buckle."

"Old habits die hard."

"Maybe the habits aren't so old. What makes you think he's *ex-*Guild?"

"If he's not already ex, he will be as soon as I find him."

Pitney resumed his tale.

"Tuck ordered twelve amber pendants that could be worn under clothing. One of the pendants was to be the keystone. It could be used to track the other eleven pendants. His main concern was confidentiality. I assumed he was forming a gang or a club. Figured it wasn't my business. It's not the first time I've handled that kind of request. I fulfilled the order, including the keystone. But toward the end my intuition kicked in. I created one more pendant, another keystone, and kept it for myself."

Lucy picked up the smaller velvet bag and took out the glowing amber pendant. "This must be the thirteenth stone."

"The standard pendants resonate with the others within a short distance— fifteen to twenty feet, max. But the keystone has a much longer range. It's basically a tracking device. Works on the surface or in the tunnels. I used it to follow Tuck from a safe distance immediately after he picked up the twelve

pendants. He drove to the Shadow Zone and stopped at one of the low-end casinos. He took a package inside. When he came out he was no longer carrying it, but the tracker indicated he was wearing one of the stones."

Gabriel watched the screen, his eyes hard and intent. Focused. Lucy recognized the vibe. The Lord of the Underworld was on another mission.

"I realized the man who called himself Tuck had given the remaining pendants to someone inside the casino, so I waited. I wanted to see who took them out. Under other circumstances I would have missed the guy, because he left from the rear parking lot. But the keystone locked onto the other pendants. I followed the vehicle. It stopped in front of a private residence in the Amber Oasis neighborhood. Here's the video I took that night."

The image of Pitney vanished. A different video appeared. Lucy watched, riveted, as a nondescript black SUV drove up a quiet street in the expensive neighborhood of Amber Oasis. The vehicle went through a set of gates protecting a high-walled estate. The house number and street name were enscribed on a discreet plaque next to the gates. The gates closed.

The video ended. Pitney reappeared.

Gabriel took out his phone and opened the mapping program.

"I waited awhile longer," Pitney said. "The signal strength of the stones weakened. I realized they were being moved again. Someone, presumably the man who had picked up the pendants, took them down into the tunnels. The house must have a hole-in-the-wall in the basement. I have no idea what is going on, but it's obvious I wasn't creating ID stones for an ordinary biker gang. I pulled up the identity of the owner of that house in the Amber Oasis neighborhood. When you do the same you will see why I'm concerned. I am going to leave Illusion Town for a while. If you find this video, I urge you to contact the police."

Gabriel held up the phone so that Lucy could see the tax records of the big house in Amber Oasis. She stared at the screen, shocked.

"Dillon Westover," she said.

"Yes."

"Now what are we going to do? We can't just confront him. We have evidence to back up my kidnapping story, but it's not proof. We need something a lot more solid."

"Agreed. We need more information." Gabriel punched in a code on his phone and set it on speaker and video.

A young man wearing a pair of black-framed glasses appeared on the screen. His hair was cut in the latest style, and his slouchy jacket and open-collared shirt were very on trend. There was loud rez-rock music playing and a wash of voices and clinking glasses. The familiar clang, buzz, and beep of slot machines could be heard.

"Yes, Mr. Jones?" he said. He noticed Lucy at the edge of the screen and inclined his head. "Good evening, ma'am. You must be Ms. Bell."

"Yes," she said. "And you must be—"

Gabriel interrupted. "Aiden Shore, Lucy Bell. Lucy, meet Aiden."

Lucy smiled. "Call me Lucy."

"Thanks—" Aiden began.

Gabriel broke into the conversation again.

"Are you in a nightclub?" Gabriel asked.

"Restaurant on the Strip, sir. Nightclubs don't get hot until midnight in this town."

"Why aren't you in the office?"

"It's almost eight o'clock, Mr. Jones. I closed the office at five, per standard Guild policy."

Gabriel frowned, clearly bewildered by the concept of regular office hours. "The Guild is on duty around the clock."

"Yes, sir, but the CEO is not in his office around the clock," Aiden said, remarkably patient. "And neither is his administrative assistant.

Once we have more staff, we will establish a proper emergency response team to handle the night shift. Until then, Jared, Joe, and myself are the closest thing we've got to an ERT. We've got our phones on. That's all we can do at the moment."

Gabriel exhaled deeply. "Right."

"We need to recruit additional staff, sir."

"Put it on my to-do list."

"It is on your to-do list. It just isn't at the top. Yet."

"Moving right along," Gabriel said in a grim voice. "I've got an emergency for you."

"Hang on while I get someplace where I can talk privately."

There was the usual screen jiggling while Aiden rose from the table and hurried into a hallway. When he stopped there was a sign on the wall behind him. EMERGENCY EXIT.

"Ready, sir," he said.

"I want you to locate a man named Tuck."

"That's not a lot to go on."

"I've got a few more details. I'm sure he's ex-Guild, so he should be in the database. We know he was in Illusion Town four months ago, and there's good reason to think he's still in the vicinity. I'll send over the only photo I've got. A few months back he was looking for a tuner who could handle rare ambers. He would have had to ask around, because he found Pitney in the Shadow Zone. Looks like Tuck killed him to keep him quiet."

"So we're talking about a man who is capable of murder and arson?"

"Yes."

"Anything else?" Aiden asked, waxing enthusiastic.

Another man eager to take on a mission, Lucy thought. She smiled to herself. Whatever else you could say about him—and there was a lot to say—you had to give Gabriel credit. He knew how to assemble a team and infuse them with his love of the job.

"One more thing," Gabriel continued. "He may be wearing a gray amber pendant like the ones I showed you today, but that's not a great clue, because he probably conceals it under his shirt and jacket."

"Is he married?"

Lucy realized Gabriel was looking at her, silently asking for an opinion.

"Unlikely," she said. "He doesn't appear to be good husband material."

"But you think he's been in town for about four months?" Aiden pressed.

"That's my theory," Gabriel said. "Where are you going with this?"

"I may be looking for a professional."

"Professional mercenary? Yes, that's exactly what I'm trying to tell you."

"No, sir," Aiden said. "A professional sex worker. He or she might remember seeing an unusual amber necklace on a client."

Lucy leaned forward. "That's a brilliant idea, Aiden."

Aiden glowed. "Thanks, Ms. Bell. I just hope it works."

"I can save you some time locating a professional," Lucy continued. "I know one who lives here in my apartment building. Veronica Star. She's a disciplinarian. Works at the Dungeon Club. Knows everyone in the business."

"Stage name, I assume?"

"Of course. I'll go down the hall and ask her to contact you immediately. I'm sure she will be delighted to do a favor for the Guild. It's obvious everyone in town wants to do favors for your organization."

"That is good to hear. It means our public relations program is rolling out the way I envisioned. I'll wait for Ms. Star's call. Meanwhile, Mr. Jones, I'll go into the Guild database and see what I can find out about this Tuck guy. But unless we get lucky, it's going to take a while. I'll call you as soon as I have information."

"Thanks, Aiden," Gabriel said.

He ended the call and looked at Lucy, who was getting to her feet.

"Where are you going?" he asked.

"Down the hall to talk to Veronica." Lucy checked the time. "It's early yet. I should be able to catch her before she leaves for work."

"I'll come with you." Gabriel smiled. "Public relations are important. The Guild wants the citizens of Illusion Town to know that we appreciate their assistance."

"If you're tempted to sign up for a half-priced package of therapy sessions, save your money. I'll be happy to accommodate you at full price."

"Deal."

CHAPTER TWENTY-EIGHT

It was only seven o'clock in the morning, but the CEO's suite was in a state of controlled chaos. Gabriel froze in the doorway. Otis, perched on his shoulder, nearly fell off. He chortled, apparently convinced the sudden stop was a new game.

"What in green hell?" Gabriel said.

Lucy managed, barely, to keep from colliding with him. She found her balance and studied the scene.

"I'm impressed," she said. "You hired an interior designer. Excellent move. You need a statement office."

"I didn't hire a designer," Gabriel said. "It was Aiden's idea."

"That figures," Lucy said. "But, hey, a CEO is known by the quality of the talent he hires, so congrats to you for having the smarts to hire Aiden."

Gabriel looked at her.

She gave him a sunny smile.

The spacious suite was crowded with workers and craftspeople engaged in measuring walls, windows, and the floor. An imperious-looking woman in a crisp business suit and heels stood in the center of the whirlwind. She was engaged in an intense conversation with Aiden.

"Mr. Jones doesn't want any loud, over-the-top colors," Aiden said. "He was very explicit about that."

"What colors in particular does he want to avoid?" the woman asked.

"Any colors that would make people think of a casino or a nightclub," Aiden said. "You must understand, Ms. Fortune, the Guild has a long and noble history. This office should reflect that. I agree we want to project a forward-thinking vibe, but the space must also invoke the history of the organization. As I'm sure you're aware, green and amber are our traditional colors. They harken back to the Era of Discord, when the Guilds were founded."

"I understand those colors are traditional, but trust me when I tell you that the combination is dreadful when it is used in a large space like this. Mr. Jones does not want a lot of green and amber."

"I'm afraid he does," Aiden said.

Ms. Fortune sighed. "We can certainly have touches of amber and green for accents, but this is a modern space. It should read *on trend*, not *old-fashioned*."

"What colors did you have in mind?" Aiden asked.

"A deep purple for the walls, I think."

"No," Aiden said. "Purple is not a good idea."

"Aiden," Gabriel said from the doorway, "I need to talk to you. Now."

Aiden whipped around. "Sorry, Mr. Jones. I didn't see you there. This is Helen Fortune, of Fortune and Associates. She's the interior designer I hired."

Helen gave Gabriel a professional smile and walked forward to greet him. "A pleasure to meet you, Mr. Jones. We're all absolutely thrilled to have our very own Guild headquarters here in Illusion Town."

Lucy nudged Gabriel. "Public relations," she whispered. "Image."

He muttered something under his breath that sounded a lot like "*I don't have time for this ghost shit*" but he managed a reasonably polite smile. "Nice to meet you, too, Ms. Fortune."

"Helen, please. I am very excited about giving your office a look that will reflect and project an aura of modern professionalism and at the same time speaks to the mission of the Guild."

"Great," Gabriel said. "That sounds terrific. Aiden?"

"Yes, sir." Aiden hurried across the room to the doorway.

Gabriel stepped back into the hall. "This is Guild business. We'll discuss it out here."

"Yes, sir." Aiden walked out into the hall and shut the door. He smiled at Lucy. "Nice to meet you in person, Ms. Bell."

"Thanks," Lucy said. "A pleasure to meet you, too. You've got a big job on your hands."

Aiden nodded with a solemn air. "I know, but it's an honor to be working as Mr. Jones's assistant."

"I was referring to the job of designing an impressive office for Gabriel," Lucy said.

Aiden got the mission-focused look that Lucy was coming to associate with people who worked for Gabriel. "Getting this office right is one of the most important items on my agenda."

Gabriel eyed the closed door. "I've got a bad feeling about what's going on in there."

"Don't worry, sir. It will be spectacular when it's finished."

"That's what I'm afraid of," Gabriel said. "I'm not the spectacular type."

"I'm sure you will grow into your new job," Lucy said.

Gabriel ignored her. "I got your message, Aiden. Tell me what you found."

"Yes, sir." Aiden rezzed his phone and studied it briefly. "As you suspected, Tuck is ex-Guild. Full name is Tucker Taylor. He's gone by Tuck since he was kicked out of the Resonance organization. Evidently he started hiring out as a so-called freelance security specialist. Worked for some shady businesses—collecting debts, intimidating customers who wanted to settle disputes in court, that sort of thing. The Resonance Guild kept an eye on him from a distance for a while, but they stopped paying attention when he left town."

"Where did he go?" Gabriel asked.

"For a time he seems to have drifted from one city to another," Aiden said. He looked up from his phone. "But all indications are that he eventually wound up here."

"There's a lot of private security in this town," Lucy said. "All the casinos, large and small, need security people around the clock. So do the nightclubs, to say nothing of the usual corporate and retail sectors. An ex-Guild man could find freelance work here quite easily."

"Who is Tuck working for now?" Gabriel asked.

"I couldn't discover the answer to that question," Aiden said. "He is evidently keeping a very low profile. He didn't show up as an employee of any of the big security agencies. Best guess is that he's working in the private end of the business. There's a lot of money sloshing around this town. Rich people always want security for their estates and penthouses."

"Is that everything you've got?" Gabriel asked.

"Not quite." Aiden's eyes gleamed with anticipation. "Thanks to Ms. Veronica Star, I was able to track down a professional dominatrix who had one session with a client who fits Tuck's description. He used the name Blue when he booked the appointment."

"What did she say about Blue?"

"Mistress Correct told me—"

Gabriel frowned. "Mistress Correct?"

"Stage name, sir." Aiden cleared his throat. "Mistress Correct said she recognized the gray amber in the pendant because she has a talent for tuning and once worked professionally in that capacity. Said there was more money in her new line. Anyhow, she commented on the stone and asked Blue where he had purchased it. Blue lied and said he had picked it up at a small shop in a town outside of Cadence."

"What made her sure he was lying?" Gabriel asked.

Aiden looked up again. "Because she recognized the style of the setting and the skill of the tuning work. She told me there was no mistaking Pitney's techniques. Mistress Correct did not push the matter, because she didn't like Blue and had already decided not to take him on as a regular."

"Was Mistress Correct able to give you a lead on Tuck's current address?"

"No, but he told her he was new in town and asked her to recommend a nightclub that would cater to a man of his tastes. She suggested the Basement. It's several blocks off the Strip in the Amber Zone. I paid a personal visit at about three this morning and talked to the manager, who said the description I gave him fit a customer who usually shows up around midnight. Stays a couple of hours watching the floor show and drinking. Evidently I just missed him. He's always alone. Always pays cash. Definitely ex-Guild, according to the manager. Here's the good news, sir: the club maintains security videos of every car that enters and leaves the parking lot. I've got a vehicle description, a license plate, and an address in the Shadow Zone."

Energy whispered in the atmosphere.

"Good work, Aiden," Gabriel said.

Aiden appeared gratified. "Thank you, sir. What's the next step?"

"Jared will escort Ms. Bell to her job in the Storm Zone. I will pay a visit to Tuck's house. With luck, he won't be home."

"Got it," Aiden said.

"One more thing, Aiden."

"Yes, sir?"

"If there is one drop of purple in my office, you will move your office into the basement."

"Yes, sir."

CHAPTER TWENTY-NINE

The small house was located in a partially abandoned neighborhood on the fringes of the Shadow Zone. The zone's Strip, with its casinos, clubs, and restaurants, was a couple of miles away, near the Wall.

Gabriel stood in the doorway of a long-closed nightclub. There was so much grime on the narrow windows, it was next to impossible to make out the interior of the place. Because of the fog, it was almost as hard to see the house across the street. There was no sign of a vehicle parked in front, and the lights were off inside. In the Shadow Zone, the lights were always on when someone was home.

It was possible that Tuck was asleep, but the lack of a vehicle indicated he was most likely out.

Gabriel left the doorway and made his way through the mist to the rear entrance of the shabby old house. The back door was locked, but that was not a problem. He rezzed the lock with a jammer.

A few seconds later he was inside. He gave his eyes a moment to adjust to the deep gloom before, flamer in hand, he began a slow, thorough walk-through. There wasn't much in the way of furniture: a small kitchen table, a chair, a mattress on the floor.

In fairness, there was more stuff in Tuck's place than he had in his own apartment, Gabriel reflected. He was going to have to do something about that one of these days. He couldn't invite Lucy over for a drink until he got a table and a couple of chairs. He needed a bed, too. Definitely a bed. Lucy's words floated through his head. *At your age, you should not be renting furniture.*

He moved into the kitchen and discovered a handful of paper plates and cups. The refrigerator contained nothing but a few bottles of Hot Amber Beer. Evidently Tuck was not into home cooking. There were paranormal footprints everywhere. Presumably they belonged to Tuck, since there was no evidence that anyone else lived in the house.

He opened his senses and took a close look at the hot prints. After a moment he went into the kitchen and fished an empty beer bottle out of the trash. More prints. He studied them, his senses open, until he was sure he would recognize them.

"Got you," he said softly.

He found a door concealed inside a closet. When he opened it, he saw a flight of steps. Tunnel heat pinged his senses. That was promising. He rezzed his flashlight and went down into the basement.

Tuck had made very little effort to conceal the hole-in-the-wall. There was a sheet of plywood in front of the opening. That was it. Gabriel moved it aside and found himself looking through a jagged rip in the quartz. Beyond was a glowing corridor.

He had to turn sideways to get through the fissure. Once inside, he switched off the flashlight and stowed it in his belt. He took out his locator. He paused to enter the coordinates of the entry point so that he could find his way back and kicked up his senses.

The faint heat of footprints glowed on the floor. Same prints as those he had found in the house. He started walking.

The tunnel sled was parked a few steps away. He had gotten lucky. The sleds looked like golf carts, and they were slow, because they used the simplest of amber-based engines. At top speed they could move only about as fast as the average person could run, but they were the only option for those who wanted to travel long distances or haul a heavy load in the Underworld.

Gabriel smiled. One of the most useful aspects of a sled was the built-in locator. It automatically recorded the coordinates of each trip.

He stepped up into the small vehicle, sat down on the bench seat, and rezzed the screen that locked in the coordinates. Most of the trips, including the last one, had been to the same destination. The location wasn't far away.

He punched in the coordinates and powered up the sled. The little engine hummed to life. The vehicle glided forward down the corridor.

Fifteen minutes later, after a series of twists and turns, it came to a halt at another jagged crack in the Wall. He drove the little vehicle into a nearby chamber to conceal it, got out, and went back to the hole-in-the-wall. There was a short tunnel through dirt and rock. At the far end, a mag-steel door guarded the route to the surface.

He moved through the tunnel, preparing to go to work with the lock pick. A strong vibe of energy from the vicinity of his jacket made him realize Pitney's tracking stone was hot. He took it out. The amber was glowing a fierce, deep blue. Pitney had not described exactly how the tracker worked, but presumably the intensity of the energy indicated that it was close to more than one signal stone. That, in turn, indicated a high probability that at least a few of the kidnappers were on the other side of the door, most likely on the surface.

He put the tracker back into his jacket, took out the lock pick, and opened the door. Predictably, he found himself in yet another unlit basement. No one rushed at him with a mag-rez or a flamer, so he left the steel door ajar and took out his flashlight.

There was a spiral staircase at the far end of the basement. When he got to the door at the top, he looked through the window and saw the faded gaming floor of an abandoned casino. Card tables and overturned slot machines had been pushed against the walls to make room for a couple of long workbenches. Three people in white coats, gloves, and protective goggles were working at one of the benches.

A clunky machine that appeared to be a cross between a fire extinguisher and a leaf blower sat in the middle of the table. Next to it was a steel rack. Three glass canisters stood upright in the rack. The contents shimmered and gleamed a ghostly shade of gray. In addition to the machine, there were a number of high-tech lab instruments and assorted power tools on the bench.

Four men dressed in khaki and leather lounged near the door at the far end of the room. They wore a lot of amber and they all had flamers and meg-rez guns, but the weapons were holstered. There was no mistaking security personnel—in this case bored security personnel.

Gabriel pulled the camera out of his jacket, took several shots through the window, and went back down the staircase. He let himself out through the steel door, rezzed the lock behind him, and moved through the fissure and into the glowing tunnel. He fired up the sled and set the coordinates to return to the hole-in-the-wall beneath Tuck's house.

He knew an off-the-books lab when he saw one. The Guild was forever taking down such operations in the Underworld. The tunnels and the Rainforest were ideal places to set up illegal businesses, but the location had one very big drawback—high-tech equipment didn't work down below. The fact that the lab he had just seen was filled with exotic instrumentation explained why it was on the surface.

The old casino didn't look like a standard drug lab. More like a weapons factory.

He considered his options. The four ex-Guild men were involved in whatever was going on in the lab. He had the authority to take them into custody and request that the police hold them for questioning. But at this point it would be next to impossible to prove they had kidnapped Lucy. He needed more information before he could act.

He brought the sled to a halt near Tuck's hole-in-the-wall and stepped down onto the quartz floor. He took out his flamer and his own locator. No sense courting trouble by exiting the tunnels through Tuck's house. Soon there would be a confrontation with the mercenary, but there was one more thing to do before that happened. It was time to take care of the public relations aspect of the case.

When he picked up Tuck, he wanted the cooperation of the Illusion Town Police and the local authorities. He could almost hear Aiden now. *It will look much better in the press if the Guild and the cops are seen as having worked together to break this case.*

Time to talk to the chief of police.

It was a good plan, as plans go—and as plans go, it went to green hell the moment he launched it.

He was about twelve feet away when the intense storm of acid-green dissonance energy flashed into existence in front of him. The whirling, pulsing ball of hot green fire momentarily seared his senses.

It happened that way sometimes. The ghosts drifted randomly throughout the tunnels. It was impossible to predict when you might turn a corner and blunder into one. That was why corporations, entrepreneurs, and research projects always hired Guild teams for protection.

The hot green fires of swirling dissonance energy were slow moving, but the big ones were exceedingly dangerous. A small version could knock you unconscious if it brushed against you. The monsters could shatter the senses—paranormal and normal—and leave the victim in a coma. A ghost that burned hot enough could kill.

But ghost hunters had some natural immunity, a side effect of their talent for handling dissonance energy. They also had the ability to sense a ghost before it got too close, assuming the ball of acid-hot flames was one of the natural sort.

This one had exploded into existence with no warning. That happened only when it had been generated by someone with a strong talent for controlling dissonance energy—another trained ghost hunter.

"Drop the flamer, Jones."

Gabriel set the weapon down on the tunnel floor. He used the move to palm the glowing blue amber, wrapping his fingers tightly around the tracker to conceal the energy. The wild flames of the huge ghost offered plenty of distraction.

"Turn around. Slowly."

Gabriel took a few steps back from the hot ghost and obeyed the command.

Tuck stood in the tunnel, flamer in hand. "Got a silent alarm that alerts me if someone accesses my hole-in-the-wall. Nice little gadget I picked up in the Guild."

"You're good," Gabriel said. "That is one badass ghost you pulled."

Tuck smiled a thin smile. His eyes glittered with energy. He was rezzed, riding the high that came with using his psychic talent at full strength.

"I was the best when I was in the Guild," he said. "But the new boss didn't appreciate my talent."

"According to the file, you were kicked out because you were running your own private pirate operation in the Underworld."

Tuck shrugged. "So? The old boss looked the other way as long as I did my job."

"You may have noticed that the Guilds are under new management now."

"Yeah, well, some of us are still old-school."

Gabriel could feel the paranormal heat from the blazing energy behind him, but the ghost wasn't coming closer. Yet. Evidently Tuck didn't want to kill him until he got some answers. That worked both ways.

"Have a nice little trip on my sled?" Tuck asked.

"I found the lab in that old casino," Gabriel said. "What's going on there?"

Tuck grinned, showing a lot of teeth. "Remember the power failure on the Amber Strip?"

"I was there," Gabriel said.

"It wasn't an accident."

"I had a feeling you were going to say that. So, you're into the weapons trade now?"

"It's not just a weapon. Don't you get it? That device took down the whole fucking Strip. My client controls that gadget and the source of the liquid crystal it uses. And I'm in charge of security for the project."

"Impressive." Gabriel opened his hand. The blue amber tracker glowed. "I see you're also into kidnapping these days."

Jolted, Tuck stared at the amber. "That's not one of my team's ID stones. Where did you get it?"

"Pitney made one more tracker before you murdered him and burned down his shop. The Guild and the local police will be able to use it to round up your gang. It's evidence that you and your pals are involved in the kidnapping of a weather channeler named Lucy Bell."

Alarm, bordering on panic, flashed in Tuck's hot eyes. "Fuck you and your evidence," he snarled. "That rock won't be a problem after you're dead."

The hair on the back of Gabriel's neck stirred. The ghost was starting to drift toward him. At the same time, Tuck finally sensed the very small ghost that was moving toward the back of his head.

He started to turn around, but he was too late. The little ball of green fire grazed him. He jerked once and collapsed.

"Size doesn't always matter," Gabriel said quietly.

He focused some heat through his ring and de-rezzed the small dissonance energy manifestation he had pulled. Then he swung around to face the large ghost Tuck had generated. The monster had stopped moving, because it was no longer under Tuck's control, but it still burned, blocking the tunnel. Left unattended, it might sit there forever, or it might start to drift.

The technique for de-rezzing a powerful ghost was similar to the one that firefighters sometimes used to stop a wildfire—a backfire. As the saying went, *it takes a ghost to kill a ghost.* He rezzed another compact, tightly controlled ball of fire and aimed it at the chaotic center of Tuck's ghost.

His hot whirlwind of controlled dissonance energy clashed with the impressive but weakly structured ghost Tuck had created. Control won, every damn time.

Tuck's flashy ghost disintegrated and winked out.

Gabriel de-rezzed his own ghost and went forward to strip off Tuck's nav amber. There was a lot of it. When he was finished, he used his captive's bootlaces to secure Tuck's wrists behind his back.

He loaded the unconscious man onto the sled and got behind the wheel. He rezzed his personal locator and punched in the coordinates of the hole-in-the-wall beneath Guild headquarters.

The first item on the agenda was to have a long talk with Tuck. Then it would be time to call in the local police and alert Mr. Smith and the members of the Illusion Club.

Public relations.

CHAPTER THIRTY

Lucy was not surprised when the other power brokers who ran Illusion Town filed into Gabriel's office an hour after receiving his request for an urgent meeting. She stood at the window, dressed in her professional Underworld gear. Otis was on her shoulder. Together they watched the VIPs enter the room.

It made for a crowd. Aiden had called the mayor's office, the members of the city council, the chief of police, and Mr. Smith, the owner of the Amber Palace. Smith had, in turn, summoned the members of the Illusion Club, which consisted of the CEOs who operated the big casinos on the Strip. The dramatic power outage two days earlier had gotten everyone's attention.

Aiden had somehow managed to produce a couple of dozen folding chairs. He stood at the entrance to Gabriel's sparsely furnished office, ushering in each new arrival and offering large cups of coffee. He had memorized every face. He greeted each individual by name and introduced the person to Gabriel.

"Thank you for coming on such short notice, Mayor Carson," he said. "Please excuse the office. We're in the midst of decorating. This is Mr. Jones, the director of the Illusion Town Guild . . ."

The mayor, a fashionably dressed woman with silver hair, exchanged pleasantries with Gabriel and took a seat.

Aiden turned to the short man dressed in a tailored white suit.

"Mr. Smith, so glad you could make it, sir. Apologies for the state of the office. We've just begun to decorate. This is Mr. Jones, the director of the Illusion Town Guild . . ."

Smith inclined his head in a gesture of respect. "A pleasure to meet you in person, Mr. Jones. I'm looking forward to hosting you and your companion in my penthouse."

Startled, Lucy glanced at Gabriel. Companion? Was Smith talking about her? Gabriel did not appear to notice her questioning look. He was busy greeting the next dignitary.

When everyone was seated, a hush fell over the crowd. Gabriel remained on his feet, subtly showing respect for his audience and at the same time conveying an aura of authority and power.

"I asked you to come here today because the Guild is on the brink of closing a case that I believe started out in the Underworld," he said. "Most of you will recall the three-day disappearance of Lucy Bell, a professional weather channeler. Ms. Bell is with us today."

Everyone in the room except Gabriel turned to look at Lucy. She nodded politely.

Aware that he suddenly had an audience, Otis chortled and waved his toy dust bunny. There were a few scattered chuckles, but the audience quickly turned its attention back to Gabriel.

"When Ms. Bell was located, she told a story no one believed," Gabriel continued, "including me. She claimed she had been drugged, kidnapped, and taken down into the Underworld. When I got her back to the surface, I made the mistake of leaving her in the hands of a clinic. She was once again drugged. Knowing no one would buy her version of events, she kept a low profile for the next two months. She had one solid piece of evidence: a pendant made of a rare gray amber that glowed blue when it was in the vicinity of another chunk of amber that had been tuned to resonate with it."

Gabriel picked up the pendant he had taken off one of the men who had attacked in the Ghost City.

"You will notice it's hot at the moment because it's resonating with another, similar pendant. Lucy?"

She opened her jacket to reveal the pendant she wore around her neck. There were murmurs of curiosity and interest.

Hopton, the chief of police, frowned. "Looks like an ID stone," he said. "Biker gangs use them. So do the members of certain clubs. Works like a tattoo. Signals the wearer's affiliation with a certain group."

"Yes." Gabriel put the pendant down. "In this case, a gang of ex-hunters gone rogue, I'm sorry to say."

Mr. Smith moved a hand in a graceful gesture that implied understanding. "These things happen, even in the best-run organizations."

Gabriel looked at him. "Don't worry, the rogues will be dealt with. But in the meantime, we have a bigger problem. That power outage on the Strip was not an accident or the result of an engineering failure. It was deliberate, and it will happen again unless we arrest the people responsible."

There were sharp gasps and murmurs of deep concern.

"Explain yourself, Mr. Jones," the mayor said.

"I will," Gabriel said. "But I think it's important that you all know how I came to my conclusion. I was able to track down the tuner who created the pendants. It turns out there were thirteen in all."

Chief Hopton spoke up. "Where is the tuner?"

"Dead," Gabriel said. "His name was Pitney. He was murdered, and his shop was destroyed in a suspicious fire. I found his vault in the tunnels. He was worried that he was in danger. He left a second tracking device that can be used to locate the other pendants and a video message. I will give you the video, Chief. It contains more evidence."

A middle-aged woman in the front row frowned. Lucy recognized her. Millicent Mitchell was the CEO of one of the largest casinos on the Strip.

"Is there something on that video that connects the pendants to the power outage?" she demanded.

"Yes," Gabriel said. "I have been able to determine that there is an illegal weapons lab operating in the Shadow Zone. A short time ago I took a rogue hunter named Tuck into custody. We had a long conversation. He gave me a lot of information, including the location of the body of an inventor named Preston Trenchard. More about that later. The important thing to know is that the people running the lab are working with crystal-based technology that can deactivate rez amber."

That news elicited a sharp gasp from the audience.

"The power outage we witnessed was, in effect, a test or a demonstration," Gabriel continued. "I think you will agree that the situation calls for the cooperation of the police and the Guild."

"Absolutely," Chief Hopton said. He glanced at Lucy. "What does Ms. Bell's kidnapping have to do with any of this?"

Gabriel folded his arms. "I can't be certain yet, but logic indicates they grabbed her because they need her talent. As I'm sure you're aware, she is one of the best channelers in the region. The weapon uses a rare liquid crystal that I think comes from the Ghost City. We can assume that whoever is running the operation is having trouble with the weather at the site of the crystal."

Mr. Smith studied Lucy with a sharp, intent expression. She felt a whisper of energy and knew he had just heightened his talent. She inclined her head slightly in recognition. He nodded in acknowledgment. Satisfied with whatever his intuition had told him, he switched his attention back to Gabriel.

"Obviously, the priority here is to take down the lab, arrest everyone connected to it, and then locate that deposit of liquid crystal," he said.

"Yes," Gabriel said. "The weapon is just the beginning. The goal of the developers is obvious. Whoever controls a power source that can shut down several blocks of casinos as well as every mag-rez gun in the vicinity will own this town."

Hopton looked uneasy. "If this gang has a working prototype and fuel, how do you propose busting the operation? Sounds like they could neutralize our communications and weapons before we can get close."

"At this point we still have the element of surprise on our side," Gabriel said. "If we coordinate and move fast, we can shut down the lab and take possession of the weapon. Once we have it in our hands, we can arrest the individual in charge."

"You know who that is?" Smith asked.

"Yes," Gabriel said. "But at the moment, gaining control of the suppressor is the priority. We can clean up afterward."

CHAPTER THIRTY-ONE

With Otis carefully tucked under her arm, Lucy walked into the Midnight Carnival with Gabriel. They were not alone. Jared and Joe were with them. They all paused to survey the bustling scene.

Researchers were scattered around the vast chamber making notes, taking measurements, and photographing the various artifacts. A woman in a white lab coat was studying a scaled-down glass conservatory that appeared to be filled with strange plants made of crystal. The sign over the entrance read LUCINDA BROMLEY'S PSYCHIC GARDEN. The researcher looked up and smiled when she saw Gabriel.

"Mr. Jones," she said. "Can I help you?"

"I'm looking for Dr. Peabody," Gabriel said.

"I believe he's inside the House of Mirrors." The researcher aimed her pen at one of the rides.

"Thanks," Gabriel said.

He led the way through the exhibits and rides. Lucy and the others followed him into a dark, cavelike structure. The interior glittered with mirrors that gave off an eerie energy. The fine hairs on the back of her neck lifted in response. Not in a good way. She knew the others experienced the same disturbing sensation. Otis sleeked out a little and muttered.

Reginald Peabody was using a flashlight to examine the small train designed to take people through the winding corridor of mirrors. He straightened when he noticed the group standing at the entrance.

Otis chortled a greeting and waved the toy dust bunny.

Peabody grimaced. "Oh, dear. Not again."

"Don't worry, Dr. Peabody," Lucy said. "I've got a good grip on Otis."

"I certainly hope so," Peabody said. He turned to Gabriel. "What can I do for you, Mr. Jones?"

"We need to borrow a few artifacts," Gabriel said, "and a couple of your security staff."

Peabody stared, appalled, but he managed to pull himself together. "Of course, Mr. Jones. Anything for the Guild."

CHAPTER THIRTY-TWO

Lucy stood in the deeply shadowed entrance of a long-closed nightclub. She was not alone. Otis was on her shoulder. Gabriel, Aiden, and Chief Hopton were there, too. They all watched the old casino at the end of the narrow street. A few architectural features remained from its semiglorious heyday. The faded sign on the marquee announced loose slots, complimentary drinks, and an Elvis impersonator.

"I remember this place," Chief Hopton said. "When I was a rookie we busted it regularly. The management was always running off-the-books, high-stakes poker games in the basement. Every time we raided the joint, the gamblers escaped through that hole-in-the-wall you found. We always lost 'em in the tunnels."

"Not this time," Gabriel said. "Ready?"

Hopton looked at the half dozen officers in heavy SWAT gear who were waiting in another doorway directly across the street. He raised one hand in a signal.

The woman in charge of the team acknowledged the signal and led the other officers toward the casino. Under the cover of the heavy fog, they took up positions. One of the team primed a small explosive and hurled it at the boarded-up front door of the casino.

There was a loud *whoomph*. Glass and wood shattered. When the smoke began to clear, mag-rezes roared from inside the casino, spraying the area around the entrance.

A guard poked his head around the doorway. He saw Hopton and Gabriel, fired two quick shots, and ducked back inside.

"It's the cops and the new Guild boss," he yelled. "We're gonna need the suppressor."

"Get out of the way," Dillon Westover shouted from somewhere inside.

He appeared at the entrance. His face was twisted into a wild, frantic mask. He used both hands to grip a strange-looking machine. He swung the barrel of the device in wide arcs, evidently searching for a target.

The machine began to glow with an ominous silver energy. The lights inside the casino dimmed and winked out.

Gabriel checked his amber. "Flatlined."

Hopton took out his mag-rez. "Dead. That damned machine really works."

Gabriel signaled Aiden and the two museum security guards.

"Go," he said.

They raised the control devices and pressed the keys.

Westover did not see Mrs. Bridewell's clockwork curiosities advancing toward the entrance of the casino until it was too late. The queen, a soldier dressed in the uniform of an Old World military regiment, and a miniature carriage drawn by two four-footed animals moved relentlessly toward Westover.

Belatedly, he heard the clanking of the killer toys and looked down.

"What the fuck?" he yelled.

He aimed his suppressor at the row of marching machines. From where she stood, Lucy could see him desperately trying to rez a trigger-like device. The weapon glowed hotter. A beam of paranormal radiation struck the clockwork weapons, one after another, but it had no effect. The queen, the soldier, and the carriage reached the entrance. The queen's head moved from side to side, seeking a target. She found Westover.

He tried to retreat, but the queen had locked onto his vibe. He realized he was in danger and tried to scramble out of range, but he went unnaturally still. He dropped the machine and fell to his knees and stared at the lethal toy in disbelief.

"I know the feeling," Lucy whispered. The memory of the cold sensation that had swept through her when the queen had fixed her gaze on her in the Ghost City was going to haunt her for a very long time.

The machine that Westover had dropped was still glowing, albeit more faintly. Unfazed, the soldier and the miniature carriage continued past Westover and went into the casino, searching for other targets. There were shouts and yells of panic.

"The tunnels," a man screamed. "We've got to get out of here."

Gabriel signaled the two Arcane guards. They de-rezzed their control boxes. There was an ominous silence inside the casino. The machine finally stopped glowing.

Gabriel checked his mag-rez. "We've got power again. We need to move fast. Their weapons will be working, too."

Chief Hopton signaled the assault team. They emerged from the fog at the side of the casino and went through the doorway.

There was another moment of silence before the team leader appeared.

"Under control, Chief," she called.

Gabriel, Hopton, Aiden, and the Arcane security guards sprinted for the doorway. Otis leaped off Lucy's shoulder and raced after the others. He was sleeked out and showing a lot of teeth.

Lucy hurried toward the entrance. The scene inside the casino was reassuring. Officers were collecting weapons and handcuffing people. Aiden was busy stripping amber off the ex-Guild men and snapping photos of the cops in action.

"We're missing two guards," Gabriel announced.

The door at the far end of the room opened. Two sullen-looking men in well-worn khaki and leather marched into the room. Their hands were in the air and their holsters were empty.

Jared and Joe followed the guards into the room. They both held flamers.

"These two made it into the tunnels," Joe said. "No one else, though."

"Good work," Gabriel said.

Dillon Westover was on the floor just inside the entrance. He was not moving. An officer was in the process of handcuffing him.

"Is he dead?" Lucy asked.

"No, ma'am," the officer said. "The doll knocked him out, but he's still breathing."

Dillon opened his eyes partway and tried to focus on Lucy.

"Should have told Tuck to get rid of you when we had the chance," he said. His voice was hoarse and blurred. "But I was afraid that if you died in the clinic there would be even more media attention. Couldn't risk it."

"So you told Tuck to give me a few more doses of the drug instead," Lucy said. She crouched beside Dillon, rage spiking. "The same drug you used at the wedding reception. Tuck and his merry band of cold-blooded mercenaries kidnapped me, but things went wrong when I escaped."

"Figured you'd never make it out of the tunnels," Dillon said hoarsely. "Shit, what were the odds? Nobody gets out of the Underworld without nav amber. But the next thing I know the local cops are calling in a Guild agent who has some special talent for tracking people down below."

"You must have panicked when Gabriel brought me back to the surface."

"I knew there was a crowd gathering in the Storm Zone. Big media event. I sent Tuck to monitor the situation. He was able to give you an injection before you were taken to the clinic and a couple more once you were inside. And then you disappeared again, you crazy bitch."

"You were afraid to make any more attempts, so you settled for ruining my reputation. You made certain everyone who worked in the Underworld concluded I was unreliable and unstable."

"It worked," Dillon said. "Until Jones came back to town as the boss of the new Guild. It's been one disaster after another."

"Depends on your point of view. From my perspective, it's been one close call after another."

Gabriel crossed the room and looked down at Dillon. "You tried to steal the clockwork doll because you were afraid the Old World technology might be impervious to your new weapon. You were right."

"I heard the Bridewell curiosities had been discovered in the museum," Dillon said. "My family was connected to Arcane back on the Old World. I knew the story of the clockwork toys. Knew they might be a problem if someone figured out how to replicate the power source. Planned to reverse engineer them."

"I doubt your team would have been successful," Gabriel said. "No one managed to do it in the old days back on Earth. The Arcane Museum staff has concluded that only someone with the same talent as the woman who crafted the toys could create one."

Dillon glared at him. "I want a lawyer."

Aiden aimed the camera at him. "Photos first. Everyone loves the perp walk. Okay, so, you're not exactly walking, but you get the idea. Smile."

CHAPTER THIRTY-THREE

Lucy put a bowl of scrambled eggs on top of the refrigerator for Otis, arranged two plates of eggs and toast on the dining counter, and sat down beside Gabriel.

She opened the morning edition of the *Curtain* and smiled when she saw the headlines and the photos.

"Aiden will be very happy," she said.

"Yeah?" Gabriel swallowed a bite of scrambled eggs and looked up from his phone. "Let's see."

She handed him the paper. He glanced at it and smiled.

"He'll be ecstatic," he said.

The headline read, *Local Police and Illusion Town Guild Create Joint Task Force to Take Down Illegal Weapons Lab.* Beneath that was a smaller headline: *Owner of Westover Outfitters Arrested.*

The front-page photo showed Gabriel and Chief Hopton standing shoulder to shoulder to announce the closure of the case. On page two there were several more shots of police officers and the small Guild team securing Dillon and the others in the old casino.

None of the pictures showed Mrs. Bridewell's deadly curiosities.

"Looks like Aiden and the crew from the museum did a nice job of keeping the artifacts out of the story," Lucy said, scanning the story and the photos. She looked up. "All in all, an excellent launch for your new Guild here in Illusion Town."

"Never forget the importance of good public relations," Gabriel said. He went back to his phone, frowning.

Lucy sighed. "Something wrong with your phone?"

"Looks like it. There are usually a lot more emails and messages first thing in the morning. The only ones I'm seeing now are those that have been forwarded by—" Gabriel stopped. "Well, damn. He did it."

"Who did what?" Lucy asked.

"Aiden." Gabriel shook his head and smiled a little. "He told me he was going to take over my business account. He said he would forward only the stuff that he thought I really needed to see."

"That's what a good administrative assistant does."

"It's like magic."

"Welcome to upper management," Lucy said. "Speaking of work, I'm going to give my boss at Storm Zone Adventure Tours my two weeks' notice today."

"Why two weeks? If you ask me, Luxton doesn't deserve even a day's notice. You never got a salary. You had to depend on tips and commissions from the sale of toy dust bunnies to make the rent. There were no benefits. Any way you look at it, Luxton took advantage of you."

"He was kind enough to hire me when I desperately needed a job."

"He wasn't being kind, Lucy. You and Otis were real moneymakers for him. He used both of you for marketing purposes. He charged extra for your tours because you guaranteed a storm event, but he didn't give you a cut."

"Yeah, well, I prefer to stage a professional exit."

"Twenty bucks says he gets so mad when you tell him you're leaving that he fires you on the spot."

Lucy shrugged. "His choice."

"Whatever. I'll drop you off at the Storm Zone on my way into the office." Gabriel tucked his phone into his pocket and started to get to his feet.

"Sit down," Lucy said.

He paused, brows lifted. "Why?"

"Aiden is handling your inbox. That means you have time for a second cup of coffee."

"Huh." Gabriel gave that a few seconds of thoughtful consideration, and then he sat down. His eyes heated. "I do have some time, don't I?"

"Yep. Get a life, Mr. Guild Boss."

"Excellent idea."

He set the phone and the coffee down on the counter, got to his feet, and scooped her off the dining counter stool.

"I'm not sure I have time for this," she warned.

"You're not due at Storm Zone Adventure Tours until nine. That gives us plenty of time. Get a life, Ms. Weather Channeler."

She smiled.

"Excellent idea."

CHAPTER THIRTY-FOUR

"Good morning, Mr. Jones." Aiden got to his feet behind his desk. "I was starting to wonder if I ought to check on you. You're usually here a lot earlier than this."

"I'm learning to get a life," Gabriel said. He slipped out of his leather jacket. "Takes practice."

"I see. Turns out your timing is excellent."

Gabriel reflected on the short but extremely hot lovemaking in the rumpled bed and the very interesting shower that had followed.

"Yes, my timing is good," he said.

"I was referring to the fact that the overnight team of designers and contractors just left. I'm happy to say that things in your office are moving along very rapidly."

Gabriel was amused. Aiden was still rezzed from his first experience as a member of a Guild emergency response team. True, the action had all been aboveground for him, but a Guild takedown was a Guild takedown whether it happened on the surface or in the Underworld. It was clear that at long last Aiden was feeling like a real Guild agent.

"Since when do decorators and contractors work overnight?" Gabriel asked.

"This is Illusion Town, sir. It runs around the clock."

"I've heard that."

"Also, Ms. Fortune and her crew are happy to do a few favors for the Guild."

"I'm starting to worry that people are going to start calling in some of those favors they're doing for us. Moving right along, that was good work you did yesterday, both in the field and on the PR side."

Aiden flushed. "Thank you, sir."

"I noticed that you cleaned up my phone. I take it we have no pressing emergencies at the moment?"

"No, sir. A number of reporters are requesting interviews, of course. I'll schedule them and make sure they are short."

Gabriel groaned. "Interviews. I never had to do interviews when I was in security."

"Don't worry, I'll coach you."

"You know, the learning curve on this job is a lot steeper than I thought it would be."

Aiden smiled. "You've got staff now, sir, and as I keep saying—"

"We need more. I know."

"I've been sorting through a number of requests from hunters who would like to transfer to Illusion Town. I'll let you know when I'm ready to recommend some people to you. I've already started hiring for the PR department, by the way. I can't continue to handle that job and maintain the level of professional service expected of an administrative assistant at the same time—not for long, at any rate."

"Staffing the PR department is as high on the priority list as hiring trained Guild agents?"

"Yes, sir. The Guild is off to a great start in terms of image and branding here in Illusion Town. We can't afford to lose that momentum."

"Right." Gabriel went toward his office. He paused in the doorway. "Speaking of actual Guild work, there are some loose ends in the weapons case that I need to take care of this morning."

"Yes, sir. Can I be of assistance?"

"We have to find the location of that liquid crystal that was used to fuel the suppressor. The hypnotist who interviewed Westover and the others we picked up says they don't know. They told him that the client supplied the fuel for the suppressor."

"What about that gray amber that was tuned for the rogues?"

"Westover discovered the amber himself. Turns out he's ex-Guild, too. Spent a lot of time prospecting on his own. The amber doesn't seem to have much use except as a signaling or ID device, but he used it to make his so-called security team feel special."

"And then ordered the murder of the tuner to make sure the pendants couldn't be traced back to him."

"Yes. We are now looking for Westover's client. There were some messages on Westover's phone, but the number went straight into the dark rez-net. It may be impossible to trace."

"What have we got to go on?" Aiden asked.

"Westover's plans and, presumably, those of the client started to fall apart when they kidnapped Lucy. I'm going back to that point to take another look at the investigation that was conducted at that time."

"Think the local cops missed something?"

"Or someone lied."

Chapter Thirty-Five

"I can't believe Luxton fired us, Otis." Lucy edged through the fissure in the Storm Zone Wall. "He was really, really pissed. Gabriel was right about how he would react to me giving notice. So much for trying to be professional."

Otis was several feet ahead of her, investigating the wreckage of a fallen tower. He did not appear to be concerned about having been fired on the spot. He chortled, waved his sequined dust bunny, and scampered through the ancient quartz ruins that littered the interior of the Dead City.

It was fifteen minutes after nine. At nine o'clock she had informed Luxton that she was giving two weeks' notice and offered to come in for occasional weekend tours until he could line up another weather channeler. He had yelled at her for ten minutes, calling her ungrateful and accusing her of a lack of loyalty, before firing her. Now she and Otis were walking home through the ruins.

"He even wanted the stupid hat back," she said to Otis. "For a minute there I thought he would demand your dust bunny, as well. Guess he figured out it looks a little too used. He wouldn't have been able to re-sell it."

Or maybe Luxton had been smart enough to realize it would be a very bad idea to try to confiscate Otis's toy. She was pretty sure Otis would have been annoyed. An annoyed dust bunny was a scary sight.

"Too early for a pizza," she told Otis. "Let's go home so I can change out of this dumb uniform. I'll pick up some of my old business cards and drop them off at a few of the smaller companies that work the Underworld. Remind them that I'm available in between Guild jobs and that, unlike Weather Wizards, I'm affordable and happy to take on the small projects. They'll love the fact that the Guild has me on retainer. Makes me look top-of-the-line."

Professionally, she was in a good position to rebuild her business, thanks to Gabriel. Her personal life, however, was looking extremely vague. Gabriel showed no signs of moving back to his own apartment, but that was not reassuring.

"I am not running a bed-and-breakfast for a Guild boss who can't be bothered to get his own apartment properly furnished," she announced to Otis.

His furry head popped up over the top of a broken pillar. He chortled agreement and disappeared.

She continued walking, dodging the ruins of the quartz towers that long ago had risen gracefully into the skies.

She was buffeted by small rivulets and occasional waves of energy as she made her way toward the crack in the Wall that opened into the Dark Zone. Some of the paranormal vibes tickled her senses; others felt like invisible shadows or the remnants of dreams and nightmares she could not quite recall.

She dodged the worst of the energy and went back to the question of

Gabriel. What was she going to do about him? The time had come to take bold action. She would not let him drift into the relationship just because it was convenient. He needed to recognize that what they had between them was special and important.

There was no doubt that the attraction between them was real. She had always known that she could trust him with her life. Literally. She wasn't so sure about trusting him with her heart, however. He appeared to be slowly but surely adjusting to the notion that he was in a position to settle down, but he would always be the mission-driven Guild man.

He had closed one very big case, and now his focus would shift back to the job of establishing the new Illusion Town Guild. He had a vision of restoring the honor and dignity of the organization he loved. He was going to be a busy man for a long time to come.

She respected his ambition and his fierce determination to rebrand the Guild image, but she was not about to become the Guild boss's lady. He might be interested in continuing the affair or even in a Marriage of Convenience, but she was not.

She wanted nothing less than a full commitment from him. If he could not give her that, she would have to end things—the sooner, the better. The longer she let the current situation continue, the harder it would be to protect herself from serious heartbreak when the end finally came.

And the end would come, because Guild bosses were expected to enter into a formal Covenant Marriage. It was tradition, even though the men at the top of the organization were notorious womanizers and rarely gave up the habit after entering a CM. Sooner or later, they got married. The two-hundred-year-old laws and conventions established by the First Generation still had enormous power throughout society. Tradition was important to Gabriel, and long-established Guild tradition held that Guild married Guild.

She was ready to get serious. If Gabriel was determined to be married to the Guild, that was his problem, not hers. She would have to move on. It was a truly depressing thought.

The bleak vision of a future without Gabriel while living in the same town and taking contracts with his precious Guild caused her to lower her guard. The psychic barrier she used to close off the most disturbing vibes of energy gave way. The shadowy fragments of dreams and nightmares crawled through the breach in her mental wall.

For a moment she was in the grip of the drug-induced visions she had experienced on the night she was kidnapped. This time, though, the images came into sharper focus. Figures in dark clothes chasing her into the ruins. The sting of the injection. Glimpses of blue amber pendants burning hot in the night. Panic, fear. The horror of knowing that she might be losing her mind . . .

Otis chortled, breaking the spell cast by the memories. She gave herself a mental shake and clamped down her psychic wall. Her mind cleared. Her senses returned to normal—or, at least, what passed for normal these days.

But in the wake of her brief lapse of control came other memories. Sharper and more focused. She recalled waking up over and over again in the chamber where she had taken refuge. Her inability to get through the doorway. Otis. Pizza. The Lord of the Underworld showing up to rescue her.

Because that's what Gabriel did. He rescued people. He protected them. And as the director of the Illusion Town Guild, he would go on rescuing and protecting people. It was his calling. His mission. She was okay with that. Theoretically. But he needed to understand that, in the end, even the most distinguished career would not be enough to extinguish the loneliness.

A thought struck her. What if he was holding back because he was afraid to let himself fall in love with a woman who felt she owed him her life and her sanity? A man like Gabriel would not want to trust a love based solely on gratitude. Maybe he was being cautious because he wasn't sure of *her* feelings.

If that was the problem, she could solve it. Gabriel had saved her once. She would try to return the favor. He was worth saving from himself. She would find a way to seize the future for both of them.

Otis reappeared just as she was about to exit the Dead City through the hole-in-the-wall on the Dark Zone side. She picked him up and plopped him on her shoulder.

"The first thing I'm going to do when the Guild pays its bill is put a down payment on a car," she said. "No offense, but you get a little heavy after a while."

Otis chortled and waved his toy.

"No," she said, "it's not your dust bunny, pal. It's you. I know, I know, it's probably all muscle."

Otis murmured agreement.

She was only a few feet away from the front walk of the apartment house when an empty cab cruised past. The logo on the side read, DARK ZONE CABS. WE CAN FIND ANY ADDRESS IN THE ZONE.

The driver looked out the window.

"Cab, lady?" he asked.

"No, thanks," she said. "I'm home now."

The cab drove down the street and vanished into a narrow, winding lane.

Lucy stopped and turned to look at the corner where the cab had disappeared.

"Otis, the cabdriver."

Otis, alerted by her tone, made questioning noises that probably translated into *What game are we going to play now?*

She took out her key and hurried toward the lobby entrance, wild thoughts tumbling through her head. She concentrated to assemble them into a logical string.

The police had maintained they had been unable to locate the driver of the cab that had kidnapped her the night of the wedding reception. They concluded he had probably been working off the books and didn't want to get involved in a missing persons investigation. After she had been diagnosed as suffering from para-psych trauma, the police had closed the case. So had the Guild.

"Can't blame them, Otis. There was no evidence to support my story. I have to admit it sounded as if I'd been rezzed on drugs and bad psi. But we have a lot more information now. It's obvious the driver must have been one of Westover's mercenaries. Naturally, the cops never found him. They were looking for an ordinary cabdriver, not a rogue hunter working with a team."

But a few weeks later someone claimed to have tracked down the cabdriver and talked to him. That same person said the driver had confirmed the cops' theory of the case, so there was no point trying to make him talk to the police or the press.

"Someone lied, Otis." Lucy rezzed the lock on the front door and walked into the lobby. "I know who."

She hurried up the stairs and rezzed the lock on the door of her apartment. Otis hissed a warning and sleeked out, but it was too late. She had the door open and she was in the front hall.

Otis tensed to spring.

"No," she said. "Not yet. Please."

Otis obeyed, but his body was shivering with battle-ready tension. A lot of teeth and all four eyes were showing.

Veronica appeared at the other end of the short hall. No makeup. No leather. She was wearing a bathrobe and slippers. Her long red hair was in a tangle. Her eyes glittered with barely controlled panic.

"Veronica?" Lucy whispered.

"I'm sorry, Lucy," Veronica said. Her voice shook a little, but she pulled herself together. "I got out of bed because I heard someone moving around in here. I knew you and Gabriel had left. I thought maybe you'd come home early because Luxton fired you. If that was the case, I knew you'd want to talk. When I knocked on your door, *she* answered."

Cassandra Keele moved into sight. She had a mag-rez pointed at Veronica's head.

"Come in and close the door," she said. "Lock it. Control the rat, or I'll put a bullet in Ms. Star's brain."

CHAPTER THIRTY-SIX

"You were Westover's client," Lucy said. "You were so good at staying in the shadows, he never realized you were the one who was using him."

"I'm the one who discovered the pool of liquid crystal in the Ghost City," Cassandra said. "I come from a long line of prospectors who have a special talent for locating crystals. I'm good. But I didn't want to spend my life in the Underworld. Decided it would be more interesting to become a private investigator. But you know how it is with talent."

"The more you try to ignore it, the more it calls to you."

"Exactly. When Coppersmith Mining opened up the Ghost City, I started hearing rumors of amazing discoveries. I couldn't resist taking a look around down there. I found my own portal. Pitney figured out how to create a key for me."

"You discovered the liquid crystal."

"A whole lake of the stuff. I couldn't stake a claim, because Copper-smith has all the mining rights, but they haven't even begun to chart that sector. It's going to take years to explore and map the territory around the Ghost City. They never knew I was there."

"How did you know the crystal was a source of power?"

"I could sense it, of course. That's part of my talent. The problem is that there's a massive tornado anchored to the lake. I managed to extract a small amount of the crystal. but it was just too risky to continue. The tornado is getting stronger by the day. I hired Westover anonymously and offered him a cut of the profits if he could find someone to handle the weather at the lake."

"He went after me," Lucy said.

"He screwed up. After that, he brought in a couple of outsiders. The first one was pretty good. She managed to fill up four canisters. She died when she went back for more. The next channeler disappeared into the lake. He didn't bring out a single canister."

"How did you find Preston Trenchard?"

"Everyone thought he was crazy, but I had read some of the articles he had written for the para-physics journals before he was fired from the lab where he worked. I knew he was the one I needed. I had Westover take a sample to him. Trenchard understood the potential of the liquid crystal immediately. He said it had the power to suppress standard rez-amber. He claimed he knew how to build a weapon that could shut down an entire city. I offered to finance his experiments."

"But things kept going wrong."

"Because of *you*." Cassandra's voice rose. "Obviously I made a serious error in judgment by letting you live. I should have had Westover take care of you when the medics took you to the clinic. But he convinced me there would be even more trouble if you died."

"Why did you come here today?" Lucy asked. "Under other circum-stances, I would have been working."

"*Yes.*" Cassandra's voice grew shrill. "*You were supposed to be working.* I came here to get rid of you and Jones."

"How did you imagine you would be able to do that? Okay, maybe you could have gotten rid of me, but a Guild boss? Westover and his whole team of mercenaries couldn't handle that job."

Cassandra gave her a savage smile. "I brought you a lovely bottle of wine. It's on your kitchen counter. A gift from your parents."

"Poisoned wine, I assume?"

"It contains the same hallucinogen that Westover put in your champagne that night. The same one that the mercenary injected you with at the clinic. But this time I used a much higher dose. One glass would have driven you mad. Two would have killed you. Either option would have been satisfactory."

"Where did you get the drug?" Veronica asked.

"I made it myself," Cassandra said. "In addition to having a lot of prospectors on my family tree, there are some very, very good chemists— psychic-grade chemists. I've been in the drug business for years. Where do you think I got the money to finance Westover and his team of mercenaries? I do very well in the investigation business, but not that well."

"You're a dual talent?" Lucy asked. "Guess that explains the instability."

"*Shut up.*" Cassandra's eyes flashed hot with rage. "One more word and your friend here is dead."

"All three of us know you're planning to kill Veronica and me," Lucy said. "You don't have any choice now. I'll bet you think you can make it look like we interrupted a burglary in progress and got shot by the bad guys."

"An interesting plan," Veronica said. "But it won't work. Gabriel Jones won't stop until he finds the killer. You're right, Lucy, she's unstable. Everyone knows what happens to dual talents."

"That's not true," Cassandra raged. "The para-psych diagnosis was wrong. *Wrong.* My file was filled with lies. The para-psych doctor didn't know what she was talking about. She didn't understand. Didn't recognize my power. She was going to have me committed. That's why I had to get rid of her."

"Yep, you sound as steady and stable as a rock," Veronica said.

Cassandra narrowed her eyes, evidently uncertain how to take the remark.

"Absolutely stable," Lucy said quickly. "But you do plan to kill us. The shots will alarm our landlady. She'll call the cops. Or maybe she'll come up here to see what's going on, and then you'll have to murder her, too. Really, it's going to be one thing after another, Cassie, and it's going to end badly for you."

"Don't call me Cassie."

Enraged, Cassandra started to swing the barrel of the mag-rez toward Lucy.

Paranormal thunder roared behind her. Shocked, she instinctively turned to see what was happening. The small bolt of lightning struck her. For a few seconds, she froze.

And then she crumpled to the floor.

Lucy cut off the small storm. Energy faded. The familiar rush hit her bloodstream. She was flying. Otis went back to full fluff mode and bounced up and down on her shoulder, channeling her excitement.

"Awesome," Veronica said. She took a deep breath and leaned down to pick up the mag-rez that Cassandra had dropped. "You're good, Lucy. But if I were you, I wouldn't let too many people know that you can pull that kind of heat aboveground."

Lucy started to answer, but the whiff of smoke cut through her sparkling senses. Alarm shot through her, overwhelming the endorphin vibe as effectively as a bucket of ice water.

Veronica looked to the side, toward the living room. "Uh-oh."

She stepped over the unconscious Cassandra and disappeared.

"Oh, shit," Lucy said.

She rushed down the hall, jumped over Cassandra, and hurried into the living room.

Smoke billowed from one of the sofa cushions. Veronica was in the kitchen grabbing towels. She tossed one to Lucy. They beat at the smoke. A small flame appeared.

"Let's get it out on the balcony," Lucy said.

She dashed across the room, yanked open the slider, and raced back to seize one edge of the smoldering cushion. Veronica grabbed the other side.

"Hurry," Veronica said.

"It's not like I'm standing still here."

They got the cushion out onto the balcony and dumped it upside down, hoping to suffocate the small fire. Smoke seeped from the top.

"Water," Lucy said. "There's plenty in the refrigerator."

They flew into the small kitchen, grabbed armfuls of bottled water, and hauled them out onto the balcony. Otis hopped up onto the railing and chortled encouragement.

The front door slammed open just as Lucy opened a third bottle of water and poured it onto the still-smoking cushion.

Gabriel appeared in the living room. Aiden, Jared, and Joe were with him. They had flamers in their hands. They came to a halt and watched the scene taking place on the balcony.

"You know," Gabriel said, "at some point in the future when we look back on this, we're probably going to laugh."

"I am not going to laugh," Lucy said.

Veronica grinned. "I will. I can see the headlines now. '*Famous Weather Channeler Sets Sofa on Fire While Taking Down Crazed Killer.*'"

Lucy glared. "Aiden, pay attention. The headline here is '*Guild Emergency Response Team Arrests Final Suspect in Conspiracy.*' Is that understood?"

Aiden hid a grin and took out his phone. "Yes, ma'am."

Lucy surveyed the others. "If anyone in this apartment says one word to the media about what happened here this afternoon, there will be more lightning. I guarantee it."

Gabriel's eyes heated. "Never argue with a weather goddess."

Veronica smiled. "You know, Lucy, if you ever decide to give up this weather channeling gig, I'm pretty sure you would be a success in my business."

"I'll keep that in mind," Lucy said.

Gabriel saw the bottle of wine on the kitchen counter. There was a pretty green bow around it. A card dangled from the bow.

"She brought wine?" he said.

"It's spiked with a hefty dose of the hallucinogen that the kidnappers used on me," Lucy said. "She said there is enough of the drug in there to drive us mad or kill us. But it wouldn't have worked."

Joe frowned. "Why not?"

"Who could resist a bottle of good wine?" Jared asked.

"Take a look at the card," Lucy said.

Jared went into the kitchen and checked out the card. "It says, *Congratulations on recovering your professional reputation. We are so proud of you. Love, Mom and Dad.*"

"I would have been suspicious as soon as I saw it," Lucy said. "My father and stepmother have never sent me a bottle of wine in my entire adult life. We're not a close family."

Gabriel picked up the bottle and held it for a moment before he set it down.

"No," he said. "We would not have opened it."

Veronica studied him. "Bad vibe?"

"Downright crazy," Gabriel said.

Chapter Thirty-Seven

"How did you figure out what was going on?" Lucy asked.

They were gathered in Gabriel's office. He was seated behind his desk. Aiden had directed Lucy to one of the two visitor chairs. He had *escorted* Veronica to the other one. Veronica had accepted the courtesy with regal grace, as if it was her due. She was wearing a severely tailored black jumpsuit and black high heels. Her red hair was bound up in a tight knot. She carried a black leather handbag.

It paid to have attitude, Lucy thought, and the right clothes. She was still wearing the stupid Storm Zone Adventure Tours uniform. At least she had gotten one of the chairs. Aiden, Joe, and Jared had to stand.

"I'd like to say that I solved the case using amazing psychic intuition and secret Guild technology," Gabriel said. "But the truth is, I went back to the start and examined the police report and compared it with the report that Cassandra Keele had given you, Lucy. When I saw that she claimed to have tracked down the cabdriver, I realized there was a problem. After all, we knew the driver must have been a fraud, not a licensed cabdriver."

Lucy groaned. "I should have tried to track him down myself."

"Why would you?" Jared said. "Keele told you he had confirmed the police report. You had no reason to doubt her investigation."

"And your own memories of the evening were blurry," Veronica reminded her. "It took you weeks to recover some of them."

"Thanks to the drugs they used on you," Gabriel said.

"After Luxton fired Otis and me this morning, we took the shortcut through the Dead City," Lucy said. "The energy seemed extra strong in the ruins today. It's like that sometimes. The weather often affects the paranormal vibe. Anyhow, today the sensations stirred up some old memories. When I reached the DZ, a cab passed us. I suddenly remembered that the police were never able to find the cabdriver. Keele told me that was because they hadn't tried very hard. But the cops told the media they had looked for him. So who was lying?"

"You decided it wasn't the cops?" Gabriel said.

"It struck me that Keele might have had a motive to lie if she was involved in the kidnapping."

"She must have panicked when you contacted her agency with the intention of hiring an investigator," Jared said. "What made you choose Keele Investigations?"

Lucy made a face. "I wanted the best. Keele Investigations is the best in Illusion Town. The really annoying part is that I paid a fortune for that investigation. It cleaned out what was left of my savings."

Veronica glanced at Gabriel and then looked at Lucy. She smiled a cool, satisfied smile. "You both stumbled onto the truth at the same time. That wasn't a coincidence. It was a classic example of a psychic intercept. It happens that way when the vibe is right between two people."

"Huh." Gabriel appeared intrigued. "My mom told me the same thing. I thought she was just putting pressure on me."

Veronica raised her brows. "Pressure to do what?"

"Get married," Gabriel said.

Lucy cleared her throat. "To conclude my story, I was about to call you when I walked in on the scene in my apartment."

"Thank goodness you arrived when you did," Veronica said. She gave an elegant shudder. "Cassandra was going to inject me with that damn drug, take me down into the Underworld, kill me, and dump my body."

Lucy looked at her. "I am so sorry you were put in harm's way."

Veronica gave her a serene smile. "No worries, friend. You saved me, and now I am going to get some excellent press. In fact, I have an interview with a journalist from the *Curtain* as soon as I finish here. He wanted to talk to me earlier, but I made him wait. It's always good to make them wait, you know."

Every man in the room except Gabriel gazed at her, transfixed.

Gabriel focused on Lucy. "Waiting is hard on the nerves."

She blinked, unsure how to respond to the cryptic comment. She sensed he wasn't referring to sex. Something else, something deeper, was concealed in the comment. Or maybe she was overthinking and overanalyzing his words. But the heat in his eyes was real.

Before she could give the matter more thought, Joe spoke up.

"Does this close out the Liquid Crystal Conspiracy case, boss?" he asked.

Gabriel sat back in his chair. "Thanks to the tracker, we've accounted for all of the members of the Blue Amber mercenary team. We've got Westover and his client, Keele, who was running the show. But there is one very big loose end."

"What is it?" Joe asked.

"We need to secure the source of the liquid crystal in the Ghost City and make sure it's under the control of the Guild. The government gave Coppersmith the exploration and mining rights to that entire sector, but they will need us for security."

"If everything Keele said is true, access to the liquid crystal is blocked by a paranormal tornado," Lucy pointed out. "You're going to need a really good weather channeler to take down that kind of storm."

Gabriel gave her his slow smile. "Luckily I know one who has the talent to do it."

Chapter Thirty-Eight

Lucy stacked her slippered heels on the balcony railing and took a sip of her brandy.

"Did you really call me a weather goddess this afternoon?" she asked.

"I did," Gabriel said.

He was sitting beside her in the second lounger, ankles stacked next to hers. It was ten o'clock. Night cloaked the city, but the glow of the quartz ruins streaked the Dark Zone in green chiaroscuro. The paranormal buzz in the atmosphere was a pleasant complement to the brandy.

Dinner at the Hideaway restaurant had involved a cozy, romantic booth, an expensive bottle of wine, and no pizza. That was not a problem, because Otis was not around to complain. He had disappeared and was off doing whatever dust bunnies did when they got together at night.

Lucy swallowed some brandy and thought about Gabriel's answer. "Did you mean it?"

"You can call down lightning to smite your enemies. Of course you're a goddess."

"Do you think I'm sleeping with you because I'm grateful to you for saving my life?"

"What the hell makes you ask that?"

"You're in the business of rescuing and protecting people. I'm sure many of them are very grateful to you. Don't get me wrong, I am grateful to you, too. Even if you did abandon me to those Blue Amber rogues."

"After which you rescued yourself."

"With Otis's help."

"You stopped those two rogues cold in the Ghost City without my help, and this afternoon you rescued yourself and Veronica. I'd say there's plenty of evidence that you can take care of yourself. By the way, you aren't the first person I've pulled out of the tunnels. I've never slept with any of the others. Just you. Where are you going with this?"

She tilted her head back against the lounge cushion. "I'm just trying to confirm that you don't think I'm having an affair with you because I've mistaken gratitude for . . . something else."

"Something else? Are you talking about physical attraction?"

"Mmm."

"We're *not* talking about physical attraction?"

"Mmm."

"I'm not good at guessing games, not when it comes to relationships."

She fortified herself with another swallow of brandy and lowered the glass. "I'm not interested in a short-term affair. I can't let this relationship continue unless I see a future for us. That means you have to see the same future."

Gabriel swept his feet off the railing and sat up abruptly. The soles of his low boots landed with a resounding thud on the floor of the balcony. His eyes burned in the shadows.

"I saw a future for us the night I found you in the Underworld," he said. "I have never stopped seeing that future. It's the first thing I think about in the morning and the last thing I think about at night."

She took her feet off the railing and sat up. They faced each other across the short distance that separated the loungers.

"I'm glad to know I'm on your to-do list," she said. "But where, exactly?"

He reached out one hand and threaded his fingers through her hair. He cupped the back of her head in his palm, leaned forward, and kissed her, a scorching kiss that aroused all of her senses. Energy heated the atmosphere around them.

He raised his head. "You're not just on the list. You're at the top. You've been there all along. Who do you think convinced the Guild Council that this sector needed its own Guild headquarters?"

Her pulse beat faster. Disbelief and excitement arced across her senses. "You?" she whispered.

"After I pulled you out of the tunnels I went back to Cadence and told my boss that opening up the Ghost City was going to bring a lot of security problems to this sector of the Underworld. I gave him a list of excellent reasons for establishing a new Guild operation here in Illusion Town. He took those reasons to the Council. When I returned from the Rainforest mission, the position of director was waiting for me."

"I was the real reason you moved to Illusion Town?"

"I had it all planned out. My strategy was in place. But when I got here, ready to pick up where we left off, I discovered that things had gone wrong. Really, really wrong. My to-do list was in chaos. But you were always on it and always at the top."

It wasn't exactly a Covenant Marriage proposal, but it was enough for now. Progress.

"I never stopped thinking about you," she said quietly. "I dreamed about you. Sometimes good dreams. Sometimes nightmares. But you were always there."

She wrapped her arms around his neck and kissed him, surrendering to the fierce urgency of the moment.

He picked her up off the lounger and carried her through the open slider, down the short hall, and into the green shadows of the bedroom.

He stood her on her feet, gripped her shoulders, and fixed her with his hot, intent eyes.

"Sometimes you scare the green hell out of me," he said.

"I think being able to scare a Guild boss occasionally is a job requirement for a goddess." She touched his hard jaw. "What was it that made you nervous? The lightning bolt in the hallway this morning?"

"I'm getting used to the lightning. What sent me into a panic this time was that conversation out on the balcony. I thought you were going to tell me you were ending our relationship."

She started to unfasten his shirt. "What would you have done if I had said that?"

"Gotten down on my knees and begged you to give me another chance."

"Hah. I don't believe that for one minute."

"It's true." He reached behind her and slowly lowered the zipper of the blue sheath. "Trust me, it's true."

"And if that hadn't worked?"

He eased the straps of the dress off her shoulders and let the garment fall to her ankles. For a moment he simply drank in the sight of her standing in the paranormal light of the ancient ruins.

"If that hadn't worked, I would have carried you down into the Underworld and made love to you until you changed your mind," he said.

"That sounds interesting." She smiled. "It would have worked."

Chapter Thirty-Nine

It was the truth, Gabriel thought. Reality slammed through him as he finished stripping off his clothes. He could not take his eyes off Lucy. She was waiting for him on the bed, the sheet drawn up over her breasts. If she had ended their relationship out there on the balcony tonight, some part of him would have shattered.

He had been living on the edge of a cliff since it had dawned on him that she wasn't going to greet him with open arms—since he had discovered what she had gone through after he had abandoned her the night he carried her out of the ruins. For a time out there on the balcony he had been afraid she was going to push him off the precipice. The future was still uncertain, but at least he had been able to take a few steps back from the edge. He was not in free fall.

He tossed the last of his clothes aside, pulled back the sheet, and lowered himself down onto the bed. He gathered her into his arms.

"You really did scare me tonight," he said.

She flattened her palm against his chest. "That wasn't my intention."

"Be careful. I'm delicate."

She laughed and pushed him onto his back. She propped herself on her elbow and began to stroke him. The feel of her warm palm, the vibe of her aura, the scent of her body thrilled him.

"Let's see just how delicate you are," she said.

She let her hand glide down over his belly and lower still. When her fingers tightened around him, he thought he would explode.

"Lucy."

"Hard as quartz," she said. "Not delicate at all."

"Okay, maybe not there, but I've got feelings."

"That's good to know. What, exactly, are you feeling at this moment?"

He pulled her down on top of him and caught her face between his hands. "I feel like making you come harder than you've ever come before."

"That sounds . . . exciting."

"Oh, it will be," he vowed. "Fascinating."

He moved his hands to her waist and then separated her thighs so that she straddled him. He found the wet heat between her legs and stroked her until he felt the small muscles clench around his fingers. The scent of her aroused body intoxicated him.

Her breathing tightened and then she tightened her legs, silently urging him to go deeper. Slowly he withdrew his fingers.

"No," she gasped.

He eased her down onto his straining erection.

"Yes," she said. *"Yes."*

He began to move, forcing himself to go slow. At the same time he stroked the exquisitely sensitive place just above her core. He could sense her climbing higher and higher. She began to fight him for control. He resisted for a while, and then he was no longer interested in control.

Her climax overwhelmed him. She came long and hard. So did he.

Lightning sparked in the shadows.

CHAPTER FORTY

"Unfortunately, the Illusion Town Project had to be shut down," Melody Palantine said.

Taggert Spooner turned away from the spectacular view of the ruins of the Dead City at the heart of Cadence and looked at his administrative assistant. Melody Palantine was young, talented, and ambitious. All qualities that would probably cause problems in the future. But for now, she was extremely useful.

Palantine was not the most beautiful assistant he had ever had, but she could manipulate the rez-net with a skill unlike that of anyone he had ever met. Even more astonishing was her uncanny ability to track down and manipulate the kind of personnel he needed for his organization. She could convince almost anyone to do almost anything. If there was such a thing as a psychic talent for running a con, Palantine had it.

"All the loose ends have been handled, I assume?" Taggert said.

"Of course, sir." Melody glanced at her notes and then looked up. "Westover and all of the Blue Amber mercenaries involved have been picked up by a task force composed of the Illusion Town police and the Guild, but none of them were aware of the identity of the client."

"Cassandra Keele."

"Yes. She was arrested when she attempted to poison the new Guild boss in Illusion Town. She suffered some sort of seizure at the scene and is now locked up in a para-psych hospital for the criminally insane. Dual talents are often unstable, as you know. She is apparently delusional."

"And the nature of her delusions?"

"She is trying to convince anyone who will listen that there is a conspiracy afoot. Seems to believe she was attempting to buy her way into the inner circles of a clandestine organization by providing it with a weapon that could suppress amber-based technology."

"You're certain no one believes her?"

"Conspiracy theories always find an audience, sir, but in this case it doesn't matter if anyone believes Keele. There is absolutely no way the Corporation can be linked to her."

"I trust you are right, Ms. Palantine." Taggert smiled a cold, thin smile. "Because this project was yours from start to finish. You were the one in charge."

An ominous energy flickered briefly in Melody's eyes. For a few seconds he wondered if she might be foolish enough to attempt to use her talent to manipulate him. That would be interesting. She had no idea of the true nature of his own talent. She would not discover that until he no longer needed her.

In the meantime, he could use her ambition to control her. They both understood that she needed him to achieve her goals. As far as he was concerned, she could be replaced. He would prefer not to have to look for a new administrative assistant, but if necessary, he would not hesitate to do so.

The dangerous light faded from Melody's eyes. He was impressed with her control.

"Keele, Pitney, Westover, and Bell were excellent choices for the project," Melody continued smoothly, as if she hadn't caught the lightly veiled threat of his words.

"Except that you lost Bell. Not only did she escape after the initial extraction attempt was made, she actually survived the catacombs, thanks to Gabriel Jones."

"Mr. Jones was a factor in the equation that could not have been predicted."

"And because of that single unpredictable factor, the entire project failed. One of these days you will learn that no matter how brilliant the plan, there is always at least one unpredictable element."

"Yes, sir."

Taggert flattened his palms on the polished surface of his desk and leaned forward a little. Just enough to intimidate. "In my experience, the unpredictable element is a human being. In the case of the Illusion Town Project, there were *two* unpredictable people involved: Jones and Bell. In the future, Ms. Palantine, let's hope you remember that individuals do not operate the way computers do. Logic, for example, is rarely involved. The real world runs on emotions, ambitions, and desires."

Melody stood very still. "Yes, sir."

"That's all for now, Ms. Palantine."

"Yes, sir."

She turned, walked swiftly across the carpeted floor, and let herself out into the hall. The heavily paneled door closed softly behind her.

Taggert straightened and went back to the window. Palantine would definitely become a problem in the future, but for now he needed her. He had ambitions, too. His ancestors had left a failed legacy behind on the Old World.

He was going to rebuild that legacy here on Harmony. This time it would be successful.

The legacy had a name: Vortex.

CHAPTER FORTY-ONE

Melody Palantine held it together until she got to her private office at the end of the hall. Once inside, she locked the door and rezzed the MEETING IN PROGRESS light.

Frustration and rage threatened to set fire to her senses. She could not allow that to happen. She took a few deep breaths, summoned up her mantra, and whispered it over and over again while pacing the room.

"You have a destiny. You have a destiny. You have a destiny."

It took a while, but she finally regained control.

When she was no longer tempted to murder the idiot in the CEO's office, she sat down at her desk, took out her phone, and opened a hidden file.

The photos came up immediately. The images were a century old. There were dozens of them. She had used a camera to record them from multiple sources—libraries, historical archives, Guild museums, and books. Each shot featured the same man. Even though the pictures dated from a hundred years earlier, it was impossible to look away. The messianic zeal, blazing charisma, and the power of his talent radiated across the years.

Vincent Lee Vance had built a cult of followers and transformed them into a militia that had fought a guerrilla war via the catacombs. The desperate times that had ensued were known as the Era of Discord.

Vance and his followers had very nearly succeeded in conquering the city-states. But in the end, the hastily assembled teams of ghost hunters had finally managed to put down the rebellion. After losing the Last Battle of Cadence, Vance's followers had surrendered in droves.

Vance and his lover, Helen Chandler, had fled into the tunnels. For years there had been speculation that the pair were still alive, still secretly plotting. Eventually they were relegated to the history books. Recently, their skeletons had been discovered by a para-archaeologist named Lydia Smith and her husband, Emmett London. There was no longer any question about how Vance and Chandler had died. They had been caught in a lethal energy trap in an uncharted sector of the tunnels.

History fades, but legends rarely do. Legends have staying power.

Once again calm and in control, Melody closed the file and tucked the phone into her handbag. Legends did not always get the details right. Yes, Helen Chandler had been Vance's lover, and yes, it had been established that they had not had offspring.

But Vance had slept with another one of his followers, a woman named Anna Mark. Anna had been a powerful talent, but she had left the cult when she discovered she was pregnant. She had hidden her relationship with Vance and managed to seduce an elderly, senile man into a quick Marriage of Convenience before her condition was obvious. Under the marriage laws, the birth of the baby had automatically converted the MC into a Covenant Marriage.

The result was that no one ever knew Vincent Lee Vance had fathered a daughter.

His talents had passed down through the family line, often skipping generations. When they did appear, the results were rarely good. Because the secret of Vance's astonishing success was that he had been a triple talent. Statistically speaking, triple talents were not only psychically unstable but often died young. Those who survived usually ended up in para-psych wards.

Melody had inherited Vance's three talents. Unlike her ancestors, she was psychically stable. She was strong. She was going to do what Vincent Lee Vance had failed to do—control the Federation of City-States.

She understood what Vance had not—there was no need to conduct an armed rebellion to build an empire. That was Old World thinking. True power in a modern society was achieved by controlling basic resources, technology, and weapons. That was the Vortex approach.

Taggert Spooner was aware she was ambitious, but he had no idea how ambitious. She was going to make Vincent Lee Vance's vision come true, and she would do that by taking control of Vortex. Spooner had a role to play. He just didn't know that yet.

She had a destiny to fulfill. Nothing would stop her.

CHAPTER FORTY-TWO

The tornado was bigger, hotter, more ferocious than anything she had ever dealt with in the Underworld. It twisted violently over a lake of shimmering liquid crystal, creating roiling, crashing waves. The combined radiation of the churning lake and the vicious twister was more than enough to keep the small crowd at a respectful distance.

Ghost shit, Lucy thought. *This is bad.*

She had braced herself for a big one, but this sucker was a real monster. Otis hunkered down on her shoulder and muttered something that was probably dust bunny for *Not a good idea.*

Gabriel studied the scene and shook his head. He glanced at Elias Coppersmith, the man in charge of the Ghost City mining project.

"No wonder those other channelers were unable to take down that thing," he said.

Elias nodded. "Worst storm we've run into down here." He looked at

Lucy. "What do you think? I don't want you risking your life over that crazy weather."

Never let the client see you sweat. She managed a confident smile. It was all about image.

"No problem," she said. She turned back to Elias. "It would be a good idea if everyone took shelter inside the buildings."

"Understood," he said. He turned to face the onlookers. "You heard Ms. Bell. Everyone indoors."

The small group retreated into a nearby structure. When the quicksilver door closed behind them, Lucy was left with Gabriel, Elias, and Otis.

She looked at the men. "Uh, maybe you two should—"

"No," Gabriel said. "I'm in charge of keeping the personnel on-site safe. That includes you and Coppersmith."

Elias smiled. "And I can't leave, because I'm the one who has to secure the liquid crystal."

Lucy knew she had no chance of talking them out of their decision to stay. "Okay, but if I say run, we all run. Got it?"

"Got it," Gabriel said.

"Understood," Elias said.

She reached up to touch Otis. "Here we go, pal. If this works, I'm buying pizza."

Otis perked up at that.

She opened her senses, searching for the organizing vibe of the tornado. Technically, it would have been possible to generate a force field strong enough to allow her to walk straight into the storm by channeling an energy tunnel. She suspected it was the way the other weather channelers had managed to haul out a few canisters of the liquid crystal. It was probably the way they had died. You never knew when a tunnel would collapse, leaving you at the mercy of the powerful forces whirling around you. No one survived such an experience, at least not with their minds and senses intact.

The secret to taking down a serious storm was to locate the source of energy that was powering it and establish a destabilizing vibe. It was a variation on chaos theory. She was looking for the butterfly that had flapped its wings and set off a hurricane—or, in this case, a tornado. You couldn't fight the storm, but if you could get hold of the damn butterfly, which, in this case, was apparently still flapping its wings . . .

She picked up the faint but steady vibe at the core of the twisting monster. Working with the exquisite care of a surgeon following an artery, she felt her way into the heart of the violent winds.

She knew it as soon as she sensed it. She could not see it because of the violent winds of gray energy, but she had done enough weather work to realize that it was some sort of resonating quartz. She sent a quick, small shock wave of energy into it, shattering it internally.

Lightning sparked and flashed inside the tornado for a moment, and then the wild winds simply vanished.

The shimmering surface of the crystal lake was fully revealed. The waves quieted. An elegantly arched bridge fashioned of gray quartz stretched from the edge of the lake to a slender pedestal that projected out of the silvery liquid. On top of the pillar stood a gray quartz bowl.

Gabriel looked at Lucy and winked. "Goddess."

She fought back exultant laughter, fixed a polite, professional expression on her face, and looked at Elias.

"That should do it, Mr. Coppersmith. Let me know if you have any more weather issues."

Elias grinned. "Call me Elias, and don't worry, we'll be in touch." He raised his voice. "Problem solved, everyone. Come on out."

The Coppersmith people emerged from the quicksilver doorway and walked forward. They gathered at the edge of the lake and studied it, fascinated.

Otis chortled enthusiastically, bounded down from Lucy's shoulder, and raced around the edge of the lake. Before anyone realized what he was after, he darted across the bridge, hopped up onto the pedestal, and reached into the bowl. He had to use two of his six paws to lift an object out of the artifact.

"Otis," Lucy called, "come here."

Otis was already fluttering happily back over the bridge. He bustled up to Lucy and graciously offered her the object he had taken from the bowl. The others gathered around her while she cautiously accepted the gift—a bar of silvery quartz that reflected light like a mirror.

"Thanks, Otis," she said.

She rezzed her senses, but there was no vibe in the quartz. She handed it to Elias. He took it and examined it briefly.

"Shattered," he announced. "This is what you flatlined, Lucy."

"It must have been resonating with the energy from the lake and amplifying it," she said. "The supercharged vibes drew the tornado and anchored it."

One of the men shook his head. "Hard to believe something that small could cause that twister."

Lucy smiled. "The butterfly effect."

CHAPTER FORTY-THREE

"I got your message, Dr. Peabody," Gabriel said. "What's the problem?"

"I'm not sure there is one, Mr. Jones." Peabody adjusted his glasses. His gray brows were scrunched together. "But considering the events of the past few days, I thought I should bring the matter to your attention."

"I'm listening," Gabriel said.

They were in the Arcane Museum, standing in front of a tunnel ride. There was no sign over the entrance.

"You're a descendant of the Jones family," Peabody said. "I trust you are aware of some of the history of Jones and Jones on the Old World?"

"I know it was founded as a psychic investigation agency. One of my cousins, Marlowe Jones, runs a branch office of J and J in one of the other city-states. Why?"

"Jones and Jones and the Arcane Society dealt with a lot of odd and dangerous cases that all had one thing in common—there were always paranormal elements involved, elements that made it difficult or impossible for the regular police departments and investigative agencies to handle. In many cases the criminal work went undetected altogether, because the crimes were committed by psychic means. Murders appeared to be deaths by natural causes. Drug dealing was impossible to prove because the chemicals were paranormal and thus did not show up in forensic tests."

"Marlowe says business isn't what it used to be back on Earth because here on Harmony law enforcement not only recognizes crimes of a paranormal nature, it has the talent and technology to deal with them."

"Yes, but back on the Old World there was one criminal organization that plagued Jones and Jones for decades. One of the legends of J and J in the twenty-first century, Fallon Jones, wrote in his journal that the group was run by individuals with particularly powerful paranormal talents. They concealed their operations behind a number of shell companies and had connections to the highest levels of government. Your ancestor notes that, while Arcane was eventually able to expose the group, they could never be sure it had been stamped out entirely."

"You're talking about Vortex, aren't you?"

"Yes." Peabody appeared relieved. "Sorry for the lecture. I was afraid you might be unaware of the organization."

"Coppersmith Mining ran into some trouble on Rainshadow Island a while back. There was evidence of a Vortex connection. The Coppersmiths and Arcane have a long-standing history. The problem was reported to J and J. So far, the investigations have hit solid quartz walls."

"Within Arcane, Vortex is something of a legend," Peabody said. "You know how it is with legends."

"They never die. But there was nothing about this recent case that appeared to be connected to Vortex."

"I'm afraid that's not true, Mr. Jones." Peabody gestured toward the entrance of the dark ride. "Will you follow me?"

"Sure."

They went through the shadowed entrance and stepped aboard the small railroad car. Peabody put the train in gear. It lurched forward and headed down the narrow tracks.

At first there was nothing to be seen. The first few feet of the journey were made in darkness, but when the train rounded a curve, an eerie luminosity appeared, revealing a diorama of an old-fashioned laboratory. Figures in white coats and goggles were at work on a disturbingly familiar device.

Peabody brought the train to a jerky stop.

"Shit," Gabriel said. He stepped off the car and moved to take a closer look at the device exhibited on the workbench. "It looks a lot like the prototype weapon that we just confiscated from Westover's operation."

"I was afraid of that," Peabody said. He left the train and walked across the small space to join Gabriel. "Notice the glass canisters."

Gabriel looked at the three tubes. "They're empty."

"The notebook that one of the figures holds indicates they are meant to contain a liquid crystal of some kind. I'm more concerned with the name embroidered on the lab coat."

It took Gabriel a few seconds to make out the old-fashioned writing, because it dated from the First Generation. The style had changed drastically after the Era of Discord.

"Trenchard," he said. He looked at Peabody. "Preston Trenchard is the name of the inventor that developed the suppressor. We found his lab and his body."

"I think this figure is one of Preston Trenchard's ancestors. According to Fallon Jones's diary, one of the scientists who worked for Vortex back in the twenty-first century on the Old World was named Harvey Trenchard. Evidently he was a genius when it came to crystal technology."

"Is this supposed to be a scene from the Old World?"

"No," Peabody said. "If I am correctly interpreting the story that Aloysius Jones was trying to tell in this exhibit, it is a warning."

Gabriel studied the scene. "A warning that a Trenchard came through the Curtain, settled on Harmony, and tried to go back into the weapons business. Apparently Preston Trenchard inherited both the technology and the talent."

"Yes," Peabody said. "There is a vast, mostly undiscovered trove of crystals and resonating amber here on Harmony, not to mention artifacts of a vanished civilization that was technologically advanced. But with so many resources available and so much potential, why go into the weapons business? That was the last thing anyone needed in the Colonial era. The city-states were struggling just to survive."

"I doubt if anyone ever went broke in the weapons business, regardless of the era," Gabriel said.

Chapter Forty-Four

The Lord of the Underworld showed up with the dust bunny and a pizza.

Lucy smiled at the sight of Gabriel standing in the doorway. He had an Ollie's House of Pizza box in his hand. Otis was on his shoulder.

"It's about time you two got home," she said. "I thought you might have had an emergency at the office."

"Ollie's was busy tonight," Gabriel said. "Long line."

She eyed the box in his hands. "You stopped to pick up pizza?"

"I thought it would make things more romantic," Gabriel said.

"Pizza? Romantic?"

"We met over a box of pizza, remember?"

"Oh. Right. How sweet." She stepped back so that Gabriel and Otis could move into the hall.

Gabriel was trying to be romantic. She had to respect and appreciate the gesture. Okay, so she did not consider the days and nights she had been imprisoned in the Underworld chamber romantic. She had been hallucinating wildly, and Gabriel had been simply doing his job when he rescued her. But apparently he looked back on the experiences in a different light.

The man might be struggling with the nuances of a relationship, but he was making a concerted effort. That's all that mattered. He was on a mission again. Focused. On her.

She smiled and then realized Gabriel was still standing in the doorway.

"Aren't you going to come inside?" she asked.

"Not yet," he said. "I have to ask you the question I wanted to ask the first time I saw you sitting there on your quartz throne."

"You wanted to ask me if I was hallucinating?"

"No."

Otis chortled and bailed off Gabriel's shoulder. He stood on his hind paws and looked up at the pizza box. He, too, was focused.

"Sorry," Gabriel said. "I promised you the pizza, didn't I?"

He gave the box to Otis, who seized it in two paws and disappeared into the living room.

Lucy raised her brows. "So the pizza isn't for me?"

"Figured you'd probably had enough for a while."

"You got that right. You said you wanted to ask me a question that night?"

"Yes," Gabriel said. "I wanted to ask you to marry me."

She stared at him, speechless for a few seconds. She finally found her voice. "What?"

"The instant I felt your vibe, I knew you were the woman I had been looking for, the one I wanted to be with forever. Maybe the word *marriage* didn't come into my head at that moment, but—"

"Uh-huh."

"I was too dazzled to follow the logic of the situation all the way to marriage, but I knew I wanted you. I knew I would never be able to forget you. I also knew I had another assignment coming up, so I wouldn't be able to stick around. Be honest—if I had told you that I wanted you in ways I've never wanted anyone else, you would have thought I was weird, possibly dangerous."

"Well, it would definitely have been a rather startling statement, under the circumstances."

"Not to mention extremely unprofessional."

"Extremely."

"I figured that when I moved to Illusion Town to start a new Guild I would have time to convince you that I was serious. Time for you to get to know me and maybe fall in love with me. But everything went wrong. When I got out of the Rainforest, I discovered you weren't taking my calls."

"I wasn't taking anyone's calls."

"It got more complicated, because your father and stepmother told me you were suffering some sort of para-psych trauma and were unable to go back into the Underworld. When I did get to Illusion Town, I discovered you were working for that low-budget tour operation in the Storm Zone. I told myself I'd arrange to meet you there and see if I could convince you to go out to dinner with me. But that's when the Arcane Museum people showed up asking me to find the clockwork doll. It occurred to me that offering you a contract might be the best way to reconnect with you."

"Strategic thinking." Lucy folded her arms and smiled. "I like that about you."

"You aren't going to make this easy, are you?"

"Why don't you just ask me the question?"

"I love you. I'm hoping you might be able to love me."

She unfolded her arms. "That's not a question."

"Will you marry me, Lucy?"

"Yes, of course I'll marry you."

Gabriel's shock stirred the atmosphere. He just stood there in the doorway, his eyes heating with a swirl of intense emotions.

"Lucy," he whispered.

She took three steps and put her arms around his neck. "Why do you look so surprised? You must have known I fell in love with you down there in the Underworld."

"You were hallucinating."

She brushed her mouth against his. "Not that badly. And I'm not hallucinating at all now."

He caught her close and kissed her with the fierce joy of a man who has been walking through the Underworld for a very long time and has finally found his way back to the surface and into the sunlight.

"You two are a never-ending source of entertainment," Veronica said from the hallway behind Gabriel.

She was dressed for work in a black corset and black leather pants.

Gabriel took his mouth off Lucy's and looked at her over his shoulder. "We're getting married soon."

Veronica smiled. "No surprise. I could have told you that."

Dazed and a little giddy, Lucy laughed and grabbed Gabriel's arm. She hauled him through the doorway and paused to speak to Veronica.

"You're going into work early this evening."

"One of the other disciplinarians called in sick."

"Have a good night."

"You, too," Veronica said. She winked. "Let me know if you need to borrow my handcuffs."

"I will." Lucy started to shut the door.

Mrs. Briggs's voice reverberated along the corridor.

"Just a moment, Ms. Bell. A word, if you don't mind."

Lucy wanted to scream, but she managed to contain herself. She summoned up a steely smile. "Don't worry, you'll have the rent money on time. You'll have to excuse me, I'm in the process of getting engaged."

Mrs. Briggs stopped in front of the doorway and saw Gabriel. Her eyes widened. "Oh, my. How nice. A Marriage of Convenience, I assume? Will you be moving in, Mr. Jones? If so, we'll have to prepare a new lease, and I'll need a guarantee from you that the Guild will be responsible for the rent."

"No," Gabriel said. "This isn't going to be an MC. It will be a Covenant Marriage."

"That's *perfect*," a male voice called from somewhere in the hall. "Absolutely perfect. I can't wait to tell the scriptwriter. She has been demanding a happy ending. The director claims that's unrealistic. Now she can argue that it *is* realistic."

Lucy leaned out into the hall and saw the stranger rushing toward the doorway. He wore snug-fitting, artificially faded jeans, a black T-shirt, and a plaid blazer. His thinning hair was cut very short. A pair of designer sunglasses finished the look.

"Who are you?" Gabriel asked.

"Xander Attwater, talent scout for Rez-Stone Studios. We're making *Guild Boss*. Delighted to meet you, Mr. Jones."

Veronica regarded him with deep interest. "You're in the movie business?"

"That's right." Xander did a double take. "Going to a costume party?"

"Nope, going to work," Veronica said. "I'm a professional disciplinarian at the Dungeon Club."

"A dominatrix," Xander said, awed. "That is *perfect*."

"If you don't mind, we're a little busy here at the moment, Mr. Attwater," Gabriel said.

He started to shut the door.

"Wait," Xander said quickly. "This is too important for you to ignore,

Mr. Jones. We all know the Guilds have an image problem. This film has the potential to totally rebrand the organizations overnight, not just in Illusion Town but in the other city-states, as well."

"He's going to shoot some of the scenes right here at my apartment house," Mrs. Briggs announced. "Can you believe it? The value of this property will quadruple after the film is released. I'm thinking I can give tours."

Veronica regarded Xander with amusement. "Did you come here to ask Mr. Jones and Ms. Bell to star in your movie?"

"No, no, no," Xander said, brushing the idea off with an impatient flick of his hand. "Don't be ridiculous. Jones doesn't have the look we want for the role. Besides, he's too old."

Gabriel grinned. "I'm too old and I don't look like myself?"

"No offense, Mr. Jones, but audiences—especially the teenage to twenty-one-year-old crowd—expect younger, more spectacular leading men. We need someone who looks like a real Guild boss."

"Right," Gabriel said. "Well, so much for that career path."

"What about Lucy?" Veronica asked.

"Absolutely not," Xander said. "We need someone with real charisma. Star power."

Lucy folded her arms. "I bet you don't get invited to a lot of fun parties, do you, Mr. Attwater?"

"Call me Xander." He refocused on Veronica. "You know, you're perfect for the role of Lucy Bell. The whole dominatrix thing works."

Veronica brightened. "Do you really think so?"

"Yes. Perfect." Xander pulled a business card out of his pocket. "Come in for a screen test tomorrow. The address is on the card. Ten o'clock. Wear the outfit."

Veronica was dazzled. She took the card and looked at it. "Okay. Thanks. By the way, here's my card."

Xander accepted the card and glanced at it. "Veronica Star. Perfect."

Veronica winked at Lucy. "Guess I'd better get to work. Congratulations, Lucy, and you, too, Gabriel."

"For not having any star power?" Lucy asked.

"For not looking like a real Guild boss?" Gabriel said.

Veronica chuckled. "You know what I mean. See you guys tomorrow."

She catwalked down the hall. Xander did not take his eyes off her until she disappeared down the stairs.

"I have a question for you, Xander," Gabriel said.

Xander spun around. "Sorry," he said. "Got distracted. It's not often you stumble across real talent, you know. What did you want to ask?"

"How did you find us?"

"It wasn't easy. Ms. Bell wasn't taking my calls—"

"I thought you were a spammer," Lucy said.

"I had a hunch that was the problem, so I asked your colleagues at Weather Wizards if they could help me contact you."

Lucy went very still. "Colleagues?"

"They assured me they could make you available because you were going to be on the Weather Wizards team. They said you were about to sign a contract with them."

"That's interesting," Lucy said. "Why were they so eager to help you?"

Xander winked. "I told them I would make sure Weather Wizards got plenty of product placement in the movie. I promised I would make certain the heroine wore the company's uniform. There would have been shots of the Weather Wizard headquarters. Walk-ons for the Roxbys, of course. And credits. There would have been plenty of opportunity for Weather Wizard merch."

"I gather that's not going to happen now?" Lucy said.

"No, the deal fell through when it turned out they couldn't get you on board," Xander said. "I tracked you down today by contacting Ollie's House of Pizza."

"Let me take a wild guess here," Gabriel said. "You offered Ollie's placement in the film, too?"

"Of course. The owner is thrilled to be a part of the project."

"Aside from telling us that we don't have the looks or the talent to play ourselves in your picture, was there anything else you wanted, Xander?" Lucy said. "Because we have plans for this evening."

"And they don't include you," Gabriel said.

"Sorry for the confusion," Xander said. "I didn't come here to talk to you about who will be playing you in the film. I'm here for the dust bunny."

Lucy stared at him. "You want Otis in your movie?"

"He's—"

"I know," Lucy said. "Perfect."

"Exactly. Plus he's already tamed."

"You don't tame dust bunnies," Gabriel said. "You form friendships with them. Or not."

"I understand they can't be domesticated in the traditional sense, but it's obvious that the one called Otis has formed a bond with Ms. Bell." Xander chuckled and looked at Lucy. "You, of course, would be our dust bunny wrangler on the set. Union scale."

"I don't think your cunning plan is going to work," Lucy said.

"The manager at Ollie's told me the creature is very fond of cheese-and-olive pizza," Xander said. "I'll make sure the caterers have it available on the set. How about a screen test tomorrow? We can do it right after we do Veronica Star."

"Who am I to stand in the way of Otis's big opportunity to have his name in lights?" Lucy said. "He'd love that. Okay, I'll bring him to the screen test tomorrow. We'll see how it goes, but I have to warn you, I'm not optimistic."

"Why wouldn't it work?" Xander demanded.

"I don't think dust bunnies grasp the concept of work as we understand it. Making a movie is hard work, right?"

"Well, sure. Long days on the set. A lot of rehearsals until the director decides the scene is right. But in the end, it's a *movie*. Thousands of people will see it. Otis will be a star."

"Fine. Whatever. Good-bye. See you in the morning."

Otis chose that moment to appear at the end of the hall. He had a half-eaten slice of pizza in his paw. He chortled.

Xander peered past Lucy. Energy shivered in the atmosphere around him.

"Perfect," he said. "Absolutely perfect."

Lucy closed the door with some force, enough to cause Xander to step back quickly.

"Ten o'clock," he called, his voice muffled by the door. "Rez-Stone Studios. Two-fifty-two Mirror Street. Emerald Zone."

Lucy locked the door and turned to face Gabriel.

"Just when you think things couldn't get more bizarre," she said.

Gabriel's eyes heated with amusement. "Look at it this way—the last unanswered question of the case has been resolved. We now know why the Roxbys were willing to go to great lengths to convince you to work for them."

"They wanted to see Weather Wizards featured in the film."

"Image and branding," Gabriel said. He went down the hall, heading for the kitchen. "Well, that's that. What do you say we open a bottle of wine and talk about our future?"

Otis chortled and vanished around the corner. Lucy and Gabriel followed.

"Wine and pizza." Lucy smiled. "To quote Xander Attwater, it sounds perfect."

Gabriel reached the kitchen first. He selected a bottle of red wine, set it on the counter, and went to work removing the cork.

"It's going to be wine and no pizza," he said.

Lucy looked at the counter. The pizza box was empty. She studied Otis. "You ate the whole thing?"

He chortled, waved the sequined dust bunny, and scampered out onto the balcony.

"Don't blame him," Gabriel said, pouring the wine. "While we were standing in line at Ollie's, I told Otis the pizza was for him but that I needed to borrow it for a while. Evidently he understood. You and I are not going to starve. I ordered delivery from the Amber Room. I'm told it's one of the best restaurants in the DZ."

"That's true. Also the most expensive. Who told you about the Amber Room?"

Gabriel handed her one of the glasses. "Aiden did the research for me."

Lucy smiled. "You are getting very good at delegating."

"I'm getting the hang of upper management, I think. What do you say we take the wine out onto the balcony? Dinner isn't due for another hour."

They went through the open slider door and sank down onto the two lounge chairs. Otis was on the railing, taking in the evening. Night landed swiftly in the DZ. The ancient green quartz Wall was starting to glow. The buzz of paranormal energy stirred the senses. The vibes were always stronger after dark.

With a farewell chortle and a wave of his toy, Otis vanished off the railing, heading for the alley below.

Gabriel watched him disappear. "How do you think he'll handle the screen test tomorrow?"

"He'll love the cameras, but I think I can safely predict that the screen test will be a disaster."

"I think you're right."

Lucy drank some wine and lowered the glass. "You really stopped by

Ollie's to get a pizza just because it made you think of the first time you saw me?"

"Since that night I have never looked at a cheese-and-olive pizza without thinking of you."

"I was right about you, Gabriel Jones. You really are a romantic at heart."

"I'm told it runs in the family."

CHAPTER FORTY-FIVE

Lucy, with Otis on her shoulder and Veronica at her side, walked out of the flashy glass-walled offices of Rez-Stone Studios. They got into the cab that would take them to the edge of the Dark Zone. From there they would get a different cab, one with a driver who knew the DZ.

Lucy took out her phone and called Gabriel's private number. She hit video. Gabriel appeared on the screen. He was in his office sitting behind an imposing new desk. Aiden was beside him.

"How did it go?" Gabriel asked.

"We have lots of good news," she said. "Then we have some ironic news. Last, a sad tale of career disaster."

"Start with the good news," Gabriel said.

"The good news," Lucy said, "actually the *terrific* news, is that Veronica got the part. She'll be playing me in *Guild Boss.*"

Veronica leaned in slightly so that she could see Gabriel and Aiden. "I'm going to be a star. I will probably turn out to be a one-picture wonder, but who cares? Even if I never get another role, I will be the most famous disciplinarian in Illusion Town, at least for a while. And the money is amazing. I'll have enough to open my own private club."

"Congratulations, Ms. Star," Aiden said.

"Congratulations," Gabriel added. "Any other terrific news, or do we move on to ironic news?"

"We do, indeed, have other good news," Lucy said. "Runner and his delivery team will also get contracts. The director wants to shoot the movie as much as possible in the Dark Zone, so the film company will need the services of people who live there and know the DZ. Also, Ollie's House of Pizza will be featured, as Xander Attwater promised."

"Ollie will be thrilled," Gabriel said.

"Great product placement," Aiden noted.

"Speaking of which," Lucy continued, "we now move on to ironic news. Weather Wizards will also get product placement and plenty of branding opportunities, because the director likes the uniforms."

Veronica leaned into the frame again. "But I don't have to wear one of their outfits, because I'll be doing all the scenes in my regular work gear."

"And now we move on to the sad story of an acting career that crashed and burned before it even got off the ground," Lucy said.

"This sad story features Otis, I assume," Gabriel said.

Otis chortled at the sound of his name and waved his sparkly dust bunny.

"Yep," Lucy said. "I have to accept some of the blame. I'm a failure as a dust bunny manager and as a wrangler."

"What went wrong?" Gabriel asked.

"All Otis had to do for his screen test was carry a box of Ollie's House of Pizza across the stage and give it to Veronica," Lucy said. "Otis was very enthusiastic when he saw the box. But things got off to a bad start, because the pizza box was empty. The director explained the box was just a prop. Otis didn't buy that story."

"You can't just offer a dust bunny an empty pizza box," Veronica explained.

"What did Otis do?" Aiden asked.

"He growled, dropped the pizza box, stomped up and down on it a few times, and began to look annoyed," Lucy said. "Never a good sign with a dust bunny. Everyone knows that by the time you see the teeth, it's too late. There was panic on the set."

"I was able to distract him with my handcuffs," Veronica said, "but he was in no mood to deal with the director and the crew after that."

"So the dust bunny is out of the picture?" Aiden asked.

"Well, yes and no," Lucy said. "Otis started playing with Veronica's handcuffs. The camera crew was able to get a lot of footage of him fluffed up, dashing around the stage and generally looking adorable while he tried to handcuff stuff. The director thinks he can work the scenes into the finished picture. They'll use fake dust bunnies or computer-generated animation for the scenes where the actual videos won't work."

"Which brings us to another bit of news that falls into the ironic category," Veronica said. "Guess who will supply the film company with the fake dust bunnies, get product placement, and also be licensed to sell dust bunny merch linked to the movie?"

"Storm Zone Adventure Tours?" Gabriel said.

Veronica uttered her smoky laugh. "Right first time."

"We were told my former boss, Mr. Luxton, signed the contract first thing this morning," Lucy said. "I'm sure he's delighted. His tour business will boom when the movie comes out."

Excitement lit Aiden's eyes. "The beauty of this movie deal is that it will take the Guild's image to a whole new level, Mr. Jones. It's bound to stimulate tourism, which is the keystone to the local economy. Everyone in Illusion Town will benefit."

"It wasn't quite what I had in mind," Gabriel said. "But I think you're right. It will probably work." He switched his attention back to Lucy and Veronica. "Where are you headed now?"

"Ollie's House of Pizza," Lucy said. "I told Otis that if he refrained from biting the director I would get him a real pizza."

CHAPTER FORTY-SIX

Runner and a couple other members of the Dark Zone Delivery Service team brought their gleaming black bikes to a halt in front of the entrance to the Dead City. Runner stepped through the gate and whistled. Otis and several dust bunnies appeared immediately.

Runner and the team began unloading the pizzas. There was much gleeful chortling.

"Here you go, guys," Runner said. "Fresh out of the oven. Cheese and olive, courtesy of the Illusion Town Guild."

Ollie's had recently ordered new boxes to update the restaurant's image and take advantage of the windfall of publicity. The label read OLLIE'S HOUSE OF PIZZA. ALL FOUR FOOD GROUPS IN EACH DELICIOUS BITE. FEATURED IN THE MOVIE *GUILD BOSS*.

Otis and his friends seized the pizza boxes, chortled thanks to the delivery team, and raced off into the Dead City to enjoy the feast. Later there would be games of hide-and-seek, followed by exchanges of interesting crystals and some hunting in the Rainforest.

The night was balmy, the desert sky was studded with stars, and the radiant ruins provided access to the endless mysteries of the Underworld. There were plenty of adventures ahead and an apparently endless supply of pizza. Life was good.

ANOTHER NOTE FROM JAYNE

If this is your first visit to my Jayne Castle world, welcome! I hope you enjoyed the ride. Those who have ventured to Harmony on previous occasions know that I also write contemporary romantic suspense under the name Jayne Ann Krentz and historical romantic suspense as Amanda Quick. They will likely have recognized a few "Easter eggs" in *Guild Boss*—bits and pieces of history from those other fictional landscapes. It seems that, although it wasn't the plan back at the start—there was no plan at the start—I have accidentally created a sort of "Jayneverse."

If you're curious about some of the elements that popped up in *Guild Boss*, here's a brief guide:

Want to know more about those dangerous clockwork dolls known as Mrs. Bridewell's curiosities? You can check out the history of the lethal toys in *Quicksilver* (written under my Amanda Quick name) and *In Too Deep* (written under my Jayne Ann Krentz name).

Craving more dust bunny books? The critters are unique to my Jayne Castle world set on Harmony. The first book in the series is *After Dark*.

Interested in the history of the Arcane Society? It starts with *Second Sight* (written under my Amanda Quick name). There's a complete list of the titles at my website, jayneannkrentz.com.

Would you like to meet more of those Jones men? They appear in all three of my worlds. Check out *Tightrope* (written under my Amanda Quick name) for a recent example.

For more information, please feel free to explore my website, jayneannkrentz.com, or meet me on my Facebook page: Facebook.com /JayneAnnKrentz/. I'm also on Instagram: Instagram.com/JayneAnn KrentzAuthor/.

Waving from Seattle,
JAYNE